SAVING

JANE

DOE

SAVING JANE DOE

A NOVEL

CAROLYN PURCELL

NEW YORK

Saving Jane Doe

Published in New York, New York, by Morgan James Publishing. Morgan James and The Entrepreneurial Publisher are trademarks of Morgan James, LLC.
www.MorganJamesPublishing.com

The Morgan James Speakers Group can bring authors to your live event. For more information or to book an event visit The Morgan James Speakers Group at
www.TheMorganJamesSpeakersGroup.com.

Morgan James Publishing
The Entrepreneurial Publisher
5 Penn Plaza, 23rd Floor, New York City, New York 10001
(212) 655-5470 office • (516) 908-4496 fax
www.MorganJamesPublishing.com

A free eBook edition is available with the purchase of this print book.

9781630476861   paperback
9781630476885   eBook
9781630476878   hardcover

Library of Congress Control Number:
2015910974

CLEARLY PRINT YOUR NAME ABOVE IN UPPER CASE

Instructions to claim your free eBook edition:
1. Download the Shelfie app for Android or iOS
2. Write your name in **UPPER CASE** above
3. Use the Shelfie app to submit a photo
4. Download your eBook to any device

Cover Concept by:
Drew Purcell

Cover Design by:
Rachel Lopez

Interior Design by:
Brittany Bondar
www.SageDigitalDesign.com

In an effort to support local communities, raise awareness and funds, Morgan James Publishing donates a percentage of all book sales for the life of each book to Habitat for Humanity Peninsula and Greater Williamsburg.

Get involved today, visit
www.MorganJamesBuilds.com

Habitat
for Humanity®
Peninsula and
Greater Williamsburg
Building Partner

For my patients

PART ONE

The EMTs found her unconscious, huddled in a corner of the second-floor hallway at the Downtowner Motel. Her hand half-held a paper cup, and orange juice spilled onto her dress. As they lifted her from the dirty linoleum floor, a rat scurried down the hall, leaving footprints in her blood. They called her Jane Doe, as the pockets of her dress were empty and her handbag, if she had carried one, had been stolen. Her flowered, short-sleeved dress was faded by many washings, but clean except for the orange juice and blood. Long sable curls loosely framed her heart-shaped face, with skin as white and delicate as Bradford pear blossoms. She looked to be about thirty years old.

Jane Doe's low blood pressure and fast heart rate suggested shock from the blood loss, so they started an intravenous line with Lactated Ringers solution. They knew what had caused the problem. Betty the Butcher worked out of the Downtowner; they had done this run before.

It was August 1971, the first week of clinical clerkships for the new third-year medical students at the University of Kentucky Hospital in Lexington, and only the second month for the interns in the emergency room. Fortunately, Bertha Jones, an experienced ER nurse, met the ambulance. Knowing the gynecology team would be needed, she caught us before we left the ER. We had just seen a woman with bleeding during her first trimester of pregnancy.

"You'll need to see another patient. They found her at the Downtowner," Ms. Jones told Dr. David Armstrong, the chief resident in GYN, as she entered the doctors' workroom.

"Did you find Betty the Butcher's red rubber catheter?" Dr. Armstrong signed the record, though you would not have known it was him from reading the signature.

"I haven't looked. I wanted to catch you before you left."

"Is she conscious?"

"No."

"What are her vital signs?"

"Her blood pressure is 90/60, heart rate is 110, temperature is 103 degrees, and respirations are 20."

"Get her ready for her exam. I'll just be a minute more here. This is Dr. Cara Land. Cara, you go watch what Ms. Jones is doing." I followed the nurse.

As a third-year medical student on call for the first time ever, I felt far from being a doctor, and nothing I had ever seen or heard prepared me for this Jane Doe. Though it was a hundred degrees outside, the emergency room's small operating room was cold—and not just in temperature. Its green tile walls stood bare except for stainless steel cabinets and equipment. The white tile floor, spotless at first, quickly became littered with bandage wrappings, alcohol swabs, and packaging for disposable sterile equipment. Bright lights glared overhead, showed every detail, and kept us from freezing.

I watched. With giant bandage scissors, Ms. Jones cut away the flowered dress, the blood-soaked slip, bra, and panties. With each cut she took Jane Doe's remaining possessions until she was left with only her failing body. Ms. Jones covered her torso with a hospital gown and sheet; her dependence was complete.

"Who is Betty the Butcher?" I asked.

"She's the woman who does illegal abortions at the Downtowner Motel. She forces a red rubber catheter through the cervix and then sends the women out. The catheter is supposed to stimulate contractions that cause the uterus to empty itself."

"Does that work?"

"Sometimes . . . sometimes not."

"What happens if it doesn't work?"

"They come here. If they are lucky they get a D&C which completes the abortion; if less lucky they get a hysterectomy."

"And if they aren't lucky?"

"Some die."

"Do many die?"

"Not many here in Lexington and not as many since antibiotics and other modern treatment, but some still do. I saw more die when I worked in Philadelphia several years ago."

"No wonder they call her Betty the Butcher. Why doesn't somebody stop her?"

Before Ms. Jones could respond, Dr. Armstrong arrived for the exam. He listened to Jane Doe's lungs and heart. When he pulled the sheet down to look at her belly, he said, "You always want to look closely for surgical scars. Ah, she has a low midline surgical scar. It could be from a number of things, but in a young woman, often it is from a Caesarean section." When he pushed on her lower abdomen, she winced. "Well, she is responsive to pain," he said. "Cara, feel how hard her belly is. This is an acute abdomen. She either has blood or pus or both in there." As I felt, it was easy to tell how rigid it was. He finished looking briefly at her legs and ankles for signs of trauma or swelling. Turning to Ms. Jones, he said, "Set her up for a pelvic exam. I'll go order blood tests, antibiotics, and a type and crossmatch for blood transfusion."

Ms. Jones opened a tray with a sterile speculum, ring forceps, and a uterine sound. She added sterile culture tubes to the tray and more trash to the floor. Then she placed Jane's feet into stirrups and pulled her body down to the edge of the table.

When Dr. Armstrong returned, looking at me, he said, "You can see best if you stand behind me. I will try to explain what I'm doing." Jane gave no reaction as he placed the cold metal speculum into her vagina. Huge blood clots rushed out, splattering his white coat, scrub pants, and shoes before creating a sticky pool on the floor at his feet. There, crawling out of the cervix like a snake out of a garden drain and not looking the vicious killer it was, lay the red rubber catheter. One end was still in the cervix, which was slightly dilated and filled with bloody-looking tissue. Dr. Armstrong clamped the tissue with the ring forceps and pulled gently. After the tissue was removed, he placed it in formalin and sent it to pathology for identification.

"What is that tissue?" I asked.

"It looks like placenta."

He touched the cervix with a culture tube and removed the catheter. Next he clamped the top of the cervix with the forceps and inserted the uterine sound through the opening.

"This measures the depth of the uterus," he said. "It is eleven centimeters." He turned the sound, and with what looked like no pressure it moved much deeper into the cervix. "Oh, she has a perforation; the sound just went through a hole. That is probably what caused her problem."

After removing everything, Dr. Armstrong finished the exam by feeling the pelvic organs between his fingers, two placed in the vagina and the other hand on her abdomen. For my benefit he said, "The uterus is eleven weeks' size and soft. There are large masses involving both ovaries. When you do an exam you always relate the size of the womb to how big it would be if the patient were pregnant, even if she's not. That way you always have a frame of reference. If a non-pregnant woman has fibroid tumors, which enlarge the uterus, we still talk about the uterine size in weeks. In this case she is pregnant, or has been. Now, you repeat her bimanual exam while I call the attending physician. She will have to go to the main operating room." Looking at Ms. Jones, he said, "Have you called her family? We will need permission to operate."

"We can't call her family. She's a Jane Doe."

"We'll have to document everything well and proceed. She will die if we wait for a court order."

"Are we doing a D&C?" I asked.

"No, she will need an exploratory laparotomy; that's an open procedure to identify the cause of the rigid belly and fix the problem. In this case that will almost certainly be a hysterectomy and bilateral salpingo-oophorectomy—removal of the uterus, tubes, and ovaries."

This was my first trip to the operating room. A nurse showed me where to change into scrub clothes, leave my things, and get a hat and shoe covers. The female doctors shared the dressing facilities with the nurses. The whole area felt like a refrigerator. In the operating room country music played as the anesthesiologist inserted an endotracheal tube and gave Jane only oxygen and pain medication. I was told that this was because she was unconscious and too sick for deeper anesthesia. Dr. Armstrong told me how to scrub my hands, put on sterile gloves, and prep her abdomen. I hadn't even seen an abdominal prep before I had to do one. Fortunately, it was simple.

I used sponges soaked in Betadine soap to wash the whole area from just below her ribs to the top of her legs, starting at the center and working my way out to the edge without going back over the center. Then I blotted off the soap with a sterile towel. In the final step I started over the incision area and in circles out from the center I painted the scrubbed area with a Betadine solution. After I removed those gloves, I put on a sterile gown and new sterile gloves.

We placed sterile towels along the edges of the incision area and clamped them into place with towel clamps. After we placed sterile sheets over the towels to cover her legs, sides, and chest, we placed one final drape over everything. It had a hole in the center to allow access.

When we were ready to start, Dr. George Gray, the attending physician, arrived. He scrubbed, gowned, gloved, and stood across the table from Dr. Armstrong. I stood beside Dr. Armstrong on the patient's left side, and the surgical nurse stood next to Dr. Grey.

Dr. Armstrong incised the skin from just below the pubic hairline up to the belly button by cutting along the sides and removing the scar. He then incised the thick fascial layer followed by the peritoneum. When the abdominal cavity was opened, a terrible odor filled the room and confirmed the infection. White patches of pus that looked and acted like glue covered her bowel, which spilled out through the incision like a white garden hose coiled across the surgical drape. The bowel was covered with a damp towel and packed into the upper abdomen, exposing the pelvic organs. The masses turned out to be abscesses involving the fallopian tubes, which were four times normal size, red, dripping pus from the ends, and stuck to the surrounding organs. A red, rough-edged hole was visible in the top of the uterus, where it had been perforated. I felt both fascinated and horrified and, fortunately, not at all sick.

After Dr. Gray explained these findings to me, he said, "We'll have to clean her out," meaning removal of the uterus, tubes, and ovaries. With that one sentence, he destined her reproductive future to the stainless steel pan sitting on the back table.

"Is there no other way?" I asked. "We know nothing about this woman. Does she have children? Does she want children, if not now, then in the future? Would she consent to this, if she could be asked?"

"She'll die if we don't. Antibiotics cannot reach areas where there is no blood supply, like these abscess cavities, and as you can see everything is stuck together so we can't really leave part."

Dr. Armstrong added, "We do know that she has at least two children, probably three."

"How?"

"Remember what I said about scars. She has both medio-lateral and midline episiotomy scars, which would suggest two children. She also had that scar on her low abdomen that may be from a Caesarean section. If she were not so infected, we would be able to tell if she had a C-section from adhesions, but we can't in this case. Besides, this situation would lead one to believe she doesn't want any more children."

"She may have lost some of those babies," the anesthesiologist added. "She has an anti-D antibody in her blood and probably shouldn't have any more babies, even if she wants to, at least not with this father. She was pregnant at least once before Rho-gam was available."

During three exhausting hours, they tediously separated the uterus, tubes, and ovaries from the attached bowel as I held a retractor. When the reproductive organs were free, they clamped the blood supply and removed them.

Dr. Gray stepped back from the table. "Dr. Land, step up here and help close the incision. I'll see you at rounds in the morning."

"Cara, this patient is too unstable to let you close the incision," Dr. Armstrong said. "Maybe next time." He failed to notice my sigh of relief.

I sat in the recovery room and then the intensive care unit (ICU) with Jane Doe most of the night and wondered if I had what it took to do that work day after day. By four in the morning her once pear-blossom skin had turned to rose-petal pink with the flush of fever. Her blood pressure was stable at 110/70; her heart rate was 120. Though she did not regain consciousness, she did breathe on her own, and the endotracheal tube was removed.

By morning rounds we were hopeful she would survive. During the day her fever reached 105 degrees, and alcohol baths barely affected it. A white blood cell count of 20,000 showed that she was fighting the infection. After receiving two units of blood her hemoglobin level, 10.8 grams and stable all day, confirmed that we had stopped her bleeding. As we monitored her vital signs, gave her antibiotics and IV fluids, measured her urine output, and watched for recurrent bleeding, I prayed.

After evening rounds, I was exhausted but wanted to stay with her. "I'll stay to check the evening labs and watch her a while," I said to Dr. Armstrong. I wanted her to wake up.

"No, Cara, you need to go home. You've been up for thirty-six hours, and you need to rest. Hers is going to be a long recovery."

I lived five minutes' walk from the hospital. Home by six o'clock, I skipped dinner, went straight to bed, and slept twelve hours.

Back at the hospital at seven the following morning, I found Jane struggling to breathe. We ordered a chest X-ray and continued rounds. By midmorning as we were paged to her bedside, she stopped breathing altogether. Her nurse called a code 500, so named in those days because it cost five hundred dollars, and breathed for her with an Ambu bag until the crash cart came. When the anesthesiologist got to her room, he inserted an endotracheal tube and placed her on a ventilator. The chest X-ray showed that her lungs were completely filled with fluid—shock lung we called it then, adult respiratory distress syndrome now. By either name, this was bad.

Every Friday afternoon off-duty medical students, interns, residents, and hospital staff gathered at Schu's, a bar across the street from the hospital. During the first two years of medical school I rarely attended this social part of my education, but I did this week, not needing a beer so much as I needed to have some fun. I sensed that I took too much of the cares of the hospital home with me. At first we all did, and then somehow we learned to relax, to leave the intensity of our work at the hospital. This Friday I was quiet but enjoyed listening to the jokes and gossip about which doctor was dating which nurse. Friday afternoon happy hour ended around seven as everyone went home to family.

Every Friday evening I visited my great uncle, Henry Land. Uncle Henry was eighty-one years old and perhaps the wisest and most loving man I have ever known. He and my Aunt Edna had been pillars in Christ Church Episcopal Cathedral. He lived in a big old mansion on Third Street over by Transylvania University. I loved his home. Giant columns accented the front porch and stood tall and white against the red brick. Since someone else had to clean up the acorns and rake the leaves in the middle of winter, I loved the pin oak trees that filled both the front and backyards and made wonderful shade in the summer.

My Aunt Edna had died four years before, and Uncle Henry was lonely. He and Aunt Edna were childless, and I was the only great niece close to them. Usually Uncle Henry and I had dinner and played Scrabble. We used the giant screened porch at the back as long as the weather allowed and the library when it was too hot or cold outside. I could rarely beat him, but I was good enough to make it a game. The Friday after Jane Doe came into the ER, I didn't even make it a game. Distracted and exhausted, I struggled to make three-letter words and excused myself to go home and early to bed. I was on call again on Saturday.

That Saturday, three days after the initial surgery, we realized Jane would need the respirator for an extended time, and because prolonged use of an endotracheal tube can damage the vocal cords, we placed a tracheostomy tube through her neck to connect the airway to the ventilator. There had been signs that Jane was about to wake up before this second surgery. She was clearly more responsive to pain; however, she had to be put back to sleep so as to prevent struggling against the respirator. For days we had to increase the pressure that forced oxygen into her rigid, fluid-filled lungs. Then, as her lungs healed slowly, we began to decrease the pressure.

Twelve days after the second operation, the abdominal incision fell apart and her bowel spilled out onto the bed. Her nurse covered this evisceration with saline-soaked towels. In Jane's third trip to the operating room we resutured her wound. This time we placed a row of large mother-of-pearl buttons on each side of the incision. A very heavy rope-like suture material connected the buttons of one row to the corresponding button on the opposite side. These retention sutures, as they were called, ran beneath the strong fascia layer that held her together and made her belly look like a double-breasted suit. If the incision did not heal this time, these sutures would prevent the disaster of a repeated evisceration. Dr. Gray criticized Dr. Armstrong for not using retention sutures during the original surgery.

With each new disaster I wondered if she really was one of the "lucky ones." Fortunately, she was spared kidney failure and she was alive, barely.

"It sure is quiet in here," I said as I sat down to write my notes in the ICU. It was Sunday of Labor Day weekend, my first holiday weekend on call, the first of years of holidays on call, and the start of my last week on the gynecology service. In one week I moved on to Psychiatry. The third year of medical school was divided into ten-week rotations. Large services, like Internal Medicine, Pediatrics, and Surgery, spanned ten weeks, but smaller services were five weeks. Obstetrics and Gynecology shared the ten weeks with Psychiatry. I don't think this was meant to imply that women needed Psychiatry more than men, but sometime in the Dark Ages someone did name hysteria from the Greek word for uterus.

"I volunteer to work holidays for this quiet," a nurse said as she emptied the catheter at Jane Doe's bedside. "I would go crazy if I had to be conscious in one of these beds for a month."

As I thought about what she said, I pictured myself in one of those beds. Bright lights burned twenty-four hours a day. There were no windows. A clock on the wall read seven, but was it morning or night? Only a thin curtain separated your bed from one on either side. With few exceptions you were in constant view of the nurses' station. People talked, laughed, cursed, cried, and died in hearing distance. Metal instruments and pans crashed onto the metal carts and tile floors. Water was turned on and off. Carts rolled in and out with medicines and equipment. There was nothing in the way of food for patients, but the aroma of popcorn was always present as workers grabbed a snack during their five-minute breaks. If the Occupational Safety and Health Administration had objections, they kept quiet about it back then.

Unconsciousness has its benefits if you have to be on a ventilator in a place like that, but my patient was about to wake up. We were giving Jane smaller doses of sedation since we were trying to wean her off the respirator and she had to assist with that process. For several days she had squeezed my hand on command. As I wrote my notes I became aware of her watching me. Because she still had her tracheostomy tube, I took a notepad and pencil to the bedside so we could communicate.

"Where am I?" she wrote.

"University Hospital, Intensive Care."

"Are you one of my doctors?"

"Yes, I'm Dr. Cara Land. I am the medical student assigned to your case."

"Who am I?"

"What? You don't know?"

"No, I can't remember anything."

"I don't know who you are. You had no identification when you came in."

"When was that?"

"August 5."

"What day is today?"

"September 5."

"I've been here a month?"

"Yes."

"What's wrong with me?

"You hemorrhaged and got an infection from an abortion that went wrong."

"I wouldn't do that," she printed with big bold strokes.

Having no idea what to say, finally I squeaked out, "You should rest now."

I went to the house staff lounge searching for Dr. Armstrong, taking the notepad with me. "Jane Doe is awake. I let her write some questions."

"Good. What did she say?"

"Look." I gave him the notes.

"She doesn't know who she is! What did you say?"

"I told her I didn't know who she was either. I didn't comment after her emphatic response as to why she was here."

"We'll need to get a psychiatry consult as soon as we get the trach tube out and she can talk."

By the end of the week Jane had been weaned from the respirator. Her tube was out and she could speak. We moved her from Intensive Care to a semiprivate room on the floor. The gynecology team got a psychiatric consultation as her amnesia continued along with her absolute denial that she would have had an abortion.

As it happened I was on the psychiatry team that came to Jane's room for the consultation. She told us the same thing she had said before. The opinion of Dr. John Whyte, the chief of Psychiatry, was that she was in a fugue state due to the physical stress of the abortion, infection, and blood loss and the emotional stress that could produce such absolute denial of the abortion. He agreed to transfer her to Psychiatry as soon as she was physically able, which was a matter of days.

Jane's room on the psych ward was a small dormitory-type room with two single beds and two chests. Flowered curtains hung at the windows, and carpet covered the floor. With the walls painted a bright yellow color, it looked less like a hospital room. As the census was down, Jane did not have a roommate.

"I'm your student doctor again," I said when I visited her on the day after her transfer. "We'll be spending a lot of time together. At least now I don't have to draw blood and keep an IV going."

"That's good." Jane was wearing a pair of gray slacks at least two sizes too large and a blue turtleneck shirt that fit. White tennis shoes with no socks completed her outfit. "How do you like my outfit?" She smiled. "I got these out of the used clothing closet. I guess I'm not the first to arrive with no clothes."

"Those pants could fit better," I said. "You've lost a lot of weight since you arrived, but I doubt they would ever have fit. How are you feeling?"

"I guess I'm better. I don't hurt. I feel a little stronger, but I'm so tired."

"That will gradually improve. It will probably take a year though before you are as strong as before."

"What is going to happen to me here?"

"Dr. Whyte says he wants to try treating you with hypnosis. The idea is that under hypnosis, you may remember who you are. Contrary to what a lot of people think, you remember what happens under hypnosis unless you are given a specific suggestion not to remember."

"That sounds reasonable. When is he going to start?"

"This afternoon."

That afternoon, Jane came to a small treatment room where Dr. Whyte performed the hypnosis. Besides Jane, only Dr. Whyte, the resident, and I were present. Dr. Whyte explained his plans for hypnosis before he began, and Jane nodded agreement. She sat in a gray overstuffed recliner. The rest of us had straight chairs. The resident and I sat on either side of the recliner, out of her direct view.

Dr. Whyte cleared his throat, leaned forward in his chair and said, "You *can* be hypnotized. Contrary to common perception, hypnosis is not about being weak and suggestible; it is about being able to focus, to concentrate on exactly what I say." Jane nodded and he continued in a low, even tone. "Now sit back and relax. Close your eyes. Feel the chair as it supports your head, your shoulders, your upper back, your lower back, your legs, and your feet." I could actually see Jane's muscles relax. She sank down into the chair, and her head rolled slightly to the left.

"Now relax your face, your eyebrows, your nose, your cheeks, and your chin." The lines in her face disappeared as the muscles relaxed.

"Take a deep breath and slowly let it out." She did. "Now relax your shoulders, your upper arms, your lower arms, your hands, and your fingers. Take a deep breath and blow it all the way out. With each breath you will feel more and more relaxed, deeper and deeper asleep." Jane swallowed. He continued in this way down her whole body. Then he said, "Picture yourself in an elevator going down. Watch the numbers as it goes down, down. With each floor you are going to be deeper and deeper asleep, more and more relaxed. You may hear a noise outside—just let it float in and out of your mind; concentrate on my voice. You have no place to go, nothing to do but be here and relaxed." A look of absolute peace came over her face.

Dr. Whyte waited a few moments. "Picture your childhood. You are four years old. Your mother is calling you to come to dinner. What do you hear?"

After a long pause, in a childlike voice Jane said, "Jessie, come wash your hands, supper's ready." I could hardly keep quiet. Her name was Jessie.

"Is there anything else?"

She paused longer this time. "No."

"Picture yourself a little older. A friend has come to visit. What does she call your mother?"

After an even longer pause Jessie said, "I can't see anything." In spite of several attempts Dr. Whyte made to indirectly approach her last name, at least her maiden name, she could remember nothing else.

"Okay, Jessie," he said in the same even tone, realizing that he would likely not learn anything else today. "Slowly, I am going to count to ten. As I do you are going to wake up. When I get to ten you will open your eyes and remember everything we said. You will also feel rested and relaxed." As Dr. Whyte said ten, Jessie opened her eyes. "It's nice to meet you, Jessie," he said.

"Thank you."

"That is enough for today. We will try again tomorrow."

"I feel wonderful," she said.

"Yes, Jessie, hypnosis has that effect."

The next afternoon Dr. Whyte proceeded in the same way. After Jessie appeared completely relaxed, he asked her name. Her only response was Jessie.

"Let's go back to your childhood, Jessie. Can you see any picture from when you were little?"

"I remember my father helping me pick green beans. My mother helped me break them and showed me how to cook them. We put them in a pot, covered them with water, and cooked them for a couple of hours. After a while, we added some bacon fat and salt. When they were finished, we ate them with chopped onions."

She obviously grew up somewhere in the South, I thought to myself.

"How old were you then?"

"Six."

"Can you remember being older."

"I remember going to church one Sunday." Jessie started to tremble. Tears dripped onto her blouse. "The preacher said when you sin, you go to hell. He said that when you are in hell, you can look up and see your loved ones in heaven."

Dr. Whyte clenched his fist and got red in the face. "How old were you then, Jessie?" His kind voice belied his expression.

"I think I was eight."

"I think this is enough for today," he said. "As I count to ten you will gradually wake up. When I get to ten, you will open your eyes and remember everything that has happened."

After Jessie left the room, Dr. Whyte said in a harsh voice, "That kind of Christianity is why she's in this shape. She can't face what she's done. Whatever happened to love and forgiveness?" I thought that Dr. Whyte must be a nonbeliever, but I learned later that he was a devout Christian.

Every weekday for the next week, Dr. Whyte hypnotized Jessie. Under hypnosis she remembered elementary school. She not only loved it, she excelled and was almost every teacher's favorite. She got to be the assistant who collected lunch money from all the classrooms and took it to the principal's office. In the seventh grade she assisted the photographer who took the school pictures. She remembered a story about her teacher who, when the photographer asked her to drop her chin, said, "Which one?"

"I love the hypnosis," Jessie told me one day. "I feel so energized. I feel confident, like I could do anything. Why can't I remember who I am?"

"I don't know." I realized how pathetic that sounded and wanted to be able to give her an answer.

"I do remember how to do things, some I haven't even told Dr. Whyte about. For instance, I know I can sew. If I had a sewing machine I could take some of the clothes in that closet and make them fit me. I'm so tired of wearing these clothes. I wonder what happened to my clothes." It was the first real complaint I had heard her utter.

"The ER nurse cut them off. They were soaked with blood."

She looked startled by my comment. "I forget that you know more about my life's history than I do."

"Do you think it would be helpful for me to go over all that happened to you here at the hospital? You know, while you were unconscious."

"It couldn't hurt . . . uh . . . . could it?"

Her medical chart, quite thick by this point, was useful to refresh my memory. I told her about where and how the EMTs found her, about her blood transfusions and three surgeries. I showed her the pathology report that proved she had been pregnant and had a perforation in her uterus. I even told her about the red rubber catheter. I told her about the scars that proved she had delivered at least two children and probably three. At that point she stopped me.

In a hushed voice, she said, "Three." She looked down at her hands folded in her lap. "I have deserted three children. How can I have done this? How can I live with it?"

16

When she said no more, I asked, "Would you like me to go?"

"Yes, please."

That evening I couldn't get Jessie off my mind. I had no children, but I could imagine that the thought of deserting three children would be a terrible blow. *Could a loving mother do what she had done? Maybe I should not have told her. No, she needs to know. She even needs to accept what she has done, if she is ever going to figure out who she is. Maybe knowing, even though it is painful, could trigger some memory of them and of herself.* I wondered if we were doing all we could to find out who she was. That was the only way we could get her back to her children. I had an idea.

As I dressed the next morning, I thought about Jessie wearing the same clothes day after day. I would have been happy to give her some of mine, but we were so different. I was short and stocky and she was tall and thin. I resolved to go shopping over the weekend, and I hate shopping. As soon as the morning staff conference was over, I went to the office of the social worker, Ann Long.

"Do you have a few minutes?" I asked when she answered the knock on her office door.

"Sure, come in."

"I'm the student doctor for Jessie Doe," I began. "I had an idea about how we might find out who she is, and I wonder if you could help me?"

"What do you have in mind?"

"Can we check with the police to see if any Missing Person reports were filed around the time she came into the hospital? She probably left home on the third or fourth of August."

"We did check. We gave a photo to the police, and at least two people failed to identify her. I can ask a friend in the police department to check again since we now know her name is Jessie."

"Would you? I hope we can find out something. I told her yesterday that we think she has delivered three children, and she became very upset."

Ann echoed my thoughts. "Maybe it will stimulate her memory."

"I had hoped so, but it didn't right away. I guess we'll know this afternoon at her hypnosis session."

The hypnosis session started as usual. When Dr. Whyte asked Jessie about any thoughts that came to mind, tears welled around her closed eyelids and she sobbed silently. The next day the session ended the same way. I felt responsible and thought I should confess what I had done.

"Dr. Whyte," I called as he was leaving the room. "May I speak with you?"

"Sure, come to my office."

He closed the door and turned to face me. "What is it?"

"I think you know that I was Jessie's student doctor on GYN."

"Yes."

"She asked me to tell her everything I knew about her medical case, said I knew more of her life history than she did. So I told her. When I told her we thought she had delivered three children, she became very upset and said she had deserted them. She asked me to leave her alone and hasn't wanted to talk about anything of importance since. That was the day before she started crying during hypnosis. I am so sorry."

"Don't blame yourself, Cara. It is important that she know as much as she can about herself. That information could just as well have stimulated a breakthrough. It still might, but I'm doubtful. I believe this sobbing indicates she had a major depression before any of this ever happened. That may be at least part of the reason she had an abortion when she has so clearly stated her belief that it is wrong and she wouldn't do it."

"I asked Ms. Long to check Missing Person reports for the time Jessie came to the hospital. She said they had checked, but it was worth checking again now that we know her first name. I hope that turns up some possibilities."

"Good thought."

"Ms. Long should know something by tomorrow."

When we discussed Jessie in the next morning conference, Dr. Whyte shared his thoughts about a previous depression being the cause of Jessie's tears. He also said we would give up on hypnosis soon if there was no change.

"Ms. Long," Dr. Whyte said, "I believe Dr. Land asked you to check on something. Do you have anything to report?"

"Yes." Ann Long had a note of excitement in her voice. "A woman named Jessica Green was reported missing on August 4. She lived in a small town about sixty miles northeast of here." Murmurs filled the room as everyone thought we finally knew who Jessie was.

Ms. Long continued. "She left home after sending her three children to school and never returned. The police asked the husband to come to Lexington to look at the photo, but he said it wasn't necessary—that his wife wasn't pregnant and would never have an abortion. I was sure it was our Jessie and called the number listed on the report. A woman named Mary answered the phone and said that Jessica Green had been found in California about two weeks after the report was filed. No one else was reported missing around that time." Our disappointment created a deafening silence.

That Saturday as I dressed for the day, again I thought of Jessie putting on those same ill-fitting clothes and remembered what she had said about a sewing machine. I had an old Norse portable sewing machine—nothing fancy, but it sewed a good straight stitch. Before going shopping, I decided to take my sewing machine and several spools of thread in different colors to the hospital for Jessie to use. Because it was the weekend, I would be able to park close to the door. The old machine was heavy and had a broken handle. As I struggled to get it into the hospital, a handsome orderly walked by with an empty stretcher and took pity on me.

"I'm taking this stretcher back to the fifth floor. Why don't you set that machine on it and I'll take a detour to your destination."

When I nearly dropped the machine on his toes, he helped me place it on the stretcher. I stood straighter and smiled. "Thanks, this is great. I'm going to the third floor."

When they buzzed us into the psych ward, he rolled the machine down the hall to the recreation room and set it on a table. "I'm off to the fifth floor," he said as he wheeled the stretcher back out the door.

"Thanks again." A big grin was his fee for service.

Jessie was standing with her back to the door. When she turned around and saw the sewing machine, I was rewarded for all the effort by a big smile. "This is wonderful! Come look through the closet with me," she said.

We found three outfits in the psych clothes closet that she thought she could alter. By Monday, she had finished a wool jumper made from a red-and-blue reversible fabric with the bodice made from one side and the skirt made from the reverse. It matched the blue turtleneck she had been wearing. With the extra fabric from where she had taken it in, she made a belt to match. She spent Monday making the gray slacks fit. She was like a woman on a mission, and by Tuesday evening a gray-and-pink blouse four sizes too large fit her like a glove. The next day a pair of black pants, again so large that she used the extra to make a little bowtie, became part of her wardrobe. She teamed them with a white cotton blouse. I went shopping after all but bought only some new panties and a bra. Nobody should have to use borrowed underwear, I reasoned.

At the hypnosis session on Tuesday afternoon, Dr. Whyte told Jessie that he intended to continue trying hypnosis for the rest of that week. "I have asked Ms. Ann Long, our social worker, to begin working on a plan for your discharge. She will meet with you today or tomorrow. I want to reassure you that even if the hypnosis does not work, we believe you will get your memory back at some point. You may see someone or someplace that is familiar, and that will trigger memories. That is not likely to happen here in the hospital. Or your memory may return after you have more time for healing and distance from this recent trauma."

Jessie's eyes looked like targets on a dart board. She gripped the chair like she was about to do a dip in a rollercoaster. "What will I do in the meantime?"

"We recognize the problems that face you, and those are the things that Ms. Long can help with."

At the first meeting with Ms. Long, which Jessie asked me to attend with her, it became clear just how big these problems were. Jessie had nothing other than the clothes she had altered—no name, no job, no money, no place to live, no friends or family, no Social Security number, no record of education, and no known job skills. She was the social worker's worst nightmare. Fortunately, Ms. Long's motherly personality and air of confidence made you feel like she could solve any problem.

"First we need to decide on a name," the social worker said. "I assume Jessie is short for Jessica, but in the absence of a last name we need to pick one. Who would you like to be?"

Jessie sat up straight, pulled her shoulders back, and made eye contact with Ms. Long. "I just read an article about the Scots clans, their crests, and their mottos. The crest for the Fergusons is a honey bee on a thistle and the motto is 'out of adversity, sweetness.' Let's call me Ferguson. I can hope for sweetness to come."

"That works for me. When would you like your birthday to be?"

"Dr. Land, what is your birthday?"

"September 17, 1947," I said.

"I suspect I'm older than that. Let's say my birthday is September 17, 1940. No. Wait." A barely perceptible frown came across Jessie's face when she remembered something of her past. It had happened every time she remembered something under hypnosis. "I don't know the year, but my birthday is April 1. I remember a birthday party when I was seven. A little boy teased me about being an April fool. Let's make it April 1, 1940."

"I doubt you are seven years older than me," I said.

"I bet I am. You said I probably had three children. You don't have any." With that statement a look of profound sadness came over her face; the light left her eyes and she seemed to shrink.

Ms. Long saw the change in Jessie and patted her hand. "I'm not sure how we will get around not having a birth certificate, but I will think of something. At any rate, the next step is to apply for a Social Security number. When you get the number, we can apply for a medical card to help with this hospital bill and you can get a job. I'll also check what living arrangements are available."

"Thank you, Ms. Long. I'll try to think of some things I might be able to do for work."

"Good idea. I'll get back to you as soon as I know anything."

Jessie heard no more from Ms. Long for the rest of the week, and as Dr. Whyte expected, nothing more came of the hypnosis. While Jessie sobbed during the sessions, she seemed upbeat and hopeful when awake. The amnesia protected her from whatever pain her past held.

That Friday when I visited Uncle Henry my mind was not on the Scrabble game.

"What in the world is on your mind, Cara? You are miles away. Care to talk about it?"

"I can't say much, Uncle Henry. There is a patient who troubles me. She has amnesia, and we don't know who she is either. She has no money, no job, no family, and no place to go and she has to be discharged soon."

"What sort of person is she?"

I thought for a moment. "She is very attractive and seems to be quite capable. You should see how she made alterations on clothes from the used-clothing closet the hospital keeps for patients who have none. By the end of the first week, in addition to the three outfits she did for herself, she had altered something for four other women. She even altered a coat for one older gentleman who always complained of being cold. All the patients seem to like her. I noticed she plays games with them, and they laugh at things she says."

"Do you trust her?"

"What do you mean?"

"Well, would she steal? Is she a gossip?"

"No, I don't think either would be true of her, but I have no way of knowing."

"Can she cook?"

"I don't know. Why do you ask?"

"I need to hire a new housekeeper. Mrs. Mason is leaving to take care of her new grandbaby in Chicago. I was thinking maybe this woman could live here in Mrs. Mason's room and work for me. I would want to meet her."

"Uncle Henry, I think she would be great. She couldn't do heavy work for a while—she's recovering from surgery—but I think she could do what you need."

Uncle Henry put M-E-M-O-R-I-E-S across two triple word scores in the right upper corner of the board. "That's 13 times 3 times 3 plus 50 bonus points, 167. If she were here, you could keep an eye on her. I can tell you are concerned about her. Find out if she has any interest in such a job. If she does, then I will come and meet her."

I hugged him. "Uncle Henry, you are the smartest and best man I know. She doesn't have a Social Security number and may not be able to get one for some time."

"That would be okay. We wouldn't need it until next year. I wouldn't pay much above room and board anyway until I see how she works out."

CHAPTER 2

Uncle Henry liked Jessie and she liked him. They made a simple contract that said she would cook, clean, and do laundry in exchange for room and board. If she got her Social Security number, then she would get a driver's license and add shopping and driving Uncle Henry to her duties. At that time they would agree on a salary in addition to room and board. Jessie left the hospital a week before Mrs. Mason vacated the housekeeper's quarters, so she stayed in one of Uncle Henry's guest bedrooms. The arrangement was perfect because Mrs. Mason was able to go over what would be expected of Jessie as well as some of Uncle Henry's idiosyncrasies.

On the first Friday after Mrs. Mason left, I went with some anxiety to dinner with Uncle Henry. I was pleased to see that the furniture and floors shone like they had not since Aunt Edna was in her prime. Uncle Henry invited Jessie to dine with us. Mrs. Mason never had, but he knew I would want to see how Jessie was doing. For his part, he seemed very happy with the arrangement. We howled at Jessie's impersonation of Mrs. Mason.

"Now, Mr. Henry likes an ice cube in his coffee. No cream or sugar, just an ice cube. Meals are to be precisely at seven, noon, and six. He doesn't like meat loaf so don't cook that. He prefers his main meal at noon, except on Fridays when Miss Cara comes to dinner. He likes something special fixed on Fridays. Miss Cara is like a daughter to Mr. Henry." Jessie captured the accent, tone, and cadence of Mrs. Mason's voice perfectly.

"Well, she got that right." Uncle Henry squeezed my hand.

"You don't have to fix special food for me," I said. "But these pork chops are delicious. How did you fix them?"

"Oh, they were easy. I just braised them in a dry skillet and sprinkled them with salt, pepper, and garlic powder. Then I made gravy, mixed it with apple sauce and the juice of one lemon, put them in the oven, and baked them, covered, at two-fifty for two hours."

"How did you know to do that?"

"I have no idea," she said. "It just seemed like a good idea."

"Jessie is a great cook, better than Mrs. Mason," Uncle Henry said. "Guess what else, Cara. She likes to play Scrabble. She's even pretty good at it, beat me once. Of course, she got all the good letters."

"Of course." I winked at Jessie. "Are you suggesting that Jessie should join our Friday night game? I'd like that." So it happened that every Friday evening, I ate a delicious meal and played Scrabble with my great uncle and my first patient. Those two became the dearest people in my world.

Uncle Henry's house had always felt safe to me, a refuge whenever life was difficult. Jessie seemed to feel that same sense of sanctuary, to be satisfied if not happy. She gained a little weight, got rosy cheeks, and recovered her stamina. Uncle Henry gave her some of Aunt Edna's clothes. They fit her, but of course they were made for an elderly woman. Jessie altered them to be rather stylish for a young woman, not that she needed them. She never wanted to go anywhere, even after Uncle Henry began paying her a small stipend and she had some money of her own. Only when she mentioned her children did her sadness show itself.

I finished Psychiatry and moved on to Internal Medicine but still had Jessie on my mind. She needed to be with her children. One day it occurred to me that if she had Rh-sensitization and complicated pregnancies, she would have needed to deliver in a high-risk obstetric unit. I made an appointment to see Dr. Steven Dunn, the head of Obstetrics. He had an interest in Rh disease and probably had a record of the patients at the university with Rh-isoimmunization. If he would let me look through the list, I could contact anyone named Jessie or Jessica. It was a long shot but worth the effort.

Unfortunately, no one was named Jessie or Jessica. I checked for the middle initial J. Nothing. I even called the University of Louisville and the University of Cincinnati and asked clerks to check, but I didn't have time to go there myself and I never got a report.

Thanksgiving came about six weeks after Jessie went to work for Uncle Henry. Since my parents were both deceased, I always spent the day with him. Jessie cooked a great meal. After he prayed, giving thanks and asking blessings on our food, Uncle Henry made his annual statement, "I declare this the official opening of the eating season." I smiled, having heard it many times, but Jessie roared with laughter. We had a wonderful day, but I felt concern that the coming holidays would be a problem for her. I need not have worried, thanks to Uncle Henry.

"Cara, when do you do your Christmas shopping?" Jessie asked during Thanksgiving dinner.

"Usually Christmas Eve. Why do you ask?"

She smiled. "I thought you might take me with you."

"Sure, maybe I will get it done sooner if I have company. I hate shopping."

"I think I don't mind, but I'm not sure."

"Christmas Day is on Saturday this year. I get off on Christmas Eve and don't start back until January 3, but I could probably find a Saturday before that."

I was on call both of the next two weekends—actually, didn't even get to stop by for dinner on either Friday evening—but on Saturday, December 18, Jessie and I went shopping.

"I'm sorry I haven't gotten over to see you and Uncle Henry. My internal medicine rotation is a killer," I said as Jessie got into my green 1967 Mercury Cougar. "I've been concerned about how you would feel about Christmas."

"I can see why you would worry, but you don't live with your Uncle Henry."

"I don't know what you mean." I pulled the Cougar away from the curb.

"He may not be a psychiatrist, but he is a wise man. One evening, right after Thanksgiving, he asked me if I would like to study the book of Luke with him. He said that he studies it in December every year. It's his favorite version of the Christmas story."

"I've heard him say that."

"I said, 'Sure, I'll study it with you,' so on December the first, right after breakfast, he said, 'Jessie, sit down. We need to start our study.' For a week we took turns reading aloud the entire book of Luke. Each day we used a different translation. He says it's important to read the whole book so that you don't take statements from the Bible out of context. 'That leads to misunderstandings,' he said. I doubt I have ever read an entire book of the Bible in one sitting before."

"I haven't."

"He said, 'Jessie, you have to be patient and prayerful. If you are, you will gain some new insight every time we read.' He's right. It's been amazing."

"What do you think helped you the most?"

"You know how people, even some churches, talk about Christmas and make it about family and friends. I agree that's better than making Christmas about getting gifts, but it's still not the point and it certainly would not have helped me this year or anyone else who is alone, for that

27

matter. Mr. Henry says Jesus' coming is all about love and forgiveness. Cara, if Jesus could forgive them for killing Him, maybe He can forgive me for killing my baby."

I turned to look at her, nearly veering out of my lane. "Jessie, I've never heard you say that before."

"I haven't, but somehow even the hope of forgiveness makes it possible."

"I thought you would get your memory back when you could admit to the abortion."

"Actually, I did too, but it hasn't happened. Mr. Henry has a theory on that too."

"So, you have told him everything?"

"Yes, he knows as much as I do. He thinks that my husband is an unforgiving man, maybe a very good, moral man, but stern and unforgiving, and I can't admit what I did to him."

"That's probably not a bad theory."

"Where are we going?"

"Turfland Mall."

"I hope they have a bookstore. Mr. Henry wants a New American Standard Version of the Bible. It just came out this year. He has five translations already, but I want to get it for him."

"What a perfect gift for him." I parked in front of the entrance.

"Cara, don't let me forget. I've made toffee for Dr. Whyte, Ms. Long, Dr. Armstrong, and Dr. Gray. I want you to take it to them on Monday."

"Wouldn't you like to take it yourself? I could pick you up at lunchtime. I'm sure they would love to see how great you look."

"I'm sure they would rather I knew who I am. No, I would rather you take it."

"Okay. It's a very nice gift. Nothing seems to please people at the hospital more than giving them food. Where did you learn to make toffee? Don't tell me. You just knew."

She laughed. "Actually, no. I found a recipe in the newspaper last week. It's really easy, surprised me. Mr. Henry loves it."

Christmas Eve was a Friday. That evening Jessie fixed dinner as usual, but instead of playing Scrabble we went to a service at Christ Church. I was exhausted from medicine rotation, so I went home early to bed. On Christmas morning Uncle Henry, Jessie, and I exchanged Christmas presents. Jessie gave Uncle Henry the Bible, and he was thrilled. You would have thought it was his only copy. I gave him a scarf and some other books I knew he wanted, but he liked the Bible best. She gave me a pair of lined wool pants that she had made and a matching sweater she had knitted.

"Jessie, these are beautiful," I said. "I'm going to go try them on."

When I came out to model them, I said, "They fit perfectly, unlike most of my pants, which are nearly always baggy in the butt."

"I could tell you were hard to fit," Jessie said.

"Thank you. They're perfect. I don't know when you found time to make them."

"It cut into our Scrabble time," Uncle Henry lamented.

"Here, open yours." I had gotten Jessie a hat, scarf, leather gloves, and boots that matched a coat of Aunt Edna's she had altered. Uncle Henry gave her a leather Bible with her name on it. It simply said "Jessie." She ran her finger lovingly over that name as big tears spilled from her eyes.

"It's mine, whoever I am," she said.

After Christmas, I invited Jessie to go to the movies or out to dinner often, but she usually refused. One Friday during the Scrabble game, both Uncle Henry and I nagged her about going out.

Uncle Henry used all his letters and scored 87. "You're a beautiful young woman. It's not right for you to spend all your time with an old geezer like me."

"You're not an old geezer, and I like spending my time with you."

"Uncle Henry's right, Jessie. Don't you want to have some fun?"

"I appreciate what you're saying, but I don't really think I should go out and have fun. I'm a married woman. Do you remember that tan line on my left hand where a wedding ring would have been? It has almost faded now, but I still know it's there. And I left my children. Are they having fun?" Jessie placed the word S-O-N on the board and did not even pluralize a word with the S.

"I'm sorry, Jessie. I hear what you're saying, but you're never going to see anyone or be anyplace that might trigger your memories if you stay in this house all the time. Don't you remember what Dr. Whyte said? You're not likely to regain your memory without some help."

"You're right. I'd forgotten that. I'll get out more when I get my Social Security number and driver's license.

"In the meantime, you could go out with me. Let's see a movie tomorrow. I'm off this weekend."

She agreed to go.

"The Academy Award nominations just came out. I saw them in the paper at the hospital."

"What got nominated? We could see one of those," she said without much enthusiasm.

A paper lay on the table beside Uncle Henry's recliner. I looked up the article about the awards. "Let's see. For best picture, it's *Cabaret*, *Deliverance*, *The Emigrants*, *The Godfather*, and *Sounder*. Do you know anything about any of them?"

"George said *Deliverance* was really scary. He read the book."

My breath caught in my throat. "What did you say?"

"I said . . . uh . . . George said *Deliverance* was really scary."

"Who is George? Is he your husband?"

"I don't know." Jessie's color blanched; her eyes grew wide and she started to tremble. I had hoped this would be the breakthrough that would trigger the return of her memory, but it was not to be. She remembered nothing more of George and that was the end of the search for a movie.

On the first day of February, I was paged to call Ms. Long, the social worker. "Is Jessie still with your uncle?" she asked when I returned her call.

"Yes. Is anything wrong?"

"I just wanted to follow up with her. Has she remembered anything?"

"We think her husband's first name, but that's all."

"So she still needs her Social Security number."

"Yes."

"I've had a terrible time trying to get it without a birth certificate. I even tried to see if I could get it through the State Department, as if she were an alien. You'd think she dropped in from Mars with as much trouble as they have given me. I hoped she would have remembered by now."

"So did I, but she doesn't go out much, so there is not really anything to trigger her memories. I can't say she is happy, but she seems to feel safe at Uncle Henry's."

"That's a blessing."

"Thank you for all this effort, Ms. Long."

"Tell Jessie I'll keep trying. It seems she has no choice but to try to build a new life and identity."

Days and weeks passed. Spring came and brought with it awareness of another passion that Uncle Henry, Jessie, and I shared. We all loved vegetable gardening. Uncle Henry lived on a large lot, a section of which he plowed up for vegetables. Not until Jessie did either of us realize how much you could plant in the area he plowed. She put green beans in with the corn so the vines could climb up the cornstalks. She put cucumbers and zucchini in cages like we had used for tomatoes so they grew up as well. Uncle Henry and I had never tried zucchini, so we were fascinated to see a small zucchini in the morning overgrown by evening. She also grew yellow tomatoes. Neither Uncle Henry nor I had realized how different and delicious they tasted. In addition to the vegetables, Jessie insisted on planting marigolds.

"My grandmother said they help to keep some of the bugs away," she said one day as we worked.

"And what was your grandmother's name?" I asked, nonchalantly.

"Mollie." Jessie's eyes widened, but this time she smiled, as if she could see her grandmother. "Her name was Mollie."

"What was her last name?"

She frowned as she thought about it. "I don't remember. I just feel like she loved me. What a nice feeling." No further memory was forthcoming.

When I told Jessie about the Social Security number, she didn't seem to mind as much as I would have thought.

"I don't want you to leave me anyway," Uncle Henry said.

"Why would I do that?"

"This isn't much of a life for a young woman. A Social Security number would give you options."

"It's enough for me until I know who I am, but I am supposed to get my driver's license and become your chauffeur as well as your housekeeper, remember?"

"That would be right. There's one other thing I want you to do too."

"What's that?"

"I want you to get your GED. You will need some documented education if you want to get another job or go to school. I won't live forever, you know."

"I hope you do."

"So do I." I squeezed his muddy hand.

Jessie took Uncle Henry's advice and asked me to find out from Ms. Long how she should go about studying for and taking the high school equivalency exam. Within the month, they were working in the garden again when I brought the mail.

"Here's a letter for you, Jessie."

"It's my GED results. Cross your fingers."

"No need to cross fingers, I already prayed about it," Uncle Henry said.

Jessie's hands trembled as she opened the letter. "I passed," she said with a smile. She made a dirty fingerprint on her letter as she twirled around and around in the yard.

"That's great, Jessie. I knew you would pass," I said. "Let me see your letter. You got it dirty. I can't believe it, fingerprints! Why didn't I think of this before? Come on, Jessie, we're going to the police station. They can fingerprint you and see if you they have a record of who you are."

"Jessie won't have a record," Uncle Henry said.

"People get fingerprinted for a lot of reasons other than arrests. It's at least worth a try."

The police were very accommodating but not hopeful. They printed all ten of Jessie's fingers and then the left and right hand fingers together. We left Jessie's address and phone number, and they agreed to call when they knew something. They told us it would be months before we would hear, but they would let us know either way. Both Jessie and I moped during dinner that Friday. We had hoped we could know something quickly, but this was twenty years before automated fingerprinting. Uncle Henry, who did not expect the fingerprinting to help anyway, told us about his plan.

"Now we need to get you enrolled in the university," he said.

"What?" Jessie and I said together.

"Jessie, dear, you are bright. You need to be educated. What do you think you would like to study?"

"I don't have money to go to school."

"I intend to send you."

"I'll have to think about this."

"Don't think too long. My friend in the College of Arts and Sciences will only hold the spot so long."

We were both stunned. He obviously had been planning this for a while. Jessie walked over and hugged Uncle Henry—just as I have countless times through the years.

The next day a catalog of University of Kentucky classes arrived in the mail, addressed to Ms. Jessie Ferguson. By the next Friday evening, Jessie said, "I have an announcement to make. I've decided that I want to go to nursing school. I think I have to do two years in Arts and Sciences and then apply for Nursing. I may be forty before I finish."

"That's okay. Who knows? Maybe someday we can work together."

"That would be nice."

Uncle Henry nodded. "Good choice. I might need a nurse as well as a housekeeper someday." His words were prophetic.

It was late June 1972 when I got a page to call Uncle Henry's home. I was working on the fourth floor; my last third-year rotation was Pediatrics.

"Cara, you need to meet me at the emergency room," Jessie said when she answered the phone. "I've just called the ambulance for Mr. Henry. I think he's having a stroke."

I was waiting in the ER when the ambulance arrived. Uncle Henry was conscious, but he had a headache, some right-side weakness, and a lopsided smile. Fortunately, his speech and swallowing seemed to not be affected. I thought Jessie's diagnosis was right.

"Jessie made me come," Uncle Henry said when he saw me. "Waste of time if you ask me."

"I guess we won't be asking you. At least you're still feisty."

"He didn't argue with me," Jessie said.

"It's the fault of that fool that nearly hit me."

"What fool would that be, Uncle Henry?"

"We were at the grocery store, and a man nearly hit us when Mr. Henry pulled out of the parking lot," Jessie explained.

"I told you I wanted you to drive me. I'm ready to quit it."

"And I said I would see if I can get around no Social Security number, get the book this week, and take the test. Don't go getting upset about that again."

"Give me your insurance card. I'll go get you registered," I said.

When I got back, the nurse had taken Uncle Henry's blood pressure and immediately left to get the doctor. "Two-twenty over one-seventy," the intern said when he came into the room. "It's a good thing you came on in. If you ladies wouldn't mind, step out into the hall. I need to do an exam."

The intern agreed with our diagnosis, and Uncle Henry was admitted. The hospital was full, but I wanted Uncle Henry to have a private room. I thought he would sleep better.

"No, no," he said. "I would rather have a roommate, gives me somebody to talk to when you and Jessie are working." So it was that Henry Land, one of the wealthiest men in Lexington, was admitted to a four-bed ward on the sixth floor.

With bed rest and blood pressure medicine, he improved and had very little residual weakness.

"You are a lucky man, Henry," the neurologist said when he came to discharge Uncle Henry. "It's a good thing you came when you did. You might have died or been paralyzed for the rest of your life if you had waited."

"I have Jessie to thank for that." Uncle Henry grinned at me as I waited to take him home.

"The nurse will bring you a prescription for blood pressure medicine. Take it twice a day. Make an appointment to see me in a month. You can leave after you get the prescription."

"Okay, doc, whatever you say. I don't want to come back here."

By the time Uncle Henry was discharged, Jessie had looked into getting her driver's license. She found it required a birth certificate and a Social Security number as we thought, and they were not willing to accept a letter from her doctor or Uncle Henry to get around that requirement.

Since the driver's license served as government issued ID, they said she would have to take it up with the Social Security office and she knew Ms. Long had already been working on that.

Uncle Henry insisted that Jessie start school in August, though both of us were hesitant to leave him alone for hours at a time. He said he could hire a nurse or "elder sitter" if necessary, but he wanted Jessie in school. About that same time, Jessie got a letter from the police stating that they did not find a fingerprint match. With her identity still in question, she saw the wisdom in accepting Uncle Henry's offer to send her to school. She rode the bus and began classes on August 16, the day I started my last year of medical school with an acting internship in Neonatal Intensive Care.

In early September, Jessie excused herself from one of our Friday evening Scrabble games. She had to write a paper for English. Uncle Henry used the opportunity for a private talk with me.

"Cara, I want to talk to you about my will."

"Uncle Henry, is something wrong?" I was concerned.

"No, dear. I'm fine. I believe you know that you are to receive the bulk of my estate. My other great nieces and nephews will receive only enough to keep them from contesting my will."

"So you've told me."

"I need to know how you feel about this house."

Now he had my curiosity. "What about it?"

"Do you want it? I mean do you have any attachment to it? You'll soon be a doctor and will inherit a lot of money. You could buy something closer to the hospital and perhaps more suitable for a young single doctor. This house is huge and a lot to take care of."

"Uncle Henry, I love to come here. I always have, but the attraction has always been you and Aunt Edna, not the house. If you want to do something with the house, by all means do it. It's yours to do with as you please."

"I want to know what you would think about my leaving the house to Jessie. She may still need a place when I'm gone."

"I think that's a wonderful idea."

"So you would be all right with it."

"Yes, of course."

"I would leave her enough money that she could take care of the house. She may not discover who she is, but even if she does, she may still need a home. It's large enough that she could take boarders if she needs more money."

"Uncle Henry, have you told Jessie?"

"No, I don't think I will."

Jessie's classes ended on December 8, with final exams the next week. When it was all over she had fifteen college hours and a 3.8 grade point average. She and Uncle Henry studied Luke again. This time I promised to read it with them. I wasn't there to read the whole book each day, but I read a chapter a day. There are twenty-four chapters, so I finished by Christmas Eve.

When I came to celebrate Christmas Eve, we read the whole book again in the King James translation. "This is my favorite translation of the Christmas story," I said. Both Uncle Henry and Jessie agreed.

"I want to ask you girls a question," Uncle Henry said at the end of our reading. "Chapter 22 talks about Peter denying that he knows Jesus. Verse 61 says, 'The Lord turned and looked straight at Peter.' My question is what do you think Peter saw in his eyes?"

Both Jessie and I were familiar with the story. One of Jesus' closest disciples, Peter, had promised that he would remain faithful even if the other disciples deserted him. Then within hours he denied he knew Jesus three times.

"I guess it would be disappointment," I said.

Jessie frowned as she did when she was thinking. "I think he would look hurt. His friend had denied he knew him."

"Ah," said Uncle Henry, "you're thinking about what you would feel. Remember, this is Jesus looking at Peter. When you really get the Christmas story, you will know that Jesus looked at Peter with love in his eyes." The Bible says Peter went outside and wept. So did Jessie.

After dinner we went to the Christmas Eve service. On Christmas Day we exchanged simple gifts. Our unlikely family seemed to have developed Christmas traditions of our own.

During my time off school for Christmas break I had a few dates with one of my classmates. He had a friend who wanted to meet Jessie, but she still refused to go out. Though the tan line on her left hand had long since faded, her commitment to that relationship had not.

_____

CHAPTER 3

In January of 1973, the Supreme Court ruled in the *Roe v. Wade* case and abortion became legal. On the good side, Betty the Butcher was out of business. On the bad side, millions of unborn babies would die and their mothers would live with the guilt and shame of it.

Saturday, January 13, dawned a beautiful, sunny winter day. Jessie and I decided to visit some antique shops in Washington, a small historic town about an hour-and-a-half-drive from Lexington. Jessie wanted an antique desk, and while I did not share her interest in antiques, I thought it would be a good way to get her out and into a new place. I was still feeling disappointed that her exposure to the university had not triggered any new memories.

We visited a number of antique shops on the main street of the charming little town. Jessie found desks she liked but none that she could afford. Her favorite was semicircular, made of wood and leather in a style designed by Thomas Jefferson. After a morning of frustration with the prices, we decided to have lunch and head home. One shop owner recommended a historic inn at the edge of town.

Built of logs in the year Kentucky became a state, 1792, the inn had been restored and renovated with electricity and running water. The owner and cook served soups, salads, and sandwiches at lunchtime and a full menu in the evening. We had finished eating and paid the bill when a couple came in.

The man was handsome in a rugged, Marlboro man sort of way. About six-feet-two, he stood straight and proud. Large square shoulders and powerful muscles stretched the sleeves of his blue shirt; blond hair curled around his collar. His big blue eyes twinkled with his easy smile. He accompanied a petite blonde woman who would have been rather plain except for her radiant smile. They sat in the middle of the room facing the door with her back and his side to us.

Jessie watched the man come in, absently fingering a curl of her long hair as she stared at him—a gesture I had never seen her do. She stopped speaking in the middle of a sentence and failed to notice when I asked her if she knew them. I touched her wrist to get her attention and found it hot; her pulse was racing and pounding so hard I could feel it through her blouse.

"Jessie, you're staring." I shook her arm. "Do you know that man?"

"Yes. I mean I don't remember him, but I know him. I am sure of it."

"Go say something to him."

"I can't."

"If you know him, he will know who you are. Don't you want to know?"

At that moment the man looked up and saw Jessie staring at him. His smile vanished and his ruddy cheeks went white. The woman, seeing his face, turned to see what had caused the reaction. He started to stand up, but the woman, who also seemed to recognize Jessie, placed a restraining hand on his arm.

"I must speak to her." With that he stood and came to our table. "Jess?"

"George?" she said in a soft voice, unlike Jessie's as I knew it. Then, in a bewildered sort of way in the voice I knew, she said, "I remember your name. I knew you."

"You knew me?" He sounded equally bewildered. "Of course you knew me. I am . . . er . . . was your husband."

Jessie fainted.

He helped me ease Jessie out of the chair and onto the floor. We elevated her feet and asked the waitress to get some smelling salts. "I'm Jessie's doctor and friend, Cara Land."

The man looked even more confused. "What's the matter with her?"

"I think she needs to be the one to tell you that rather than me. But I will tell you that she has amnesia. You are the first person she has remembered in a year and a half."

At that point, the blonde woman stood and in a meek little voice said, "I'll wait in the car, George."

"I'll just be a moment," he said with kindness in his voice.

"What did you mean 'was your husband?'" I asked.

"I divorced Jess about seven months after she left. When she left, I filed a Missing Person report and looked in hospitals all over the country. It wasn't like her to disappear like that. Then I got my credit card bill. She had paid her way to California on my credit card, and I'm still paying it off. There were charges for a baseball game in St. Louis and a bullfight in Colorado. Jess would never have done those things unless she was with a man. My lawyer said I should cancel the card and that I could divorce her after six months, so as not to be responsible for any more of her bills. Kentucky law says that after six months a marriage can be declared irretrievably broken if both persons agree or if one claims it and the other person doesn't contest. Since I heard nothing from Jess, the judge ruled on the divorce."

"I see." With a sinking feeling, I asked, "What is your last name?"

"Green. Look, I have to go. Mary is waiting in the cold."

"I don't know what will happen when she comes to. Can you tell me how she can reach you, in case she doesn't remember?"

"She doesn't need to reach me. I remarried six months ago."

"What about your children?" I asked as he walked away.

"I have full custody," he said as the door closed behind him. The waitress arrived with the smelling salts, and Jessie came to.

"Is he gone?"

"He had to leave," I said.

She was able to get up and sit at the table. I could only guess what might be going through her mind. At length, she said, "I assume he divorced me. He said 'was your husband.'"

"Yes, he said seven months after you left."

"It didn't take him long."

"He thought you had deserted him and gone to California with another man."

"Why in the world would he think that?"

"He got a credit card bill that paid for a trip across the country and events you would not have done alone."

"Oh, God. I had a credit card in my purse, and I didn't know to report it stolen. I'd only thought about an ID."

"Jessie, it's even worse." I nearly choked on the confession. "I never told you, but the hospital checked for Missing Person reports for the time you would have left home. We already knew your name was Jessie, and Ms. Long found a report that a Jessica Green was missing."

"Yes, Green. That's right."

"When she called to see if it could be you, someone told her that Jessica Green had been found in California. We didn't pursue it. If we had asked how they knew you were in California, we could have known then who you were. I am so sorry."

"You didn't know."

"I wish I had at least mentioned the name to you. It might have triggered something."

"Cara, I'm not sure I would have remembered if you had. I must have needed this time and distance from my life."

"Do you think you can walk? Let's get out of here."

"Can you take me by the house? I want to see the kids before we go back to Lexington. I need to stay with Mr. Henry until he can find somebody, but then I will be home at last."

Of all the painful things I had to tell Jessie, this may have been the hardest. "Jessie, George remarried six months ago. You can't go home."

She took deep breaths, like she couldn't get enough air. Her hands clutched the green-and-white plastic tablecloth like a lifeline for a drowning woman. "Mary Johnson, is that who he married?"

"I guess if that's the woman he was with. He called her Mary, and Mary was the name of the woman who told Ms. Long that Jessica Green was in California. She was at your home that afternoon."

"She would have offered to watch the children after school."

"She probably brought casseroles too," I said. That caused a momentary smile. "Well, he is an attractive man."

"Did George say anything about the children?"

"Only that he has full custody."

"I wonder what I can do about that."

"I don't know. Surely a judge will reconsider when he knows what really happened?"

"Can I tell a judge I had an illegal abortion? He might put me in jail instead of giving me custody of my children."

"I don't think most states prosecute women who have illegal abortions. I think it is just the people who do them."

Jessie loosened her grip on the table and stood. "At least I know who I am, who they are, and where they are. I will figure something out."

While we were in the café, the sunny sky had turned gray and snow mixed with sleet had begun to fall. The temperature dropped thirty degrees. Highway 68 from Washington to Lexington was a two-lane road, built by asphalting over a trail made by buffaloes as they walked to the salt licks along the Licking River. There were so many hairpin turns one wondered if the buffaloes had been into Kentucky bourbon. The normal ninety-minute trip back to Lexington took three hours. For the first hour Jessie said nothing. Finally I asked, "How much do you remember?"

"Everything." Some minutes later, she continued. "I remember meeting George. I was a sophomore in high school and he was a senior. He played on the basketball team. We met at the Dairy Queen after a basketball game. I thought he was the most gorgeous man I had ever seen. He pretended he wasn't interested in me, but he asked me out the next week. After he graduated, he went into the Marines for two years while I finished high school. We were married right after I graduated, and I got pregnant on our honeymoon. I lost that pregnancy but got pregnant again within a few months." After a little gasp, she began to cry. "Oh my babies, my babies."

I had so many questions, but I was afraid to ask them. Something had kept her from these memories for months. I wasn't sure she was strong enough to bear them even now. After another hour of creeping over ice-covered roads, Jessie spoke again, this time with a smile as she remembered her children.

"Jeff was twelve when I left home; Ellen was ten; Grace was six. Though Jeff was the boy, he was most like me. Ellen was her father's daughter, strong, outspoken, saw things in black and white. Grace was unlike any of us. She seemed self-contained. It was terrible punishment to send Jeff and Ellen to their rooms, but Grace didn't care. She would suck her thumb and retreat into her own little world. What must they have thought when I didn't come home?" Only the sounds of snow and ice hitting the car roof and windshield wipers scraping the window filled the silence that followed.

After two more miles of treacherous roads, Jessie continued. "Cara, I had three stillborn babies. The first one was between Ellen and Grace. We knew I had the Rh problem, but Ellen had not had much trouble and we were short on money, so I didn't get to the doctor early enough. With

Grace, I got in right away and she had intrauterine blood transfusions. Then after Grace, even that didn't save them. I had two more stillborn babies in three years. I couldn't bear to have another one."

"Is that why you had the abortion?"

"Yes. I told myself it was a pregnancy, not a baby. It was easy to believe since I didn't expect to have a baby at the end. You've never had children so you may not realize this, but the joy of feeling a baby move inside you is indescribable. I remember the first time I felt Jeff move like it was yesterday. I was hanging clothes out on the line to dry, and I felt this little quiver. I ran into the house and called my mother."

She smiled at the memory. "Mom told me she was making apple butter when she first felt me move. It wasn't long until Jeff was doing somersaults. He was very active all the way to the end. Ellen was a very active baby too, but she slowed some toward the end of the pregnancy. She was beginning to get sick. My first stillborn, a little boy, moved about ten weeks and then quit. Grace was active for only six weeks then she slowed down. They told me she had heart failure, and I almost lost her, but the intrauterine transfusions kept her going. She was the one delivered by C-section." Jessie turned away from me and stared at the snow falling in the woods along the side of the road.

"With the stillborn babies, they would begin to move and then stop. The sense of doom I felt when they stopped moving was as indescribable as the joy was when they started. I know it sounds crazy, Cara, but I couldn't bear to feel another baby move only to have those movements slow, slow more, and then stop altogether. I asked the obstetrician to do the abortion, but he refused. I worked in our little hospital as a nurse's assistant in the operating room. Once in a while we would have to do a D&C on someone who had an abortion. I thought that was the worst that could happen, and it would make the doctor do what I asked."

"Where did you deliver your children, Jessie?"

"At the perinatal unit at the University of Cincinnati. Why do you ask?"

"It occurred to me that you would need a perinatal unit since you were Rh sensitized, so I checked all the Rh cases at UK but didn't find you. I even called the University of Cincinnati, but they never got back to me. I wish I had pursued it more. I'm sorry."

"Cara, you did more than any doctor could have been expected to do. You have nothing to be sorry about."

"Did you tell George that you wanted to have an abortion?"

"No, he wouldn't even let me use an intrauterine device for birth control because they think that some pregnancies are aborted before you even know you're pregnant with that method. I knew he would never approve."

"Why didn't you take birth control pills?"

"I did after Jeff was born. After just nine months, I got a blood clot in my leg. They took me off, and I had Ellen within the year. I was willing to risk another blood clot, but they wouldn't give them to me after she was born. Pills were in really high doses then. I used a diaphragm with some success for a while before the first stillborn, but I got pregnant with that because I had it in wrong. They said the position of my uterus made it really hard to get it in right. The diaphragm and the stillborn are the reasons there are four years between Ellen and Grace. Then after so many deliveries, the diaphragm was uncomfortable."

"George could have used condoms."

"He did sometimes."

"Since Grace had heart failure, I assume the stillborn babies were because of Rh disease?"

"Yes. Every pregnancy was complicated, even with Jeff. The doctor said I got sensitized with the miscarriage. Usually people don't have a problem with the first pregnancy, but even Jeff was jaundiced and had to have an exchange transfusion. Ellen was delivered three weeks early and had the same problems with jaundice. Grace was delivered at thirty-two weeks by C-section after four intrauterine transfusions. With immature lungs as well as the jaundice, she had a respirator and four exchange transfusions."

"Why didn't they tie your tubes during the C-section?" I probably should not have asked, but this lesson in the horrors of Rh disease was terrible to hear.

"George is Catholic and he was against it. With the last two stillborn babies, I had intrauterine transfusions, but the babies died at twenty-five and twenty-two weeks. Labor was induced and I didn't have C-sections for those deliveries."

Jessie was quiet for a long time. My eyes were glued to the ice-covered road, so I couldn't see her face, but I heard her soft sobs and occasional sighs. At length she continued. "They told us we might have an Rh-negative baby; the chances were either zero or one in four, depending on George's parents' blood types. They were both Rh-positive, so I had no hope even though there was still a small chance. I had seven Rh-positive pregnancies, none negative. Only after the abortion did it occur to me that the last baby might have been Rh-negative."

I wondered what she remembered about the abortion itself, but I was afraid to ask. As if she read my mind, Jessie said, "That was the last thing I remember thinking before I passed out in that hallway."

When she said no more, I changed the subject. "Tell me about the rest of your family. Where do your parents live? Do you have any brothers and sisters?"

"My father lives in Illinois. He remarried soon after my mother died of breast cancer. She was only forty-seven years old. I lost her about six months before the first stillborn. She died in our home. Her suffering was horrible to watch, and she hated taking the pain medicine. Dad was good. He helped me take care of Mom, but as soon as she died he started seeing a woman he had known during high school. She lived in Illinois, so he moved there. With the stillborn babies, work, and the activities of the other kids, I haven't seen Dad since he moved. It was like losing both of them."

"I'm so sorry." Obviously, that wasn't a good change of subject.

"I have one much younger brother," she said. "He was still in high school when Mom died, so he moved with my father. He came to see me once after he came home from a tour in Vietnam but then decided to move near my father. I wonder if they even know I was missing."

After a period of silence, Jessie said, "Do you want to know something truly amazing? My maiden name is Ferguson."

It was dark by the time we got back to Lexington. I offered to come in with Jessie, but she said no. Guilty about being relieved at that response, I drove home and thanked God I could sleep through anything.

Unlike the usual Kentucky snowstorm of two inches, gone in a couple of days, this one produced four inches and stayed on the ground for almost a week. Sunshine on the white snow would have made it look cheery and fun, but the skies were gray. It was the kind of week in winter that makes one question Kentucky's place as a Southern state. Public schools closed, but the university did not, so Jessie showed up for class on Monday. Actually, she showed up through Thursday, but by Friday the weather had warmed and the roads were clear. She cooked chili for our dinner, borrowed Uncle Henry's car, and went to see her kids. I would have gone along, worried that she might faint again and need me, but in the end she insisted that she had to do it alone. She knew her driver's license had not expired as she had renewed it the April before she left home. While she was at home, she intended to pick up her birth certificate and social security card so she could get a replacement.

"How is she, Uncle Henry?" I asked as I arrived for Friday dinner.

"She doesn't talk about it. She's done all of her usual work, which keeps her busy, but then she stayed up late into the night cleaning out closets and washing curtains. I don't know if she is preparing to leave or just doesn't want to lie down and try to sleep."

"I'm worried about her. I should have gone with her when she went home the first time."

"What do you think you could do?"

"Uncle Henry, she fainted when she saw him. What if she isn't able to drive home?"

"Cara, it was a shock when she saw him. She's had all week to think about it. She'll be fine."

"What if he's abusive?"

"Do you think he is?

"No, he seemed nice enough. It's just . . . well . . . you never know."

"Cara, since you were a little girl, you've thought that you had to fix everything. You can't fix this. Jessie knows who she is now, and she knows what her life was before. She has to accept that her life can't be the same. She made a new life and so did her husband. She has to figure out how to bring the old and new together."

"What if she can't?"

"Then she will have to make a new life, different from both."

"I hope she comes in before I have to go home." I made three-letter words in that night's Scrabble game.

"I'm glad you're still here, Cara." Jessie saved me from the worst game I had ever played when she got home at nine o'clock.

"So am I. I wondered what happened today."

"I had to see my children."

"Did you see them?" I followed Jessie around as she hung her coat in the hall closet, put the teakettle on, and got chamomile tea, teapot, and cups from the cabinet.

"Yes, I saw them, but Jeff and Ellen wouldn't talk to me. They came home from school, saw me sitting in the living room, and went to their rooms. They didn't even say hello. Before I left, I went upstairs and knocked on their locked doors. They wouldn't let me in."

"I am so sorry, Jessie."

"Grace was Grace. She ran, threw herself into my arms, and clung to my leg the whole time I was there. She was always an independent little girl. This has affected her in a different way than it has Jeff and Ellen. They're angry with me, and Grace seemed afraid I would leave her again. She had never been afraid of anything. She cried when I left." At that, Jessie wept. "Why couldn't I have gone home before George married again?" What could anyone say to that?

After she collected herself, Jessie continued, "Mary wanted me to leave before George came home from work. Imagine that in my own house! Anyway, I insisted that I needed to talk to him about the children and I wouldn't leave. Finally, George came home. I couldn't tell him much with Grace on my lap, but I did say that my purse and credit card were stolen while I was unconscious. I nearly died and came to in the hospital with no memory of who I was or how I got there. He wanted to know what was wrong, and I said that I preferred not to go into it all in front of Grace. Then he wanted to know what I was doing there. I told him I wanted to see my children. He sneered and said, 'It seems they don't want to see you.' But Grace said, 'I want to see Mommy.'" The teakettle whistled interrupting Jessie's report. She made the tea then slumped in a chair at the kitchen table.

"George told Mary to take Grace upstairs. She cried and screamed as Mary took her away. George said, 'I think it's time for you to go.' I asked when we could talk, and he wanted to know what we had to talk about. When I said 'our children,' he said they were his children. 'No judge will ever give you custody,' he said. 'That may be true,' I told him, 'but I have a right to visit them.' Finally, he agreed to meet me in Paris next Friday to talk about it. Jeff has a middle school basketball game there. George will come early and talk to me before the game. Ellen and Grace will stay with Mary, and Jeff will be with his team."

I took the teabags from the pot and poured two cups of tea. "I'm glad you'll have a chance to talk alone."

"I want you to go with me, Cara."

"Why?"

"He will have questions about what happened to me in the hospital. You still know more about that than I do." I wondered if she was afraid to meet George alone.

I asked to leave early the next Friday afternoon, and Jessie and I drove to the picturesque town of Paris. We met George in a diner on Main Street, up the street from the courthouse. He was waiting when we got there.

"Why did you bring her?" he asked as soon as he saw me.

"She knows more about what happened to me than I do. I thought she might be able to answer questions that I couldn't." Jessie and I hung our coats on a coatrack attached to the booth where George sat with a cup of coffee in front of him. We sat side by side opposite him. Jessie looked beautiful. She had taken care to apply her makeup and fix her hair. She wore a beautiful purple cashmere sweater and black slacks. George, dressed in jeans and a UK sweatshirt, had not shaved.

"Okay, Jess. Level with me. Why did you go to the city?"

"I went to have an abortion."

"You what?" he said. "You were pregnant?"

"Yes, and I just couldn't do it."

"You could've told me."

"Could I?"

"Well, I never would have allowed you to murder our baby." He was red in the face and raised his voice when he spoke.

"Please, George, keep your voice down. I knew how you felt. I thought I could take care of it and you wouldn't know. I'm sorry. I was wrong. I never dreamed all this could happen."

"What did happen?" Before Jessie could answer, the waitress who had been standing by the counter listening came to take our order. She glared at Jessie as we asked for coffee. When she left, Jessie continued.

"After the woman performed the abortion, I started to bleed. At some point I passed out and someone stole my purse. When I woke up after a month, I was in the hospital and couldn't remember any of it. I even denied I had an abortion until Cara showed me the pathology report."

"Was this baby Rh-positive?"

Jessie looked at me. "Cara?"

"We didn't check a blood type."

"So you could have killed a healthy baby."

"There's a very low chance of that, but yes, I guess I could have. That didn't occur to me until after the fact."

"Why did you get amnesia?"

"The psychiatrist said they thought because of the multiple stresses, physical and emotional."

"Jessie nearly died, George," I felt compelled to add.

"What happened?"

"She got an infection, then shock lung. She was on a respirator for a month."

"Who's paying for that?"

"I am trying to get Medicaid. That will pay for most of it," Jessie said.

"I'm not paying a dime."

"I'm not asking you to."

"What are you asking me?"

"I want to share custody of our children."

"When hell freezes over. They're staying with me. You deserted them for a year and a half, and your cockamamie story about amnesia won't cut it with any judge in this country. Are you going to tell the judge you had an illegal abortion and then expect him to give you your children? He ought to send you to jail." The waitress brought the coffee in time to hear that remark.

"George, please. I know what I did was wrong, but you know I love our children, and you know they need their mother."

"Yes, I know better than you do. I know what they went through when you left, what we all went through. They have a new mother, and they are better now. I will not have them upset again, and I will not let you tell them that you killed their little brother or sister as an excuse for leaving them."

"I wouldn't tell them that, but they need to know that their mother loves them and didn't desert them on purpose."

"They don't want to be with you. Didn't they make that clear?"

"Grace does."

"What makes you think you could take care of them anyway? You surely don't think a judge is going to let you have the kids and make me pay child support after what has happened."

"I just know that I am their mother, and I want to be with them."

"Oh, you know that now do you?"

"I have a job as a housekeeper." Jessie's coffee sat cold and untouched.

"Where have you been living?"

"In the housekeeper's quarters."

"Do you think your employer is going to let you keep three children there?"

"No, well, I don't know. I will have to look into where we could live."

"Get back to me when you work that one out."

Jessie's arguments got less and less convincing as they talked. It seemed like she was actually shrinking. Finally, she said, "Please, George. Let me see them."

"Okay, Jessie. I'll make you a deal. You let this custody thing drop, and I'll let you take Grace every other weekend. I won't make Jeff and Ellen go with you when they don't want to. If they change their mind, they can visit you too. That's the best a judge would give you anyway."

Desperate for whatever she could get, Jessie said, "Can I get Grace next weekend?"

"No, you can pick her up the weekend after that. Next weekend is her birthday, and Mary has planned a party for her."

Jessie gasped and seemed to shrink even more. In a voice so low I could hardly hear her she whispered, "I'd forgotten that." Then after a pause, she raised her head and squared her shoulders. "I'll be there in two weeks then. Let's go, Cara."

I thought we would go straight home, but Jessie had another idea. "Would you mind going to the basketball game? This is Jeff's second year on the team, and I've never seen him play. Playing basketball was all he talked about the summer before I left. That fall was the first year he was old enough to play."

The gym was small, only ten rows of bleachers on each side of the court. At one end, tables were set up to sell popcorn and soda in cups with no ice. The teams were warming up when we got there. We were given a mimeographed sheet with each team's players, positions, and numbers. Jeff, number ten, was by far the tallest boy on either team. While Jessie had seemed excited about seeing Jeff, she became more reticent as we got to the gym.

"Maybe I shouldn't let him see me," she said. "I don't want to upset him before the game. Let's sit on the home side. His team is visiting, so he wouldn't expect me to be there."

I started to argue that he needed to know she cared enough to be there, but in the end I just took my seat and said nothing. Jessie didn't watch the game. She watched Jeff when he played and when he sat on the bench. If he saw her sitting on the back row, he didn't show it. Being a big Kentucky Wildcat basketball fan, I was used to watching really good basketball. This grade school game was different. Jeff's team won with a score of sixteen to twelve. He scored ten of the sixteen points. It reminded me of a story Uncle Henry used to tell about the first game he ever played. His team won five to three, and he was the high scorer for both teams.

I suggested we go and congratulate Jeff after the game. "It won't upset him to see you now," I said. I wish I had not.

We waited outside the locker rooms. When the team came out, two boys said, "Hello, Mrs. Green," but Jeff walked by and looked the other way. It may or may not have upset him, but it certainly upset her.

Jessie skipped class all week. When I arrived on Friday evening, Uncle Henry's furniture had lost its shine. Jessie came to dinner with unkempt hair, a wrinkled blouse, and red, swollen eyes. Dinner was delicious, chicken in a mustard-mushroom sauce with wild rice and a green salad. She was still taking care of Uncle Henry, if not herself. She ate only a few bites. Conversation was slow. Jessie spoke only when spoken to. Finally, I asked Uncle Henry if she had talked to him about having the children come every other weekend.

"I think we should try it," he said. "This old house hasn't had children playing in it since you were a child, Cara."

"I knew you wouldn't mind."

"There is plenty of room. They can use the two small bedrooms beside Jessie's room. I wouldn't even have to know they were here if I didn't want to."

"I can't wait to meet them."

"Well, you will get to meet Grace. I doubt the other two will come," Jessie said.

"All in its own time," Uncle Henry said. "That's in Ecclesiastes, you know."

"Yes, we know. What have you planned to do, Jessie?"

"If the weather is nice, I thought we would go to the park. If not, then I thought we could go to the library and get them cards so they can have books to read here that they don't have to carry from home."

"I told Jessie that she should go through the attic and see if she can find some of the children's games we kept for you, Cara. Grace may not want to play Scrabble."

"I played Scrabble with them at home. They didn't score like you do, Mr. Henry, but they liked to play."

When it came time for us to play Scrabble, Jessie asked to be excused. "I'm going to look for jobs when I go to Washington next week to pick up Grace. I ordered the Maysville paper, and it came in the mail today. I need to check the help-wanted ads. I applied for an official name change from Jessica Green to Jessica Ferguson, so I can use my old Social Security number and keep the college credits I earned as Jessica Ferguson."

"So you've decided to move back?" I said.

"It would be best. I could be there for the children's activities and see them more, even if I don't have custody."

"Where would you live?"

"That's the problem. There are very few apartments there, and I doubt I can make enough to rent a house."

"Jessie, I hope you know you can stay here as long as you want," Uncle Henry said. "Plus, you can use the car as much as you need to go there for the children."

"Thank you, Mr. Henry. I do know that, and I can't thank you enough."

Jessie went to class that next week but skipped on Friday. She left early for the job search, picked up Grace, and was back in Lexington by the time I came for dinner. Uncle Henry had suggested pizza for dinner. I was to pick it up at Joe Bologna's, an Italian restaurant near the university. Though that was not his favorite food, Uncle Henry thought Grace would like it and Jessie wouldn't have to cook. Ellen was at home, but as expected she refused to come, using ballgames and homework as excuses. Jeff was not even at home.

Unknown to Jessie, Uncle Henry also asked me to pick up an ice cream cake at Baskin Robbins. He decided that Grace should have a birthday party with her mother as well as the one she had at home.

Grace was adorable, a tiny little girl, much smaller than you would expect for her age. She had her mother's dark curly hair and blue eyes. She was so pale she reminded me of the way her mother looked in the ER. She noticed everything and asked questions nonstop. Uncle Henry delighted in showing her around the house. Her favorite room was his favorite, the library.

"I like to read." She ran into the room. "Oh, does the fireplace work? We have one at home, but we can't use it."

"Why, yes, it works, Grace, but I haven't had a fire for a long time. Would you like to have a fire?"

"Oh, yes, please, could we?" We were all warmed by that fire and by the child who suggested it. I wondered why we had played Scrabble by that fireplace for two winters and never had a fire.

Grace did like the pizza. She chose the one with onions, mushrooms, and green peppers along with pepperoni instead of the plain cheese which I expected she would choose. She ate one piece of pizza and a small slice of birthday cake. Uncle Henry had balloons delivered, which helped to make a party. He even had a present for Grace, a small gold heart necklace that had a Celtic cross engraved on it. It had belonged to Aunt Edna when she was a child. Jessie was as pleased as Grace with this second birthday party.

After Grace went to bed, Jessie told us about her job search. "First I checked at the hospital where I worked before. They had filled my job after a couple of weeks and didn't have any openings. The paper listed a receptionist job in an insurance agency, but that one was filled on Monday. The other jobs were in fast food restaurants, and they didn't even pay minimum wage. There never have been many jobs there for women with no skills. The best jobs are for nurses and teachers."

"Maybe you should stay here in Lexington long enough to finish your nursing education," I said. "You would be able to make a better living."

"That's true," Uncle Henry said. "You can bring the children here for weekends."

Grace and Jessie had a wonderful weekend. Saturday was a bright winter day, unseasonably warm. They went to the park and the library.

On Sunday they went to church with Uncle Henry and then Jessie took her home.

I had hoped that Jessie's sadness would lessen after she had a weekend with Grace, but just the opposite happened. On Monday, Uncle Henry called me as I was finishing in the clinic.

"Cara, I think you need to come and check on Jessie."

"What's going on, Uncle Henry?"

"She's been in her room all day, didn't go to class, and hasn't eaten. I'm worried about her."

"I have another patient to see. I'll come by in about an hour. Do you need me to bring dinner?"

"Chinese would be good."

When I got to the house, Uncle Henry answered the door. "I'll put the food in the dining room," he said. "Go see about Jessie."

When I knocked, a cold draft coming from under Jessie's bedroom door raised the hair on my arms. "Jessie, I brought Chinese for dinner. Come have something to eat."

"I'm not hungry."

"May I come in?" When there was no answer, I tried the door and discovered that it was not locked. Inside I found the window open with Jessie sitting on the ledge.

"Don't come any closer, Cara. I need to jump, but I'm afraid."

"Jessie, please come back into the room and let me close the window. It's freezing in here."

There were no tears, no frowns. She raised her head and looked at me momentarily before looking back at the ground below. Her eyes were as cold as the room—empty of hope, steeled in determination. "I can't live with what I've done."

"Please come in. We'll call Dr. Whyte. Maybe he can help you."

"There is no help for me. I've ruined everything. My children are better off without me."

"Grace isn't. She loved being with you."

"And it broke her heart when I left her, again."

"She'll get used to going back and forth. She can at least have you part of the time. Come on, Jessie. Give it some time."

Uncle Henry stepped into the doorway. "What's going on here?" When he saw Jessie on the window ledge, his voice changed and had an authority I had not heard before. "Jessie, you get off that ledge and back into this room this minute."

Jessie raised her head and looked into his eyes. He held her gaze for what seemed like hours but was in reality a few seconds.

"I should have died in that hallway, Mr. Henry."

"That's your opinion, but God has a different one. Besides, if you had died then, I might have died from that stroke. Come in, Jessie. This is as wrong as anything you've ever done."

Jessie pulled her legs up and turned to bring her bare feet back into the bedroom. Slowly, she jumped off the window ledge and took a step into the room. I slipped behind her and closed the window while she stood shivering. Uncle Henry took her into his arms, holding her as he had held me when I was a child and something hurt me.

"Get a blanket, Cara. She's freezing."

I stripped a blanket from her bed and wrapped it around her shoulders. Uncle Henry led Jessie downstairs to the library to sit by the fire.

I said, "I think I should call Dr. Whyte."

Jessie shook her head. "He can't get my life back for me."

"No, but he might give you some medicine to help you sleep and eat. That would help you deal with it. Don't you want to be able to enjoy Grace when she comes?"

"I'm not sure I should have Grace come anymore."

"Jessie, don't say that."

"I thought I was depressed after the stillborn babies. I should have been grateful for the ones I had. Now I've even lost them."

"You haven't lost them. Your relationship with them has changed, yes, but they are still your children, and they need you." I looked at Uncle Henry for help.

"You still have things to be grateful for," he said.

"Like what?" Jessie snapped. For the first time, she seemed irritated with Uncle Henry.

"Well, one or all of your children might get sick or die. Would that be worse than this?"

"I'm sorry." She hung her head. "You're right. That would be worse. I wouldn't be in this mess if I'd been grateful for what I had before. Cara, would you call Dr. Whyte?"

"Uncle Henry, if you will stay here with Jessie, I'll call him now." I left the room to make the call. Miraculously, I was able to speak with Dr. Whyte after evening rounds. He was concerned when he heard about the resolution of Jessie's amnesia and her suicide attempt.

"Dr. Whyte wants to admit you to the hospital."

"When?"

"Tonight."

"All right." Jessie stood and walked toward the stairs. "I'll pack a few things. At least I won't have to get my clothes from the psych closet."

Dr. Whyte saw Jessie in the ER and admitted her to Psychiatry. He was not at all surprised by her depression and started an antidepressant as soon as she got to her room. He wanted her to take the medicine for at least six months. Dr. Whyte did not consider shock treatments, which were a common treatment for depression at the time. He felt she had already had shock enough. Uncle Henry and I stayed with her until bedtime.

"I think we need to study the Psalms," Uncle Henry said, opening his Bible. "King David knew something about sorrow for making a mess of his life. The good thing is that God can bring good from the mess."

"I don't see how that will happen."

"That's the problem," he said. "You don't see, but someday you will. Do you remember the story of Joseph, the one with the coat of many colors that shows up in children's Bible storybooks? Next to Jesus, Joseph is my favorite person in the Bible. He was arrogant and favored by his father. His brothers were jealous and sold him into slavery. Then his owner's wife accused him of adultery, and even though he was innocent, they threw him into prison. Through all of this, he was faithful to God, who helped him rise to a position of power. In the end, he forgave his brothers and told them that what they did for evil, God used for good. You see, he saved his whole family because of the position he was in when a famine came. Someday, Jessie, your children will need you in a way you can provide now that you might not have been able to provide before."

"I can't imagine that."

"I know you can't, but God will redeem this." Even Uncle Henry was surprised at how soon we would see evidence of his prediction.

Uncle Henry visited every day. He brought his Bible, and the two of them studied the Psalms. Whether from the Bible study, Uncle Henry's wise counsel, professional counsel, or the medication, by the time Grace was due to come again, Jessie was sleeping better and eating some. Dr. Whyte agreed to release her on Thursday so she could pick Grace up on Friday.

CHAPTER 4

On Friday morning, Jessie cooked spaghetti sauce and meatballs for dinner, knowing it was one of Grace's favorites. After lunch she took Uncle Henry's car for the ninety-minute drive to pick up Grace. Before Jessie was back with Grace, Uncle Henry had built a roaring fire in his library. He wore a blue sweater, just the shade of his eyes. His full head of white hair was worn a little longer, and he looked ten years younger than usual. He seemed as excited as Jessie to have Grace visit.

I arrived shortly after Jessie and Grace got home. The three of us talked and finished dinner. Grace washed salad greens; Jessie cooked the pasta, and I mixed a box of brownies and baked them while we ate. Grace wore green corduroy pants and a sweater of the same shade. Having just had my color palette done, I wondered if Grace was a "winter" like me. I couldn't wear that shade of green, and Grace shouldn't either. Her face looked a pale yellowish-green color, not unlike the sweater, and she had dark circles under her eyes. She seemed energetic enough, but it crossed my mind that she might be sick.

After dinner, Grace joined in our Scrabble game. As she sat by the fire, her cheeks pinked up a bit, so I didn't think more about her color until I got home and tried to catch up on my journal reading. I kept seeing that pale green face. When I awoke on Saturday morning, I had this nagging suspicion that something was wrong. I hadn't planned to see them over the weekend but decided I needed to act on this concern. Even as a medical student, I had learned to pay attention to that intuition.

When I arrived at Uncle Henry's, Jessie opened the door and looked somewhat surprised. "I brought Spaulding's," I said.

"Cara, what are you really doing here? You hadn't planned to come today."

"Grace can't come to Lexington without having the city's best donut." I smiled at the little girl, who had joined her mother at the front door.

"And?" Jessie asked.

"Where's Uncle Henry?"

"In the library," Grace said. "Can I take him a donut?"

"Yes, Grace. That would be nice."

"Okay, Cara. What is it?" Jessie said after Grace had scampered off.

"I want you to take Grace to the doctor."

"What? This is only my second weekend with her? Why should I do that?"

"I'm concerned because she is so pale."

"She has always been fair."

"It looks like more than fair skin to me. Will you let me do a little exam when she comes back? I'll just look at her eyes and feel her neck." When I saw her hesitation, I said, "Jessie, please."

"What are you looking for?"

"Her eyes will tell me if she is just fair or if she's anemic. I would be checking her neck for enlarged lymph nodes."

"Okay."

When Grace returned from the library, Jessie asked her to let me check her neck and eyes. Her conjunctivae were nearly as pale as her skin. She had several small soft lymph nodes at the back of her neck.

"Jessie, I think Grace is anemic, and she has some enlarged lymph nodes."

"What does that mean?"

"I'm not sure. It could be a number of things."

"What do you want to do?"

"The pediatric clinic is open on Saturday morning. They could do a complete blood count, an exam, maybe some viral tests. They need to check her liver and spleen. It shouldn't take long. If I am wrong you'll still have most of the day."

"Grace, have you been to the doctor at home?" Jessie asked.

The little girl shook her head. "No. Am I sick?"

"Dr. Cara thinks you might be. We would like you to see a children's doctor."

"Will you be with me?"

"Yes, honey."

Fortunately, the clinic was not very busy and we got in right away. She saw Dr. Greeley, the chief of Pediatrics. After the exam and blood work, he reported.

"Grace's hemoglobin is very low, indicating that she is anemic as Dr. Land suspected. The red cells are very small, suggesting that this might be an iron-deficiency anemia. Her white cell count is slightly elevated. Her mono test is negative. My concern is that she has some atypical lymphocytes on her blood smear. I think we need to admit her to the hospital and do a few more tests."

Jessie's face blanched. "Admit her? What do you think is wrong?"

"I'm not sure at this point."

"Well, what do you think?"

"I think we need to rule out leukemia."

Jessie hugged Grace, who was sitting on her lap. "I will have to call her father. We are divorced, and he has custody."

Jessie called George and explained the situation. At first he tried to deny that there was anything wrong, accusing Jessie of trying to keep Grace with her.

"You speak to the doctor," she said as she handed the phone to Dr. Greeley.

When Dr. Greeley finished, George agreed to admission and said he would be there by afternoon. Grace was admitted to room 413, and Dr. Greeley consulted the pediatric hematologists.

Jessie and George both spent the rest of the weekend in Grace's room. Uncle Henry came to visit and invited George to change and shower or stay at his house for as long as Grace was sick. The next day, George accepted the shower. The only test completed before Monday was a spinal tap. Jessie held Grace during the procedure, and while her lip quivered, she did not cry. For a bone marrow biopsy and a lymph node biopsy, which were done on Monday, they sedated Grace and gave her a local anesthetic. By Thursday, when all the test results were back, George, who had gone home on Sunday evening for work, came back to the hospital. I was visiting when the pediatric hematologist, Dr. Greta Campbell, came to report. George frowned when Jessie asked that I be allowed to stay and hear the results, but no one disagreed.

"The good news is that the spinal tap results were completely normal and the lymph node biopsy showed benign reactive changes as children often have. Unfortunately, the bone marrow biopsy indicates that Grace has acute lymphocytic leukemia." Dr. Campbell paused to give them time to process this diagnosis. "This is an ominous diagnosis," she continued, "but there are some extremely good prognostic factors in Grace's case. One is that the anemia is from iron-deficiency, not from the leukemia, or at least not totally. While there are tumor cells in the bone marrow, they are not completely replacing the bone marrow. The other good prognostic factors in addition to the normal spinal fluid are the relatively low white count and the normal liver and spleen. This appears to be an early diagnosis, and we find the earlier the diagnosis, the better the response to treatment. You should be very glad that Grace's anemia was checked."

"What is the treatment?" George asked.

"She will get chemotherapy for at least six months. Hopefully, that will induce a remission. The length of the remission is variable. There are cases where it has been as many as seventeen years, but honestly, those are extremely rare."

"How long will she need to stay in the hospital?" Jessie asked.

"She will be in and out the whole time, probably more in than out. Before we start the chemotherapy, we need to give her a blood transfusion. You might want to donate some blood for her."

"I can't. I have antibodies," Jessie said.

"She has my same type," George said. "I can give."

"That would be good. She may have to be transfused more than once, and some people consider family-designated blood donations safer."

"Her brother and sister are the same type too," Jessie added. "How old do you have to be to give blood?"

"I'm not sure. We can check with the blood bank. How do you know so much about their blood types?"

"I had Rh disease." Jessie frowned and looked past the doctor as if she could see the lost babies. That evening George gave blood for Grace. While at the blood bank, he learned that the minimum age for donating blood is sixteen with parental permission. Thus even Jeff was still too young.

When George got back to Grace's room, I was about to leave. To my surprise, he said, "Dr. Land, I guess you are responsible for Grace's early diagnosis. Thank you."

"You're welcome, George, but please call me Cara. I am your friend here, not Grace's doctor."

"George, I've been thinking," Jessie said. "When Grace gets out of the hospital, would you let her stay with me? She will need to be in and out getting tests and chemotherapy. It will be easier on her not to have to make the trip back and forth from Washington."

"That might be best," he said. "The trips would be hard, and I have to work."

"Mr. Henry said you could stay at the house when you want to come and see her."

"He seems like a good man."

"He is."

"I guess we could try that arrangement for a while. She can't go to school anyway."

Jessie took incompletes in her classes and dropped out of school for the rest of the semester. George came every weekend to visit, and Jessie used that time to take care of Uncle Henry's home and cook his meals. During the week she stayed at the hospital. Grace had chemotherapy for six months. She was often sick, her little arms and legs covered with bruises. Her lips and gums bled. She had to be transfused several times, and her veins collapsed. Still, it was Grace who cheered everyone else. She found joy in the smallest things. When she could be out of the hospital, she spent hours in the library with Uncle Henry, who read to her. They plotted what they were going to do when she got well. They watched out the window as Jessie got a start on the spring garden. Uncle Henry held her in his lap and prayed for her.

On one occasion Jeff and Ellen came with George so they could see their sister in the hospital, but they did not stay with Jessie. Grace was overjoyed to see them, and while they were warm and loving with her, they were very cold with Jessie. This was only the second time she had seen Jeff. George seemed so grateful for help with Grace that some of his anger toward Jessie dissipated.

By the end of summer Grace was finished with her treatment and in remission. While her spinal test was negative, Dr. Campbell knew that the central nervous system was often the site of residual tumor that could end a remission. She asked permission for a course of chemotherapy applied into the spinal canal. This was not standard of care at the time, but something that was being considered and has since proved useful. George and Jessie agreed, and with that Grace's treatments came to an end.

In the meantime, I graduated from medical school on June 10, 1973. Uncle Henry came and took pictures. After we celebrated with dinner at the Coach House Restaurant, we went to the hospital to see Jessie and Grace. Since I was undecided about what specialty I wanted to pursue, I stayed in Lexington for a rotating internship, which I started on July 1 in the emergency room. I scheduled enough Internal Medicine and Pediatrics in my internship that the year would count toward either residency. In the end, I chose neither. I decided that Obstetrics and Gynecology was the perfect specialty, a combination of medicine and surgery, and endocrinology was my favorite part of medicine.

Come fall, Grace did not want to go home, and Jessie didn't make her. She argued that if Jeff and Ellen didn't have to visit her because they didn't want to, then Grace should be able to stay with her because she wanted to. In the end, Grace and Jessie won that battle. Jessie enrolled her in elementary school in Lexington, and Grace went the other way for visits every other weekend.

Jessie confided, "I think if we knew the truth, Mary wanted Grace to stay with me. George didn't want to fight both of us. Mary is afraid Grace will get sick again. Jeff and Ellen are old enough to take care of themselves, and Mary has a new baby. At least Mary is Rh-positive, and she had a healthy baby girl."

While Jeff and Ellen's attitudes toward Jessie may have helped her get Grace, they did not help Jessie's longing to be with them. Every other weekend she called to see if they would come for a visit. Basketball, football, baseball, and track all kept Jeff busy. Ellen was in cheerleading, the band, and 4-H. Finally, Jessie gave up hoping they would come to her and started asking if she could come and just take them to dinner. They did not agree to that either.

Most of what she knew about her two older children, Jessie learned from Grace and from their local newspaper. The *Daily Independent* arrived a day late, but she read every word looking for information about the children and their school events. When she took Grace for her weekends with her father, Jessie often stayed to watch a ballgame or listen to the band, but she rarely talked to them.

Grace, Jessie, Uncle Henry, and I spent that Thanksgiving Day together. After the prayer, Uncle Henry announced the opening of the eating season, and this time Grace laughed. Jessie and I just smiled. Most of our gratitude was for Grace. She seemed happy in her new school, and she did well. Her leukemia was still in remission, at least for the time being. Jessie was back in school and doing well. We were all learning to appreciate each day. Grace reminded us of that. The next day Grace went to spend the rest of Thanksgiving weekend with her father.

On December 1, Grace joined Uncle Henry and Jessie for their annual study of Luke. Uncle Henry told me one Friday evening after she had gone to bed that Grace's comments and questions were exceptional. "She adds a fresh perspective that makes this the best study I have ever done."

That Christmas Jessie had one of her children with her for the first time since she left home, and Uncle Henry had a child in the house for the first time ever. When I was Grace's age, I still lived with my parents. Grace stimulated a whirlwind of activity, decorating, baking, and even bell-ringing. Uncle Henry had been on The Salvation Army Advisory Board for years, and the board had a day to stand at a kettle and ring the bell to raise money. Uncle Henry had thought himself too old to do it until he thought it would be a good experience for Grace. In deference to his age, he was allowed to take a stool to sit during his hour of ringing. Grace loved it, and they attracted a crowd of givers when she and Uncle Henry sang Christmas carols. They had the largest kettle collection of the season, but probably because Uncle Henry slipped in a five-hundred-dollar check. As soon as they finished, Grace made plans to do it again the next year.

Grace and Uncle Henry found a lighted nativity set in the garage. They had to replace the lights, but it looked lovely on the lawn, and neighbors called to tell Uncle Henry how much they enjoyed seeing it again. Grace helped Uncle Henry pick out a real Christmas tree, which they decorated with Aunt Edna's antique ornaments. They bought four red stockings with white fur tops and hung them on the mantel.

Jessie baked sugar cookies, and Grace helped decorate them. She also made pounds of toffee and gave it to the mailman, the paperboy, the garbage men, Grace's teacher, her hairdresser, Grace's doctors, and the neighbors. Jessie and Grace glued glitter on the stockings to make our names.

Gifts were simple that year. Uncle Henry gave Grace a Bible. Jessie got her a doll and dollhouse, and I got extra doll clothes and furniture for the house. Uncle Henry and I bought Jessie a camera. She requested one with a zoom lens. "I want to record as much of Ellen and Jeff's lives as I can, and they don't let me get very close," she said.

January 1974 began a relatively uneventful year. I missed lots of Friday nights during that year and felt grateful that Uncle Henry was not alone. Grace went for regular checkups but miraculously remained in remission. Jessie worked extra hard in school to make up for the semester she lost during Grace's illness. Before we knew it, it was holiday time again.

On December 28, 1974, Jessie, Grace, and I went to Frankfort for the inauguration of Julian Carroll as governor of Kentucky. While the temperature was close to zero, the day dawned bright and sunny. We set off early in the morning to get a place on the front row to see the inaugural parade and take pictures. Ellen's band was one of many high school bands marching in the parade. Ellen was in middle school, but the band was newly formed and they needed the middle school children to make a respectable number. George and Mary had not planned to attend.

We found a perfect place to watch, just before the bridge over the Kentucky River on the street leading to the capitol. Dressed in blue and white uniforms the school had bought used, Ellen's band marched near the front of the parade; she played clarinet. The lines were crooked, and many were out of step. Plenty of squeaks came from the clarinets along with wrong notes from every section. Some of the younger kids stared at the crowd more than the crowd stared at them.

The bands marched up to the bridge, stopped, and walked across. I remembered from my own marching days that bands don't march over bridges. The vibration of being in step is supposed to make the bridge fall. I thought Ellen's band could have marched over the bridge with no problem. They were exactly what you would expect of a new high school band full of middle school kids, but that was not an acceptable excuse for Ellen. When the band was finished and allowed to meet family and friends, she ran into Jessie's arms in tears.

"We were terrible," she wailed. "I don't know why we have to go places like this until we learn to play better."

Jessie tried to console her. "It wasn't so bad, and now you will always remember that you played in the inaugural parade."

"I don't want to remember this."

Jessie held her and let her cry. She had tears in her own eyes as she said, "I'm sorry, baby. I'm so sorry." Ellen couldn't see her face, but it said she was sorry for a lot more than the poor performance of the band.

After a time Ellen pulled away. She stood with her head down, scuffing her shoes on the sidewalk. She seemed a bit embarrassed that she had let down her guard toward her mother, but it had not escaped her attention that she had needed her mother and this time her mother was there for her. Neither had it escaped Jessie's attention that this was the first time Ellen had embraced her since that fateful day when she left home three years before.

"How much time do you have before your bus leaves for home?" Jessie asked.

"We have two hours."

"Let's find a place to get warm and eat some lunch," I said.

"That sounds great," Ellen said. "I'm freezing."

Grace, who seemed nearly as happy about seeing Ellen as Jessie, said, "I want chili."

Jessie put and arm around each of her girls as we walked down the street. "The hotter, the better," she said.

Jessie smiled all the way home. I wish I could say that everything was good between Ellen and Jessie after that, but it was not to be. Ellen was thirteen and destined to have a difficult time as a teenager; still, it was a start. On rare occasions she came to visit Jessie at Uncle Henry's, but she seemed unhappy everywhere. Mary's new baby girl, Erin, was getting too much of her father's attention, and she was still cautious, not really trusting her mother.

Jeff still refused even to talk to Jessie.

CHAPTER 5

In May of 1976 Jessie graduated from nursing school. Uncle Henry, Grace, and I attended her graduation and took her out to dinner to celebrate. She got a job working in Labor & Delivery at the University Hospital, but she kept her other job, housekeeping for Uncle Henry. Two months later, I entered my last year of residency. Two of my fellow residents had been in my medical school class and helped care for Jessie when she was in the hospital. I was amused at their response to her. Neither of them remembered that this intelligent, capable, hardworking nurse was the Jane Doe whom we had on our GYN service five years before. I certainly wasn't going to tell them. Of all the admirable adjectives I could use to describe Jessie, compassionate was the most accurate. She had an uncanny ability to sense someone's pain, fear, or guilt. I wondered at her sensitivity. It made her a fabulous nurse.

One Friday evening in early July, I arrived for dinner with Uncle Henry and Jessie. Grace had gone to her father's for the weekend. I hadn't seen Uncle Henry since Jessie's graduation and was the first to admit that I spent too much time at the hospital, missed too many Friday nights of Scrabble. The sight of him stunned me; he had lost thirty pounds, and he had not been overweight.

"Uncle Henry, you are so thin. What's wrong with you?"

"Cara, I didn't want to worry you, but I have cancer."

"What? Where?"

"Colon cancer and it's in my liver now."

"How long have you known?"

"Just a couple of weeks."

"You should have called me. What are they going to do for it?"

"Nothing. They say it is too advanced."

"We need a second opinion."

"I've already done that. Everybody's opinions agree, so we signed me up for hospice. Jessie has agreed to take care of me."

I looked at Jessie, still reeling from the news.

She nodded. "Yes, even if it means I have to take a leave from my job."

"What can I do?"

"Just come when you can."

"I'll help Jessie take care of you," I said, feeling helpless and afraid.

"I can still spell," he said. "Let's have a game of Scrabble.

Two weeks later, Uncle Henry developed a bowel obstruction; so, in spite of his plan to do nothing, he underwent a colon resection. While there was no plan that it would be curative, we hoped it would make his passing less painful. It did. It also made it happen more quickly. One night in the hospital after he had recovered from the anesthesia, I asked him if there was anyone he wanted me to call or anything he wanted to do or have me do.

"No," he said, "but there is something I want to tell you. I guess really I want to confess."

"Confess? Uncle Henry, you are the finest man I know."

"That's it, Cara. I am a man, and we all sin."

"You don't need to confess to me, Uncle Henry. I'm sure you have already confessed to God."

"Yes, I have, to God and to Edna."

"Aunt Edna? Are you telling me you had an affair?"

"I would hesitate to call it an affair, but I was unfaithful."

"Why are you telling me this?"

"I am telling you because I want you to know about my life's most important lesson, the lesson that made me the man I am today."

"All right, Uncle Henry, I'm listening."

"We'd been married about five years when your Aunt Edna's namesake, an unmarried great-aunt of hers, became ill with, of all things, colon cancer. She had no one to care for her except Edna. I was working night and day on a project at the time, so Edna's being gone a lot seemed not to be a problem. There was a woman working with me who shared my passion for the work. As it turned out, she also had a passion for me.

"I was flattered and lonely, so we started spending more time together. I did not feel that I was being unfaithful having late-night dinners, but at length I crossed the line. I broke it off after one time, but she didn't want it to end. She thought if she told Edna, our marriage would end and we could continue our affair. I was tempted to lie to Edna and deny it. It is hard to tell the truth when you know it will hurt someone you love, but you should think of that before doing the hurtful thing. Anyway, that is not the lesson, though it's a good one." Uncle Henry twisted in bed and winced.

"The fact is I told Edna the truth. I told her I loved her, begged for forgiveness, and promised to be faithful. Now, here is the lesson, Cara. She forgave me. Edna loving me was a wonderful thing, but her forgiving me was so much more. That forgiveness is the glue that held us together. It was the source of the strength it took to remain faithful ever after. It made me love her even more than I did before. Cara, love is a wonderful thing, but when you add forgiveness to it, you come closest to the kind of love God has for us and wants us to have for each other. I'm telling you because I want you to know: there is power in forgiveness."

I could see the relief he felt from unburdening himself. "Thank you for sharing that, Uncle Henry. I always thought you were the most forgiving person I have ever known. I guess maybe that accolade should go to Aunt Edna."

"It helps a person to be more forgiving when they recognize their own need for forgiveness."

Three days later Uncle Henry died. He got up to sit in a bedside chair and collapsed with a blood clot in his lung. The doctor said it was merciful that he didn't have to suffer from the colon cancer, but at the time that seemed like a hollow blessing. I made it through his visitation and funeral in a state of numbness. Mourners stood for two hours in a line that stretched around the room, out the door, down the hall, and through the outside door of Kerr Brothers Funeral Home. Everyone had a story about Uncle Henry and something he had done for them. Through it all Jessie was there to support me. Some cousins showed up for the funeral, but Uncle Henry's passing seemed no great loss to them. They hadn't seen him in years, claiming they lived too far away to visit.

Grieving Uncle Henry's death was like grieving for my parents all over again. He had become my guardian when, at age fifteen, my parents were both killed in a car wreck. For fifteen years, half my life, he had been the only parent I knew. I loved him like I loved my real parents, maybe more, because he was all I had left. I realized then some of the disadvantages of being an only child.

Two things gave me comfort. One was shared grief with Jessie, the way siblings share grief at the loss of a parent. I realized that for five years Uncle Henry had been like a father to her too. Jessie had gone from patient to friend to sister. The second thing was my faith. I believed that Uncle Henry was in heaven with Aunt Edna, and that was a comfort for me.

Those cousins who couldn't visit had no trouble traveling the distance to be present for the reading of Uncle Henry's will. They did have trouble swallowing the results. Uncle Henry left each one of them two hundred and fifty thousand dollars. He left everything in the house to me with the stipulation that anything I didn't want should be offered to Jessie

before it was offered for sale. He left his car and the house and lot to
Jessie. He also left Jessie five hundred thousand dollars to be used to
endow maintenance of the house. Beyond that, the money was to be used
as Jessie saw fit, perhaps to help educate her children. The rest of his
sizable estate, including stocks, bonds, and commercial property, he left
to me.

Uncle Henry's attorney explained that if anyone contested the will,
they risked losing even that which they had been given. Two hundred and
fifty thousand dollars was enough that, furious as they were, none of them
wanted to risk losing it to contest the will. Uncle Henry and the lawyer
had known the amount required to satisfy their greed. Jessie was surprised
when she was asked to be present for the reading of the will, even more so
after hearing it.

"Cara, I'm shocked. What was Mr. Henry thinking? What do you
think?"

"He was thinking that you and Grace were a wonderful gift to his
final years, and he wanted to help you after he was gone. I think he was a
wise and generous man."

"Did you know?"

"Yes, I knew. He decided not long after he had his stroke."

Jessie was silent for a moment. "I have to do something to honor
him."

"He knew you would, and I'm sure you will."

Going through someone's personal effects after he dies is a difficult
thing. I don't think I could have done it without Jessie. We cried and we
laughed at the things he had saved. I knew I wanted a few pieces of
furniture that I had loved since I was a child; one table in particular was
octagon shaped with swirled legs. I had no idea if it was a valuable antique;
I just liked it. I didn't know what to do with most of the furniture. Some
of it I knew I would want in my home later, but it would not fit in my
apartment now. Some I wanted to leave for Jessie to use, but she was
hesitant to take the obviously valuable antiques. I called and offered the

cousins the opportunity to look through some of Uncle Henry's personal effects to see if they wanted a keepsake.

When the last one refused even to look, Jessie said, "That was a mistake."

"Yes," I said. "They will be sorry they didn't look." His personal effects included diamond cuff links, rings, some of Aunt Edna's jewelry, sterling silver mint julep cups worth two hundred dollars each at that time, and many other valuable things. "I guess they didn't think I would offer them anything of real value."

"That's because they wouldn't have offered you anything of real value."

"Uncle Henry left me more money than I will ever need. I would rather have him."

"Me too." Jessie looked up from the box she was going through. "Cara, I've been thinking. This house is so big, and I will rattle around in it. You want more of this furniture than will fit in your apartment. Would you want to move in here and be my roommate?"

"I hadn't thought of moving."

"I know you don't need to save the money, but you might like some company sometimes. The house is mine, but the furniture is yours. I would feel better about using your furniture if you used my house."

Her words made me smile. "It would solve my problem about what to do with the furniture I know I want to keep for later, and I spend most of my time at the hospital or with you as it is. I'll think about it."

This actually seemed like a great idea, the more I thought about it. I wouldn't feel so awkward about leaving things in Jessie's house if I lived there. It seemed that neither of us wanted to change much about the house. It was as though leaving Uncle Henry's things would somehow keep part of him with us. It would be a good situation while I finished residency and decided where I would practice.

I decided to move in at the end of October. We painted, changed the carpet and drapes, and bought new linens for Uncle Henry's room, which became mine. Jessie insisted that she was very comfortable in the housekeeper's suite. She still did not seem used to the idea that the place was hers. My commute to work was a little longer, but I enjoyed the company and shared meals. While I loved Jessie's cooking, I wasn't thrilled about the five pounds I gained.

I was grateful that the OB/GYN residency at the University of Kentucky did not require the residents to do abortions. After 1973 some residencies did. So I was not prepared for a patient who came to the hospital that November.

One evening, Jessie noticed that I was not myself. "Are you thinking about Mr. Henry, Cara? You seem so sad."

"No, I was thinking about a patient I saw this week."

"Can you talk about it without names?"

"I suppose. She reminded me of you."

"She had amnesia?"

"No, she was Rh-sensitized and wanted to have an abortion and be sterilized."

"Oh."

"She came in scheduled to have a hysterectomy, and I was the resident who was next up to do the procedure. I had never seen the woman before. I talked with her and then with the attending physician who scheduled her. He told me that the procedure would be much like a Caesarean-hysterectomy, which at some time in my career might be a life-saving procedure. What we did not talk about and what I did not really think about was the fact that this was a life-*taking* procedure. Everyone treated this as though the baby was already a stillborn, and I did too."

"So you did the procedure?"

"Yes. It was more difficult than a normal hysterectomy. The tissues were soft, swollen, and friable. I never saw the baby, but today the report came back from the lab. I read where they weighed it and measured it. It was a boy. They did everything but check his blood type. What if he was Rh-negative?"

Jessie took a long time to respond. "I live with that question every day, Cara. I'm sorry that you will have to as well."

"Jessie, I don't think I can do this again. Some people argue that it's an OB's responsibility to do abortions for their patients if they want it, but I can't."

"Cara, you will refer patients for other reasons. I guess you will have to refer these as well." I had no idea how soon this issue would arise again.

Two weeks before Thanksgiving, when Grace came home from visiting her father, she said that Ellen had asked if she could spend Thanksgiving with Jessie. George wasn't thrilled about it, but Jessie had not spent a holiday with Jeff or Ellen since she left over five years before. Jessie began making plans for what they would do to celebrate.

"Is Jeff coming too?" she asked excitedly.

Grace's negative response took some of the joy out of the occasion, but Jessie, grateful for even the slightest opportunity to spend time with either of her two older children, continued her planning with a smile on her face.

Jessie cooked a fabulous, traditional Thanksgiving dinner with turkey, dressing, fresh cranberry salad, scalloped oysters, candied yams, mashed potatoes, and giblet gravy. Ellen seemed withdrawn, like she had something on her mind. None of our conversation or questions drew her out. She barely smiled as Grace made Uncle Henry's Thanksgiving pronouncement. After we stuffed ourselves, we bundled up and took a long bike ride. Grace chattered the whole time about the birds she saw, the horses grazing in the fields, and the beauty of a grove of blue spruce trees.

"I wish all trees could stay green," she said.

"Then we wouldn't have the beautiful colors in the fall," Jessie responded.

"Hadn't thought of that," Grace conceded as she put on a burst of speed, pedaling hard down a hill.

"Careful!" Jessie called after her.

That evening Grace was exhausted. We all were, but she went to her room unusually early. Later I wondered if Grace sensed that Ellen didn't want to talk in front of her. Her sensitivity to people continued to amaze me and was perhaps even greater than her mother's. She had just had a checkup, and her leukemia remained in remission.

No sooner was Grace out of the room than Ellen blurted out her fear. She sat on the sofa and twisted a Kleenex. "I think I have cancer."

"What? Why do you think that?" Jessie asked, her eyes wide with alarm. She sat beside Ellen, taking her hand.

"I have these growths."

"Where?" Jessie and I were a duet.

"Down there."

"Can you see them outside?" I asked.

"Yes."

"Will you let Dr. Land look?" Jessie said.

"Now?"

"We could wait. I can see you in the clinic tomorrow."

"No, look now," Ellen pulled down her jeans enough that I could see.

"They're warts, Ellen, not cancer. They can be treated."

"Where did I get them?"

I looked at Jessie, knowing that she knew as well as I did. "Usually from having sex with someone who has the virus," I said.

"But I haven't," Ellen said.

"Ellen Marie, you will not lie to us. Dr. Land is trying to help you, and she has to know the truth."

Ellen raised her chin in a defiant pose. "So what if I did? We love each other, and we are going to get married after I get out of that pathetic school."

"Who is this boy?"

"Mark Jones."

"Pete and Jane Jones' son, the one that's Jeff's age?"

"Yes."

"You may be out of school sooner than you think if you keep this up. What did you use for birth control?" Jessie asked, displaying a calm that I doubt she felt.

"He used condoms except once."

"Ellen, one out of every four times you have unprotected sex, you get pregnant," I said. "When was your last period?"

"This Monday, I just finished today. I'm not pregnant."

"If you can come by the clinic tomorrow, I'll treat the warts and do a Pap smear."

"Why do I have to have a Pap smear?"

"Because when you have warts, you have an increased risk of getting cervical cancer."

"Oh."

"I'll call you tomorrow when I get to the clinic and let you know the best time."

"Thanks, Cara. We'll be there," Jessie said.

Ellen turned pleading eyes to her mother. "Do we have to tell Dad?"

"I think he would be very disappointed in you, Ellen. I know I am. You are too young for this, but I am not going to tell him. You will have to do that yourself."

After Ellen went to bed, Jessie asked, "Do you think she needs to be on birth control pills? She's so young."

"Yes," I said. "She doesn't sound like she intends to stop, and she will get pregnant. You know we get girls younger than her in Labor Hall every day."

"Do you think pills make young girls have sex more?"

"No, I don't, but I do think pills keep them from getting pregnant. They do what they want to do with or without them. Sometimes if a young girl holds out and makes the boy use a condom every time, she does decrease her chance of getting a sexually transmitted disease, but Ellen has already failed that test."

"When could she start?"

"Since she just had her period, I can give her samples tomorrow. She can start Sunday."

"Well, one good thing will come from this."

"What's that?

"She'll have to come see me more." Jessie smiled.

"You always find the silver lining."

Ellen was happy to use pills. She admitted that her boyfriend had been pressuring her to get them, but she had not wanted to tell anybody she was having sex.

George had refused to do any of the driving required for the children to visit, and Jessie was so glad for the chance to see them that she didn't argue. Thus, it was a surprise when he knocked on the door during the week before Christmas. Jessie had picked up Grace two days before. As he pushed his way past Jessie, he threw the birth control pills on the hall table and screamed at me, "What do you mean giving Ellen birth control pills?"

"What has she told you?"

"She said she loves that Jones boy, and you gave her pills."

"She was having unprotected sex, George. What did you expect me to do? Do you want her to get pregnant?"

"I don't want her sleeping with every boy that comes sniffing around."

"I don't either, George," Jessie said, "but she says it has only been this one boy. You have already forbidden her to date him, and that didn't stop her, so what do you think you can do?"

"I'll put her out."

"Yes, I guess you would, but I fail to see how that would stop her."

"Well, she's not taking these."

Jessie's countenance and voice changed. "George, what about letting Ellen come and live with me? It would get her away from that boy, and I would love to have her."

"No, you've been a bad enough influence already." He stormed out.

Christmas was grim that year. We decorated the house because Uncle Henry had liked it decorated and because Grace liked it decorated, but my heart wasn't in it. On December 1, Jessie and Grace started their study of Luke, but I didn't join them. Grace spent Christmas with her father, and both Jessie and I missed her. Jessie reminded me of what Uncle Henry had taught her that first Christmas she was there, that Christmas is really about God's love for us, His sending His Son for us, not just about gifts or even family. I knew that message had been important for Jessie that first year and always would be, but it didn't comfort me as I grieved for Uncle Henry, still felt guilt over the abortion I had done, and dreaded the coming winter.

CHAPTER 6

I had six more months of residency. As a chief resident, I was allowed to take calls from home. My last six months included three months on Pathology, the least demanding and time-consuming part of the final year. I decided to take a class in finance. While Uncle Henry had left his money, now my money, in good hands, I felt I needed to understand more of the subject even to be able to speak to the professionals.

My finance class started on Tuesday evening, January 11. The teacher, Jon Parker, was a graduate assistant who had an MBA from Wharton School of Business and was working on his PhD in finance. He was a Vietnam War veteran and a Wall Street veteran who had made enough money to retire at thirty-two. A wonderful teacher, he had that perfect combination of book knowledge and experience. Tuesday and Thursday nights came too slowly and finished too quickly. He was older than the other graduate assistants, actually thirty-three years old.

In school I was almost always the teacher's pet. Because I was nearsighted and did not find out until medical school, I always sat on the front row. Because I was focused to a fault, I always paid attention. Because my face is like an open book, one slight frown at something I did not understand would cause the teacher to stop and explain. One is fortunate when the teacher gauges the whole class's understanding by your understanding. I found myself hoping I would be teacher's pet again.

Unlike some women, I have never had a strong preference for either blond or brunet men. I like both. Nor do I have a preference for tall or short men, blue or brown eyes. Jon was perfect. He appeared to be about six feet tall with a lean athletic build. He had no hair as he carefully shaved the little hair left by his baldness. It created a striking look, made even more so by the long hair styles of the time. His hazel eyes flashed with quick wit. I didn't know whether I wanted class to be over so I wouldn't be his student anymore, or whether I was afraid for class to be over because I wouldn't see him anymore.

During January, Jessie repeatedly tried to talk to Ellen, but she, like Jeff, was never at home when Jessie took Grace. Then one extremely cold and snowy Thursday night near the end of February, George knocked on the door again. "Is Ellen here?" he asked as Jessie invited him in.

"Of course not," Jessie said, her eyes registering alarm. "You mean you don't know where she is?" She began pacing back and forth across the living room.

"I discovered that she was not in her room this morning. I don't know exactly when she left." George stood in the middle of the room, looking down at his hands as he twirled his brown hat in a circle.

"Was anything wrong?"

"Not that she said. She never talks to me anymore. I don't like her friends, and I don't let her see that Jones boy. I thought maybe she talked to you."

"When would she have talked to me? Did you check with the boy?"

"Yes, she was not at his house, but he wasn't there either. She didn't go to school today. I thought maybe she had come here."

"Have you checked with the police?" I asked.

"No, I wanted to check here first."

Jessie went to the phone and called the police. "I need to report a missing person." When she hung up, she said, "They said I have to come down there and file the report."

"I'll go home and file a report with the police there. I'll check with some other friends too, now that I know she's not here."

"George, will you please let me know if she comes home? I'll call you if she comes here."

"Yes," he said as he turned and headed for the door. "Ask Grace if she has any ideas. Ellen did talk to her last weekend."

Jessie called Grace downstairs after her father left. "Ellen seems to have run away from home, Grace. Do you have any idea why or where she might have gone?" By this time Jessie had sat on the sofa. She held out her arms for Grace to come sit beside her. They each seemed to need the touch of the other.

"I told her she should ask to come home with me."

"What was the problem?"

"I don't know exactly. She and Dad either fight or don't talk at all. I told her you would listen and that you would be there for her."

"That was good advice, Grace. I would, but so would your father."

"Maybe, but he's more critical than you."

"Maybe he has more right to be critical, Grace. Do you have any idea where she might have gone?"

"She said she needed to talk to her boyfriend."

"Is that still Mark Jones?"

"Yes."

"Did she say what she needed to talk to him about?"

"No."

"Thanks, honey. You let me know if you can think of anything else that might help us find her. I have to go to the police station to file a report. Cara, could you stay with Grace until I get back?"

"Sure." I built a fire.

Grace had gone back to her room to do homework, and Jessie had been gone about an hour when Ellen knocked on the door. She stood on the porch alone, shivering. Icy tears dripped from her chin and a frown crossed her face when she realized it was not her mother who answered the door.

I heard a deep rumble from the muffler as an old car pulled away from the curb. "Come in, come in. Your mother will be so relieved to see you. How did you get here?"

"Mark brought me, but he left. Where's my mother?"

"She's gone to the police station looking for you."

"She knows I ran away?"

"Yes, your father has been here. Come, sit by the fire and I'll call and let her know you're here. She's worried."

Ellen sat by the fire and looked at her hands when she spoke. "Would you wait, Dr. Land? I want to talk to you."

"About what?"

"I think I'm pregnant?"

"When was your last period?"

"About six weeks ago."

"Have you been regular since you stopped the pill? Sometimes they can make you a little irregular when you first come off them."

"I've only had the one."

"Have you been using condoms?"

"No."

"Have you had any abnormal bleeding?"

"Yes, about two weeks ago I bled a little, but it wasn't a normal period, not even as much as the light period on the pill."

"It sounds like you may be right."

"Do I have to tell my parents?"

"You don't have to. If you are pregnant, you are an emancipated minor, which means that you can make decisions for yourself regarding the pregnancy, but you are hardly in a position to take care of yourself. I think you should tell your mother."

"My friend said I should have an abortion. She said nobody would have to know."

"Ellen, you would know. That's enough, but whatever you decide, you should not be alone in this." As I said that, we heard Jessie open the back door. "Please tell your mother."

When Jessie came in, Ellen ran to her like she had that day in Frankfort. Though she was not, in so many ways she seemed like the same little girl. Jessie held her a moment then pushed her away to look into her eyes. "Ellen, where have you been? How did you get here? Why did you run away from home?" She pulled her back into her arms, closed her eyes, and took a deep breath as though she had been unable to breathe before. I wondered if she had pictured Ellen alone, unconscious in a dirty hallway.

Ellen chose the easiest of this string of questions to answer. "Mark brought me."

"Why didn't he stay? I would like to meet him."

"He said he had to get home." After a pause, she added, "He broke up with me."

"What? Why?"

Ellen looked at me, and Jessie followed her look. "Why?" she repeated, her voice a little higher in pitch.

Ellen walked away from Jessie. She raised her chin, turned, and made eye contact.

"It's Dad's fault."

"What did he do?"

"He wouldn't let me take pills. Now I'm pregnant."

Jessie's shoulders dropped with the weight of Ellen's words. She walked to her but hesitated short of touching her. She waited until Ellen turned and melted into her arms. "Cara, have you two talked?" Jessie asked me, looking over Ellen's shoulder.

"Yes."

"Do you think she is?"

"Yes, it sounds like she is."

"When can you see her?"

"I'll work her in tomorrow." During our last year of residency we could have a few private patients. It looked like I had my first one. How ironic it should be Jessie's daughter. "You two have a lot to discuss. I think I'll go to bed."

As I left the room I heard Jessie say, "I need to call your father and tell him you're here."

"Please," Ellen said a little too quickly, "don't tell him I'm pregnant."

"We'll see the doctor first. I'll tell him that I will bring you home on Sunday."

I lay awake most of the night thinking about my conflicted convictions about abortion. *I'm glad it's legal; don't ever want another poor woman in Jessie's position or that of other women who try to abort themselves. The Supreme Court said that until the age of viability the decision should be between the woman and her doctor. Ellen is my first private patient. What will I do if she decides she wants to be aborted? The Supreme Court's decision doesn't change the morality issue. Pro-choice? Pro-life? God loves mother and baby.* I decided I would refer Ellen to an abortion clinic if that was her choice and fell into a troubled sleep.

Jessie called work the next day and took off for a "family emergency." Then she and Ellen came to the clinic at eleven o'clock to see me. Except for the blood transfusions at birth, Ellen's medical history was unremarkable. Her general exam showed a healthy fifteen-year-old. Her uterus was consistent with a six weeks' pregnancy, and she had a four-centimeter ovarian cyst on the right. I wasn't worried about the cyst, but Ellen's would be a high-risk pregnancy because she was fifteen.

"It looks like you are about six weeks pregnant," I said when I finished her exam and she had dressed. "We date the pregnancy from your last period, even though we know you conceived two weeks after that. You are due October 24. Your exam is normal except that you have a small ovarian cyst on the right side." Jessie and Ellen both gasped. Ellen reached for Jessie's hand.

"What does that mean?" Jessie asked for both of them.

"It's very common to find a cyst at this point. At ovulation, when the ovary makes an egg, a cyst is formed normally. If you get pregnant the cyst usually takes about two and a half months to go away. Often we can feel it, if we check carefully."

"What do we need to do about it?"

"We just watch it. I want to repeat a pelvic exam on each visit until it has gone away. You need to be seen once a month," I said to Ellen. "Usually I only do this whole exam the first time."

"Is there anything we need to watch for?" Jessie asked.

"The cyst can rupture, and that can cause some pain. Let me know if you get any sharp pain on your right side." Ellen's eyes got wide and she twisted the tail of her sweater. "Don't worry, Ellen. Even if that happens, it's usually only painful for a few hours and then you are fine." She relaxed a little but still looked fearful.

"Don't worry, honey. You'll be all right," Jessie said, reassured by my comments.

"Jessie, Ellen mentioned that some of her friends said she should have an abortion. Did you discuss that possibility last night?"

"Yes. We did. I told her I was absolutely opposed to it, and I knew her father would be, but I assured her that I will be there for her whatever she decides. In the end, it is her decision."

"He wouldn't even have to know," Ellen said. Jessie looked at me. I knew she was thinking how wrong she had been in thinking the same thing years before.

"He might find out; besides, that's not the point. You are the one who will have to live with the decision and the consequences. Guilt and grief will be lifelong burdens that will get heavier as time goes on." Jessie spoke with a voice of experience and sadness that took us both back a few years.

"Ellen?" I waited for her response.

"When do I have to decide?"

"With modern techniques, it is relatively safe within the first ten weeks. After that the risks increase. You should decide within the month. I want to go over what you can expect during pregnancy and how you should take care of yourself. Before I do, do you have any questions?"

"Will my baby die like Mama's did?"

"Ellen, you were young," Jessie said. "I didn't realize you worried about that."

"It was terrible, Mama. It affected all of us."

"I'm so sorry, honey. I was so wrapped up in my own grief I didn't see what it was doing to you."

"I'd rather be aborted than have that happen to me." Jessie was silenced by that comment.

"No, Ellen, you don't have to worry about that," I said. "The problem with your mother's blood type that caused her stillborn babies doesn't happen to Rh-positive women, and we know you are Rh-positive. There are risks though, especially since you are so young, but most of them are related to how well you take care of yourself, so let's go over that."

That evening, after Ellen and Grace had gone to their rooms, Jessie said, "How about a drink?"

"That bad is it?" We didn't drink much. "Do we even have anything here?"

"There's a bottle of wine."

"Let's open it." As Jessie got the wine and glasses, I got the corkscrew. "When you and Ellen talked, did you tell her about your abortion? After her comment today about the stillborn babies, I wondered."

"No. George was adamant that I not tell the children why I was sick and didn't come home, so I didn't tell her, but I was stunned today when she said what she did. I had no idea she was so affected by those stillbirths."

"It sounds like she might have been more forgiving of you leaving if she had known the whole truth."

"Perhaps. Maybe I will tell her sometime. You know, Cara, if I don't tell them the truth, I can't really expect them to forgive me, and I need them to forgive me."

When Ellen got up Saturday morning, she seemed more mature. She had dressed, combed her hair, and put on boots while the rest of us sat around in our bathrobes.

"I'm going for a walk," she announced. "My doctor"—she smiled at me—"says I need to stay active with exercise, like walking, bicycling, or swimming. Sure can't swim in this weather."

"I also said you should have regular meals. Don't you want to have breakfast first?"

"No, I'll eat as soon as I come back. I won't be long. I have to work up to long walks."

"It sounds like she may have made a decision," Jessie said as the door closed.

When Ellen returned, over a poached egg and whole wheat toast she informed us that she wanted to have her baby. The mood lightened as if someone had pumped helium into the air. Jessie hugged her and Grace jumped up and down. "I'm going to be an aunt!"

When the excitement settled a bit, Jessie said, "Ellen, what exactly did Mark say when you told him you thought you were pregnant?"

"He said if I was, it wasn't his."

"Is that possible?"

"No, of course not. Mark is the only one ever. Why do you ask?"

"Ellen, I know your father. He's going to want to make Mark marry you. I was just trying to see what Mark might say about that."

"He said it isn't even his. I doubt he'll want to marry me."

"I think you're right. The question for me is do you want to marry him?"

"I did, but now I don't know. I thought he loved me, but if he did he wouldn't say it wasn't his baby. I don't want to marry someone who doesn't love me."

"And I don't want you to either. Cara, how long will it be before Ellen's pregnancy shows?"

"The average for a first pregnancy is about sixteen weeks, but it's sooner in short women and sometimes later in tall ones. With Ellen's height it might be eighteen or twenty weeks, especially if she is careful about weight gain."

"That would be the end of May or the middle of June. Ellen, you could finish this year of school."

"But I don't want to go back to school."

"Well, you don't get everything you want. If you are going to be a single mother, you need to finish school. You've already done six weeks of this semester, and it would be crazy to waste it."

"Can't I go to school here?"

"It's better if you stay where you are. You don't have to discuss the pregnancy with anyone. When school is out, you can tell your father you want to spend the summer with me."

"Are you going to tell him I'm pregnant?"

"No, I am going to leave that to you."

"I want to wait until it shows. If everyone can see, maybe he won't try to make me marry Mark."

"That's up to you. I just have one request. Don't lie to him. If he asks you, you tell him the truth."

Ten days later, just as Jessie and Grace got home from choir practice, Ellen called in a panic.

"Ellen says she has some bleeding," Jessie said to me as she held the phone.

"Ask her if it is as heavy as a period."

"She says no."

"Does she have pain?"

Jessie shook her head. "No."

"Tell her there is nothing we would do at this point. She should rest as much as she can and call if she has heavier bleeding or pain. I'll check her when she comes this weekend."

Jessie picked up Ellen early that Friday and brought her to the clinic. At this point the bleeding had stopped and there was still no pain. Ellen's exam was normal except for the cyst, which was much smaller.

"I think everything is fine, Ellen. The cyst is nearly gone. As a matter of fact, the cyst dissolving may be the reason for the bleeding. Sometimes there is a drop in the level of the hormone your body makes to maintain the pregnancy when the hormone production changes from the cyst to the placenta. It happens at about eight weeks, so that may be what happened. Anyway, everything looks good now. Let's not worry."

"I was afraid for me, but I kind of hoped I might lose the baby," she confessed. The sentiment did not surprise me so much, but Ellen's being so straightforward about it did. "I'm going to be a terrible mother."

Jessie put her arm around Ellen's shoulder. "It's not surprising you feel that way now, Ellen. Right now the baby is an interruption in your life. Give it some time. Soon it will become your baby and not your pregnancy. That makes a difference. Having had that thought doesn't mean you will be a terrible mother."

I didn't worry until a month later when Ellen bled again. The uterus had grown appropriately and there was no dilation of the cervix. I could hear the baby's heartbeat and let Ellen and Jessie hear it as well. That reassured all of us, and it went a long way toward making this Ellen's baby and not just her pregnancy.

I am a terrible liar. If I think it, whatever *it* is, the idea arranges itself on my face, like an artist putting a painting on a canvas. When Ellen bled again at sixteen weeks, this time a large amount, I was very worried and both Ellen and Jessie could see it.

"What's wrong?" Jessie asked.

"I'm not sure," I confessed. "In the absence of pain, the most likely thing is a low-lying placenta."

"What does that mean?" Ellen asked.

"It means that the afterbirth has attached to the uterus down close to the cervix, perhaps in front of the baby. I think we need to get an ultrasound to be sure."

Fortunately, we got the ultrasound that afternoon. In those days, ultrasound did not show anything like the detail we have now, but it was still amazing for Ellen to see the baby moving and the heart beating. She was as excited as I was worried. The placenta was indeed lying in front of the baby's head. It was slightly off to the left side, giving me some hope that as the uterus enlarged, the placenta would grow up the side of the head. Still, this was the most central placenta praevia that I had ever seen.

"Ellen, this does show a placenta praevia. That means the afterbirth is lying between the baby and the cervix."

"What does that mean?"

"It means that you will probably have more bleeding. It means that we will not be doing any more pelvic exams. It means that you must not put anything in the vagina, like tampons, if you bleed. It means that you must not have sex. It means that you may have to have a period of bed rest toward the end of the pregnancy; you may need to have blood transfusions; you may have to be delivered early, and you may need to have a Caesarean section for delivery."

"Will my baby be all right?"

"Yes, I think so. The baby's biggest risk would be early delivery." I didn't tell her that the greater risk was for her life.

"What should I do about PE class? I was jumping on the trampoline in class when I bled this time."

"You should avoid strenuous activity. I will give you a written excuse."

"I only have two more weeks. I'll be glad when this school year is over."

"So will I." I wanted Ellen close to the hospital.

CHAPTER 7

_____

That spring was crazy busy. I was due to finish my residency at the end of June and had decided to stay in Lexington in private practice at Good Samaritan Hospital. A new doctors' office building had been built right across the street from the hospital. Space was available for lease. Since it was in walking distance of the hospital, the location was perfect.

The space was fourteen hundred square feet, with no internal partitions and bare concrete floors. I found a contractor who would build the office from plans I drew myself. I had read that all exam rooms need to be identical to improve your efficiency. The contractor didn't want to do it that way because he wanted to back up the plumbing, but I stood my ground. Fortunately, Uncle Henry's money made it easier to stick to my wishes. I had a friend who was an interior decorator and just starting her new business, so she helped with the décor. I was especially grateful for Uncle Henry's money because, had I needed to borrow the money to build the office, interest rates would have been twenty-one percent.

Busy as I was, I still never missed a finance class. Not only was I learning a lot, but I was having fun—until one week before final exams. As the class waited for our teacher, a stranger came into the room and announced that he would be finishing our class. Our teacher had some sort of medical emergency and would be gone the rest of the semester. After class, we asked for more information. All we were told was that it concerned a disease related to exposure to Agent Orange in Vietnam. When I called Jon's office the next day, I found that he had not only left the university, he had left the city.

Also, thanks to Uncle Henry's money, Jessie was able to take a leave from her job at the end of May. She had spent all her free time that spring learning how to homeschool Ellen. She figured that if she could homeschool through the summer, then Ellen could have the fall semester off when the baby was born. At that point, they could either homeschool the second semester or enroll Ellen in school in Lexington. In either case, Ellen wouldn't get behind in school.

Now that I knew I would be staying in Lexington, I began looking for a house to buy. Ellen would be moving to Jessie's and would soon add a baby to the household. I knew I would be in and out of the house at all hours—it would disturb everybody. Having a roommate was good for the time of grieving after Uncle Henry died, but I was ready for a place of my own. After about a month of looking, I found a lovely old house on Ashland Avenue. The backyard had shade trees but also one sunny spot for a garden. The house needed a lot of work, but now that I had found the contractor who was doing my office, I was undaunted by that.

I made an offer for less than the asking price, and after some haggling—probably because of a large deposit and a cash payment—the offer was accepted. I used the same decorator and contractor to get my home ready for me to move. They estimated it would take three or four months. I set a goal to be in my home by Thanksgiving.

Ellen came to live with Jessie on May 30, 1977. It was Memorial Day and graduation day for Mason County High School, Jeff's graduation day. Jessie did not get an invitation or reserved seats with the family, but Grace told her when the graduation would take place. She arranged to leave Grace for the summer and pick up Ellen on that Monday so she could be there for graduation. It was some comfort for Jessie that both Grace and Ellen chose to sit in the back of the gymnasium with her rather than in the family's reserved seats, but Jeff remained aloof. He did accept the gift she brought—a leather briefcase with MGJ, his monogram, on it—but he refused to open it in her presence, depriving her of a chance to see his reaction.

Through Grace Jessie had learned that Jeff wanted to attend the University of Louisville to study accounting. He made it very clear that he did not want to be in Lexington. U of L was more expensive than UK, and Jeff had been denied a scholarship. Jessie offered to pay his tuition but he refused, telling her that he did not want anything from her. George was not so uncompromising. He accepted the money from Jessie, and Jeff did not know how his father had come up with the funds for him to attend the school of his choice.

With Jessie's attention to Ellen's homework every other weekend and with the decrease in Ellen's social life that accompanied her pregnancy, her grades improved. She got a 3.2 GPA that semester before she came to live with Jessie, the best she had ever done in high school. However, the best thing about Ellen's education was Jessie's homeschooling, which started the first week in June. After reviewing required subjects and discussing with Ellen what she wanted as electives, they decided on five subjects: English, driver's education, Kentucky history, home economics, and band. She arranged the driver's education through a local driving school, scheduled Ellen for private clarinet lessons, and had her audition for the youth orchestra. The English, history, and home economics she taught herself.

Jessie may have made a mistake being a nurse instead of a teacher, because she had a gift for making the subjects come alive. For instance, in home economics she taught Ellen how to sew by having her make maternity clothes. At first Ellen objected to the idea of wearing homemade clothes, but Jessie convinced her that they would not look homemade when they finished. They bought patterns for maternity tops, skirts, and slacks, and Jessie taught Ellen the basic steps required to make the garments. Then she taught Ellen how she worked her magic. They added buttons, bows, appliqués, and top-stitching. In the end, Ellen was the best-dressed pregnant teenager in Lexington. They made baby clothes too. Jessie even taught Ellen how to make curtains and a matching skirt for the crib in the baby's room.

Sewing was only part of Ellen's home economics class. Jessie had her take the diet sheet I had given her for healthy eating during the second half of pregnancy and plan her own meals. She took her shopping and taught her how to cook. We all ate healthier. I even lost the extra five pounds I had gained. Jessie gave Ellen an allowance and taught her the basics of budgeting.

Home economics was not Jessie's only inspired class. She made Kentucky history come alive as well. She had researched possible textbooks, finding one that was readable. She set up a schedule that would have Ellen finished with the reading by mid-September, but the field trips were the best part. I even enjoyed some of them. We went to Blue Licks Park and visited the site of the last battle of the American Revolution, which Ellen learned took place in Kentucky.

Jessie researched where Civil War reenactments were done, and one weekend we went to Perryville to learn about the Civil War battle that took place there. Jessie took Ellen to Cheapside, site of the slave market in Lexington. She even got Grace in on some of the history lessons. Grace spent the summer with her father, but she did come to Jessie every other weekend. Jessie had Ellen and Grace decide which side they would take in the Civil War. They were not allowed to choose the same side. Jessie wanted to make them understand what it was like for families to be divided by that struggle, emphasizing Kentucky's unique position as a border state.

As part of history and English, Jessie introduced Ellen to the Lexington Public Library and the reference department there. She taught Ellen how to find original newspaper reports of events that she read about in the history book. She had Ellen write a paper supporting her choice of sides in the war. Grace wrote one too, just for fun.

I finished my residency at the end of June and started to work in my new office on July 1. My schedule was full from the very beginning, probably because I was the only female OB/GYN physician in private practice in the city. It bugged me that women wanted to see me because I was female. I wanted them to see me because I was a good doctor, but that remained to be seen. Since the few private patients I had attended as a resident were not due to deliver until later in the fall, my evenings were usually free. I did have a coverage arrangement with another doctor so that I had to be on call some weekends for his patients who were due. Still, it was a nice break from the grueling schedule of residency and allowed me to share some field trips with Jessie and Ellen.

When Ellen came to live with Jessie at the end of May, George expected that she would come home to visit him every other weekend. When she refused, he was not as accepting as Jessie had been. Still, Ellen refused to go home. Jessie suspected that Ellen had not told George about the pregnancy, but she stayed out of it. The healing that was taking place in her relationship with her daughter was visible. While neither of them had been thrilled about the pregnancy in the beginning, both Ellen and Jessie had moved on to focus on the coming baby, and they found joy in that. Jessie did not want to risk the fragile rapport she had with Ellen by insisting she tell George about the baby. Ellen would have to deal with that on her own.

One very hot Friday evening in mid-July, George came unexpectedly to get Ellen for a visit. Ellen still had no intention of spending the weekend with him. A nice breeze cooled the back porch, where we all relaxed after dinner and watched Ellen model the latest outfit she had made. It was a pair of khaki culottes with a darker brown top. Ellen had designed this one totally on her own, and Jessie was proud of the result. Ellen had taken the same brown fabric as the rest of the top and made a large pocket right in the middle. Then she had used several different fabrics to make a head, body, ears, and eyes of a baby kangaroo, which she had appliquéd just behind and coming out of the pocket.

Jessie and Ellen were gently swinging in the old-fashioned porch swing, and I sat at the table playing solitaire when George walked around the corner of the house. We had not heard him knock at the front and were surprised to see him; still, we weren't nearly as surprised as he was when he saw Ellen. The look on his face left no doubt that Jessie's suspicion had been right. He went red. I was afraid he was going to strike either Jessie or Ellen, but he controlled himself with clenched fists and teeth. He was furious with both of them, perhaps even more with Jessie than with Ellen.

"Did you not think her father should know about this?" he said to Jessie.

"Yes, I thought you should."

"Then why didn't you tell me?"

"I thought it was her place to tell you. Besides, we don't talk much."

"Who's the father?" he asked as he glared at Ellen, still clenching and unclenching his fists.

"Mark Jones."

"I'll make him marry you."

"She doesn't want to marry him." Jessie rose as though to make a buffer between George and Ellen.

"I don't care what she wants. No daughter of mine is going to have a baby out of wedlock. Does he know you're pregnant?" he said to Ellen.

"I told him I thought I was, and he said it wasn't his. It is, but I don't know how I can prove it. If he loved me, I wouldn't have to. I didn't tell anyone after I knew for sure." Ellen's voice had a note of maturity that I had not heard before.

"He will marry you."

"It's not like Ellen is the first single girl to have a baby," Jessie said.

"Well, the others aren't my daughter. This is your fault."

"My fault?"

"Yes, this would not have happened if you had been a decent mother to her."

"I tried to put her on birth control pills."

"And you gave her permission to whore around." Jessie gasped and bent in the middle, like she had taken a belly punch. She stared at George, speechless. George, ignoring Jessie, turned on Ellen.

"If you don't marry that boy, then you will not be welcome in my house."

"I am not going to marry him."

"Don't come knocking on my door when you need help."

"Don't worry. I won't." Ellen screamed at her father's back as he rounded the corner of the house.

On Friday morning, July 24, I saw Ellen for a prenatal checkup. I was thrilled that her urinalysis and blood pressure were normal. Her weight gain and the baby's growth were good. She was twenty-six weeks at that point.

"Everything looks good, Ellen. I'm relieved that you've had no further bleeding. Still, I want you to continue your precautions. We'll do another ultrasound when you get closer to delivery."

That afternoon, Jessie drove to Washington to pick up Grace for the weekend, leaving Ellen at home. She had planned a field trip for Saturday. The four of us went back to Frankfort; this time we were there to tour the capitol and visit the old governor's mansion. We couldn't help but remember the inaugural parade as we crossed the bridge leading to the capitol. Ellen laughed about it, and it was good to see her laugh. We did a lot of walking that day, and Ellen seemed a little tired by early afternoon, so we decided to call it a day. We were in the car, almost back to Lexington, when Ellen said, "I think my water just broke." Grace was in the backseat with Ellen as Jessie drove.

"It's too early for that," I said. "Are you having any pain?"

"No."

It was Grace who noticed that it was not fluid. She gasped as she stared and pointed at Ellen's blood-soaked pants.

"Jessie, go to the hospital, quickly!" I said. This time there was a lot of blood.

Jessie ran a stop sign right in front of a policeman. When he put on his light, we screamed out the window that we were going to Good Samaritan Hospital, waved for him to follow, and kept going. With gratitude and relief, we watched as he pulled around and kept his light and siren on leading the way. Grace and Ellen were both sobbing in the back and the policeman didn't relieve their distress, but he did relieve mine and Jessie's as she flew through stoplights.

As soon as we got to the emergency room, I ran in, had an orderly take a stretcher for Ellen, and told the clerk to admit her directly to Labor & Delivery. I called the lab to order a stat complete blood count and type and crossmatch for four units of blood. When they came in with Ellen, I went with her to L&D while Jessie and Grace parked the car. I had already learned that you should only give a patient two fingers to squeeze when they need to hold your hand, but I guess it was a measure of my own distress that I gave Ellen my whole hand to hold as we flew down the hall. By the time we reached L&D my hand was numb. This was typical placenta praevia bleeding, extremely heavy and painless. Ellen was terrified. So was I.

The Labor & Delivery suite was a third-floor wing of the 1954 building. A waiting room was the first door on the left before double doors opened into a wide hallway. On the left were three labor rooms and a small delivery/operating room at the back. On the right a little used labor room was first, followed by the nurses' station and two delivery rooms. We took Ellen to the second labor room on the left, directly across the hall from the nurses' station. It was the place most easily observed by nurses and doctors alike. The operating room, a few feet down the hall, was made ready in case we couldn't keep up with Ellen's blood loss. I noted with relief that no one was there in labor. It would be quieter and the nurses would have more time for Ellen.

Ellen undressed and put on a hospital gown. By the time she got into bed, the lab technician came to draw her blood. When he finished and while the nurse checked Ellen's vital signs, I started a sixteen gauge IV, apologizing as I did it. "I'm sorry, Ellen, this is going to hurt, but you need a big IV for a blood transfusion."

Her face looked pale. "Do you think I'll need a blood transfusion?"

"Yes, I'm almost certain of it. The test she just drew will be a baseline. We will repeat it in about an hour to see how much blood you are losing. Sometimes it seems like more than it really is." I did not even believe that myself, though it was true.

Ellen's blood pressure was low, and her heart rate was faster than her usual. I wasn't sure if it was because she had lost a lot of blood or because she was frightened. Perhaps both. Donna Lane, the L&D nurse, let Ellen listen to the baby's strong, normal heartbeat, and that seemed to calm her a bit. Still, every ten minutes, when Donna checked and had to change another blood-soaked pad, Ellen's eyes widened and she clenched the sheets even harder.

Jessie and Grace had waited for me in the doctors' lounge before, so I expected they would be there. It was located up the hall from the L&D suite, across from the nursery. As soon as Ellen was settled in the bed, her IV started, and my orders written, I went to tell Jessie she could come in with Ellen. I found them in the lounge, but Jessie was not in a position to go to Ellen. She held Grace in her arms as the child sobbed, saying over and over "Ellen's going to die. Ellen's going to die." Jessie's face was as white as Ellen's, and her eyes were wide as saucers. She said nothing and looked as though she believed Grace was right.

"No, Grace," I said. "We are not going to let that happen. This bleeding usually stops on its own when you get off your feet."

"What if it doesn't? She was bleeding so much."

"If it doesn't then we have to deliver the baby, but we really don't want to do that yet."

"It's too little, isn't it?"

"Yes." That brought on a new wave of sobs. "Jessie, I can stay with Grace for a few minutes if you want to see Ellen. Then you might want to take her home. Maybe Mrs. Applegate could stay with her if you want to come back. I need to stay here." Mrs. Applegate was Grace's Sunday school teacher, a retired schoolteacher who lived up the street from us.

"That's a good idea. I'll call her when we get home."

"Turn left at the end of the hall, knock on the double doors, and tell the nurse you want to see Ellen," I said as Jessie left the room.

In one hour when Ellen's blood count was rechecked, it showed her hemoglobin level had dropped one gram from her baseline level on admission, suggesting she had lost a unit of blood. Donna checked the bleeding and found it had not slowed.

"It's time to transfuse her," I said. "Let's hang the first unit. We don't want to get too far behind this bleeding."

After the transfusion was started, Ellen started to shiver. "I'm cold," she said. Donna covered her with two warm blankets.

"That's not surprising," I said. Transfused blood comes straight from the refrigerator. "We'll put a warmer on it. I need you to let me know if you feel anything else unusual while you are getting the blood."

When Jessie returned, Ellen's lip trembled and she cried as her mother held her. She quickly got herself together and seized on the one reassuring thing. "The baby's heartbeat sounds normal."

"That's good, baby," Jessie said. "I hoped we could avoid that." She pointed to the blood as it dripped into Ellen's arm. She knew the risks of blood transfusion as well as I did.

"Unfortunately, I suspect this is the first of many, if we hold off delivering this baby."

"Are you thinking of delivering her?"

"I've decided to give her eight hours for the bleeding to slow. At that point I'll have to consider it. I'll be right here at the desk if you need me."

As I sat at the desk, dictating my admission note and writing orders, I heard Donna talking with Jessie and Ellen. She had a wonderful way of relieving fear and tension.

"That was a really cute maternity top you were wearing when you came in, darlin'," she said to Ellen. "My daughter is pregnant, and I think she would love that. Where did you get it?"

Ellen had been wearing the kangaroo baby top. "I made it." She grinned at Jessie.

"Surely not," Donna said, obviously surprised. "Why, it's adorable. Did you have a pattern?"

"Only for the basic top. I designed the pocket and the baby kangaroo from a photo I saw in the encyclopedia."

"That's amazing. You could sell those."

"I hope it isn't ruined with blood."

"I'll just go soak the bloody part of your clothes in ice water. That'll do the trick. We're used to getting blood out of things here."

When Donna left the room, Ellen said, "Mama, you said no one would know my clothes were homemade."

Ellen bled very heavily for six more hours while Jessie and I sat by her bed, frowning every time Donna changed a blood-soaked pad. Periodically, Jessie went to the lounge and called to check on Grace and let her know how Ellen was doing. At seven o'clock, Donna came in to say that she had asked the cafeteria to send up dinner for Jessie and me. It was in the doctors' lounge. Ellen wasn't allowed to eat until we were sure she would not have to be delivered. Jessie said she wasn't hungry, but Donna insisted she needed to keep up her strength. She didn't have to ask me twice.

"You look worried, Cara," Jessie said when we got to the lounge.

"I am, Jessie. I hate to give her so much blood, but the baby won't make it if I have to deliver her now."

"I know."

We had just finished eating when Donna called the lounge. "You might want to come and see this."

We hurried back to the labor room where Donna stood holding a half-soaked pad. "It's slowing down."

Ellen grinned. "Don't squeeze me too hard," she said as Jessie hugged her.

With the bleeding stopped completely after twenty-four hours, I felt it was safe enough to move Ellen for another ultrasound. Ultrasound machines were much bigger and less portable in those days. Jessie went along to watch. She had seen ultrasounds at her work, but this was her grandbaby.

"What does it show?" Ellen wanted to know.

The radiologist told her. "The placenta is centered over the cervix in front of the baby's head. That's why you bled. The baby's measurements are consistent with twenty-six weeks. It looks like it is developing normally."

"Is it a girl or a boy?"

"I don't see external parts, so that suggests a girl, but I could just be missing it."

Ellen smiled. "I'd like a girl."

"This is a bad one," the radiologist observed out of Ellen's hearing. "I've seen a lot of praevias, but never one as central as this."

"I haven't seen one as central as this either. I hope as the uterus grows, this placenta moves a little bit toward the back."

"Why's that?"

"If it doesn't, even a C-section will be difficult."

"I don't envy you taking care of this."

"What a way to begin my practice, huh?"

On Sunday evening, Grace called the hospital. Her father had phoned wanting to know why Jessie hadn't brought her home after the weekend visit.

"I completely forgot that I needed to take Grace to George's," Jessie said as she hung up the phone in Ellen's room. "He wants me to call him."

"Please, don't tell him I'm in the hospital," Ellen said.

"I have to, Ellen. I have to explain why I didn't take Grace, and besides, he's your father and he loves you."

"He didn't act like it this summer."

Not having a response for that, Jessie stood and kissed Ellen on the cheek. "I need to go call him."

Jessie called George and explained what had happened. When he didn't offer to come to visit Ellen and get Grace, Jessie agreed to take Grace on Monday while Ellen was still in the hospital.

When Jessie got back from George's on Monday, she came straight to the hospital. Neither she nor Ellen discussed the fact that her father had not come to see her. If Ellen was disappointed, she didn't show it. Jessie, on the other hand, wore a thoughtful frown, closed doors a bit harder than necessary, and avoided eye contact with Ellen. She didn't want to increase Ellen's unhappiness by showing her irritation with George.

"There's no question that you will bleed again," I said as I discussed the ultrasound with Ellen and Jessie on Monday evening. "As you get further along in the pregnancy, the changes that take place in the cervix make it inevitable. Even complete bed rest will not prevent it, but rest will help you bleed less. The question is, do we do the bed rest in the hospital or let you do it at home?"

"I'd rather be at home," Ellen said, even as Jessie blurted, "I think she should stay in the hospital." They both laughed uncomfortably, and Ellen looked at me. "What do you think?"

"I think since you live here in town and since your mom is not working and can stay with you all the time, we can try letting you go home. Jessie, you will need to do your errands when I can be at the house. Someone who can drive Ellen to the hospital must be immediately available at all times. No more out-of-town trips."

George refused to bring Grace back two weeks later. At that point it was almost time for Grace to begin school, so Jessie had to pick her up. Grace liked her school in Lexington and had no intention of living with her father all the time. I stayed with Ellen, who made it through another week before she bled again.

Solo private practice was very different from residency. In residency we shared call and the workload. In solo practice both the call and the work were all mine. Unless I left town or made special arrangements, I was on call all the time. I made two rules for myself. One was for the office and one was for my life outside the office. The office rule was that I could not sleep at night until the paperwork was done, the phone messages all checked, and phone calls made. Even if I had to leave for a delivery or a meeting, I had to go back to the office if I hadn't finished. That rule kept me from having things hanging over my head that I didn't like to do. It protected me from my tendency to procrastinate.

The life rule protected my patients. No matter what celebration, birthday, wedding, Super Bowl party, Derby party, or whatever else came along, I could only have one drink. I never broke it, and there were plenty of times I was thankful for it. One was the next time Ellen bled.

I had a rare date to a football game with a friend from residency, Tom Porter. We tailgated before and after the party at the med school alumni tent. I had a beer with food before the game. After the game, beer flowed freely but I declined, remembering my new rule for life. About thirty minutes later, the ER paged me. Ellen was there.

When I called the ER, I gave them orders to admit Ellen directly to Labor Hall. Then I asked the nurse to transfer me to Labor & Delivery. I didn't have another quarter, and this was long before cell phones. I gave orders to draw a complete blood count, crossmatch more blood, and start an IV. Then I asked Tom to take me to the hospital. Jessie could take me home from there.

When I got to the hospital, I was disappointed to find Ellen in the third labor room and four patients laboring in the other two. It was noisy, but Ellen and Jessie seemed calmer this time. They had been through it before and Ellen was not bleeding quite as heavily, probably because she hadn't been walking all day. They had her IV going by the time I got there, and the fetal monitor showed the baby was fine. During the next six hours, Ellen, Jessie, and I listened as the laboring patients began to push and were rolled into the delivery room.

After three hours, Ellen's bleeding seemed to decrease. I was optimistic until a laboring patient had to be admitted into the second bed in Ellen's room. She was in hard labor, terrified and out of control. She screamed with every contraction and cursed her husband in between contractions. The curtain between their beds failed to prevent a visible effect on Ellen who turned away, pulled her knees up, and assumed a fetal position. In a small voice she asked, "Is that how it's going to be?"

"No, it's not going to be that way for you, and it isn't that way for most women. Some Lamaze classes would have helped her know what to expect and how to deal with it. Part of her problem is that she's afraid the pain is going to get worse or that the contraction isn't going to go away. The pains last about forty-five seconds and then you have a couple of minutes to rest."

"I haven't been able to go to my classes because of this bleeding."

"I know, but you don't need to. Because of this bleeding, you won't go into labor. You will have a C-section long before that." I was surprised that the thought of a C-section could be so comforting, but Ellen smiled and Jessie sighed with relief.

That time Ellen did not bleed quite as long or as heavily, requiring only two units of blood. She stayed in the hospital about three days and then begged to go home again. The baby had grown well, but it was still premature enough to have a very difficult time in the nursery. I let her go.

I overheard one of my colleagues say he thought I should have delivered Ellen. They were the experienced ones, so I doubted myself. I didn't know at the time that none of them had ever dealt with a central placenta praevia or that I never would again.

On Sunday morning, two weeks after Ellen's last bleed, Grace's youth choir sang at church. Jessie wanted to hear her and do a video recording with her new video camera. I made rounds before church so I could be home with Ellen. I had nobody due to deliver, but I was on call for another doctor that weekend. He had no one in labor, so I thought it would be safe. Jessie planned to be gone only about an hour and a half.

She had been gone twenty minutes when I got a call from the hospital. A patient, pregnant with her second baby, had come into the hospital, completely dilated on admission. I needed to go immediately. I checked to see that Ellen was not bleeding and left the number for the ambulance by the phone. I told her to call the ambulance if she saw one drop of blood, and I left the door unlocked so they could get in and she could stay in bed. I had no choice but to go. When I came out of the delivery room, where this second-time mother delivered a nine-pound baby boy after pushing for only twenty minutes, Ellen was in a labor room, bleeding again.

"The ambulance brought me. I left Mama a note."

I could hardly believe this was the sullen, irresponsible teenager from only a few months before. She bled for about eight hours before abruptly stopping again, and she required two more units of blood. Even so, she remained slightly anemic. Ellen was thirty-one weeks now, and I was fairly certain the baby was still too immature to be delivered without risk of serious respiratory disease.

"Ellen, I need to find out how mature your baby is," I said.

"How do you do that?"

"I stick a needle into the uterus, draw out some fluid, and test it for the ratio of lecithin to sphingomyelin; it's called an L/S ratio. It needs to be two before I deliver your baby."

"Does that mean I won't have to wait until the end of October?"

"It sure does."

"Then let's do it."

Ultrasound confirmed the placenta location was unchanged; it lay directly in front of the baby's head, which measured consistent with the estimated thirty-one weeks of gestation. Normal changes in the cervix as labor approached would increase both the frequency and the quantity of bleeding.

"Look at this, Ellen, boy parts."

"Really? Let's not tell Mom."

"That will be your call."

As I expected, the L/S ratio was only 1.6, indicating that the baby's lungs were immature and he would likely have to be on a respirator to survive. Since I had proof that this baby would have difficulty if delivered, and since I had already garnered the criticism of my colleagues, I decided to wait again. Because the risk of more frequent and heavier bleeding posed serious risks for Ellen, this time she stayed in the hospital with two units of blood held ready in the lab for transfusion at a moment's notice.

Almost miraculously, Ellen did not bleed again until thirty-four weeks, at which time a second amniocentesis showed the L/S ratio at 1.9. That was close. I wanted it over 2.0.

"Ellen, I'm going to deliver your baby by C-section on Monday in two weeks if you don't bleed in the meantime," I announced. "If you do bleed, I'll do a C-section immediately, but I prefer to have it scheduled so the pediatricians can be better prepared for the baby."

"Will he be all right?"

"Yes, I think so, but the longer we can wait the better for the baby, though with greater risk for you."

Ellen waited one more week before she bled again. It was the autumnal equinox, Tuesday, September 20. Jessie and Grace were visiting at the time. I had just finished in the office. I called the pediatrician and we went to the operating room. Current hospital rules allowed Jessie to be present, and Grace waited in the doctors' lounge. In the interest of speed, Ellen got a general anesthetic rather than an epidural. It took a minute longer, but I made a low transverse skin incision. I figured I could handle criticism for that and the scar would never show. I did make a low vertical uterine incision, knowing that the placenta was attached over the part of the uterus we normally incise at C-section. The top of the vertical incision could be extended upward if more room was needed and the bottom came to the edge of the placental attachment. I placed my hand between the placenta and head and gently pulled the head through the incision; the body easily followed. A four-pound, six-ounce baby boy screamed as I handed him to the pediatrician.

"He looks good," she said. Jessie's attention immediately went to the baby. She and the pediatrician stopped to show the baby to Grace on the way to the nursery while I delivered the placenta, checked for bleeding, and closed the incisions.

I waited to check Ellen's hemoglobin level after delivery before giving more blood. We had been able to deliver her so quickly that I hoped she wouldn't need it. When it came back seven, she got one more unit. Fortunately, with the autotransfusion you get with delivery, she did not need more.

The baby required ultraviolet light for jaundice but had no breathing difficulties and no feeding difficulties. He looked like a carbon copy of Ellen—blonde hair, blue eyes, and the same ski-jump nose. Since Ellen looked just like her father so did this baby. *How ironic*, I thought. *I wonder when his grandfather will see him.*

Ellen surprised me again. She took her pain medicine every three hours for twenty-four hours and then never asked for it again. She was hungry almost immediately and tolerated regular food on the second day. Maybe it was because she had been on bed rest for so long, but for whatever reason, she bounced in and out of bed like nothing had happened.

When I stopped by for evening rounds on the second day, Jessie and Grace were visiting. "Your chart looks good—you look good. How're you doing?" I asked Ellen.

"I'm fine. When do I get to go home?"

"Tomorrow, if your blood count stays up and this food stays down."

"Will Henry get to go home then too?"

"Who?"

"Carl Henry Green." She beamed. "I named him for you and your Uncle Henry."

"But you didn't know him, Ellen."

"Yes, but Mom talks about him all the time. My baby has a life because of you, and we have a home because of Mr. Henry." So it was that the first of many babies was named for me, and my precious, childless Uncle Henry had a namesake.

Though it was early fall, the day was very chilly. At home that evening Jessie and I built a fire, which always reminded us of Grace and the first night she had stayed in that house. What a miracle it was that her remission continued. Grace went to her room to do homework, while Jessie and I talked about Henry, the new and the old.

"You know, it was Ellen's idea," Jessie said.

"What was Ellen's idea?"

"The name."

"I was amazed."

"Are you pleased?"

"How could I not be pleased? It is truly an honor for me. I don't think it will ever cease to be, even if a hundred babies are named for me, but I may be even more pleased for Uncle Henry."

"Do you think he knows?"

"I hope so." We sat in a comfortable silence for a while. "Jessie, do you remember what Uncle Henry once told you?"

"There were many things. What are you thinking?"

"I was thinking about how he told you that God would redeem what happened to you, that from the bad He would bring good. I wonder what would have happened to both Grace and Ellen if you hadn't been in a position to help them the way you have."

"I'm grateful every day that I have been able to help the girls. I wish I could have done more for Jeff. I've given money so he can attend the college he wants, but he doesn't know, and now that he's in college I probably won't have much opportunity to see him."

I realized that as involved as I had been with Jessie's family, I had only seen Jeff that one night after his middle school ballgame.

"I need him to forgive me," Jessie said almost to herself.

After Jessie and Grace left to visit Ellen at the hospital, I continued to sit by the fire. When the phone rang, I was startled from an unplanned nap. "May I speak to Cara Land," a vaguely familiar bass voice said.

"This is she."

"Cara, this is Jon Parker, you may not remember me."

"Of course I remember you. I'm glad you called, though I didn't expect that you would. Are you well?"

"Yes, thank you, I am."

"I called your office the day after you left class and learned that you had not only left the university, but even Lexington."

"Yes, I'm in the Air Force Reserves, and I left to have tests at an Air Force hospital in California. I was a member of Air Force Operation Ranch Hand, the unit responsible for the aerial spraying of Agent Orange in Vietnam. Any time we have a problem, they want to investigate. I was there all summer."

"Someone mentioned Agent Orange and I gave you leukemia. I hope I was wrong. You know the curse of being a medical doctor."

"Yes, you were wrong, thankfully. I had a terrible skin reaction, more common and less deadly."

"I am so glad to have been wrong."

"I was wondering if you would go out with me. I'm going to be tied up for a couple of weeks, but the fall meet at Keeneland opens on October 7. Would you like to go with me? It's a Friday so I know you may be working."

"I'd love to go. With this much notice, I may be able to arrange to be off. My only problem would be if I have already scheduled somebody for surgery."

"I understand. I wouldn't want my doctor to change my surgery to have a date."

"Since I just started my private practice this summer, I don't have much surgery scheduled. Can I call you tomorrow after I check at the office?"

"Sure. My number is 255-6323." I memorized the number, and we talked until the fire died and Jessie and Grace came home from the hospital.

Ellen went home on the fifth postoperative day. She could have gone sooner, but she stayed so she could take little Henry with her. It seemed that all was going to be well for the fifteen-year-old mother, her baby, and her inexperienced doctor, but Ellen had gotten one transfusion too many.

CHAPTER 8

On October 7, a perfect autumn day, Jon Parker and I went to opening day of the fall race meet at Keeneland. The sky created a bright blue background for the red and gold trees spread around the grounds. Summer rains had kept the grass emerald green. I thought again how there were few places more beautiful than Kentucky in October.

Jon looked gorgeous, wearing khaki pants, a light blue shirt, and a navy blazer. His navy tie was covered with jockey silks that represented some of the more famous stables. I had been to the races before, but not often. I didn't know much about the horses or betting, but Jon had come to Lexington because he loved horses. He explained how he read the racing form and admitted that he knew a few of the trainers, who had given him some tips. First time out of the gate, we won the daily double. It paid thirty-nine dollars for a two-dollar bet. We split our bets and won a few more races, but that first ticket was special, as was the whole afternoon.

Jon walked down to the paddock to look at the horses while they warmed up for each race. As he watched closely, he talked about conformation, ankle taping, and demeanor. I didn't know whether it was better for the horse to be calm or excited, but it was clear that Jon was there because he loved them.

At dinner after the races, Jon told me about growing up all over the world. His father, a career pilot in the Air Force, had been stationed in Germany, Hawaii, and a number of other states. Fluent in both German and Spanish, he had traveled all over Western Europe. As he talked I sensed that he was aware of the advantages that living in and traveling all over Western Europe brought, but he said it had been lonely at times. His parents were now retired to Florida.

"I love to travel," I said, "but I have always lived here."

"This has to be one of the most beautiful places in the world."

"I agree, but I think you may be influenced by those big animals you love so much."

He smiled. "Could be, but you need to see my farm if you want to see beautiful."

"I didn't realize you live on a farm."

"Yes, three hundred acres, just over the Fayette County line on Paris Pike."

"That is some of the area's best farmland."

"Would you like to come to dinner tomorrow evening? I'd love for you to see it."

"Sure. I will even arrange to be off and come without a pager."

If I were not already falling in love with Jon Parker, I would have been after that evening in his home. The drive out Paris Pike was a buffet for the senses. The air was crisp as I drove with the windows down to let the wind blow my face and hair. The stone walls and white fences stood against a background of gently rolling green pastures. Red and gold leaves covered the mature trees that lined the two-lane road. No wonder there was a movement to prevent widening it. That battle would be waged for years.

After just a few miles, the noise of the city was gone. I turned off the radio to listen to the silence of the country. As I turned into the driveway lined with white wooden fences that led to Jon's restored century-old house, I smelled the charcoal grill already burning.

Jon's house was a wonder of understated masculinity. There were no pictures of flowers on the walls, but neither were there deer heads. I did note a number of paintings of horses in races, in green pastures, and in barns. The dark brown leather sofa and chairs in his den were complemented by dark walnut tables, but the woodwork was painted white and the walls were covered with grass-cloth paper in muted shades of green.

During the restoration the wall between the kitchen and den had been removed, making a great room. A huge stone fireplace stood in the center of the wall opposite the kitchen, flanked by built-in bookcases filled with books on subjects as diverse as horse breeding and world history. A bar with four stools separated the kitchen from the living area. The centerpiece of the kitchen was a commercial gas range with six burners and two ovens. I wondered if Jon did serious cooking.

When Jon came to the door, a little dog accompanied him—not a breed familiar to me.

"Hi, Cara, come in. I want you to meet Pippen." Pippen was barking and jumping on my leg. "Down boy," he said. The dog settled.

"Hi, Pippen, you're a cute one. What kind of dog is he?"

"He's a Norfolk terrier. In recent years they were made a separate breed. Previously, they were drop-eared Norwich terriers. They're rare, less than three hundred born a year in this country."

I guessed Pippen's weight. "You gotta love a man who lives in a big house on three hundred acres with a thirteen-pound dog."

"He thinks he's a big dog," Jon said with a deep chuckle that would warm my heart for years to come. "He once went after a Rottweiler. Fortunately, they were both on leashes and he didn't get him."

"Pippen. Is that for Peregrin Took?"

"Yes, so you know *The Lord of the Rings*."

"I spent one of my spring breaks in college reading it."

"What? No bikini-clad fraternity parties on a Florida beach?"

"This has never been a bikini body."

"I like the curves."

"And I like bald."

I moved into my newly restored old house during the first week of November, and Jon helped me. We had just finished carrying in the last box when Jessie called.

"Cara, I need you to come," she said as soon as I answered the phone.

"Where are you?"

"I'm at UK hospital with Grace. She fainted at school earlier today, and I brought her into the ER. We just saw Dr. Campbell, and she admitted Grace to room 413."

"Do they think her leukemia is out of remission?" I was sick to think that as soon as Ellen delivered, Grace might be ill.

"We don't know. They've drawn a lot of blood, but no results are back yet."

"What can I do?"

"They said she may need to see a gynecologist."

"Oh . . . why?"

"Her first period started about two weeks ago, and she's still bleeding heavily."

"Maybe that is all that's wrong with her. She looked good when I saw her two weeks ago."

When I got to the hospital, I found Grace looking pale. Her heart rate was rapid, and her blood pressure dropped when she sat up.

"How much are you bleeding?" I asked.

"Mom got maxi pads, and I have to change about once or twice an hour."

"That seems pretty heavy. How long have you bled like that?"

"The whole two weeks."

"This all may be from acute blood loss," I said as I offered a prayer that it was not a recurrence of her leukemia. "I think you will need a pelvic exam, but let's wait until we get the blood work and I can talk to Dr. Campbell. Since she's the attending physician, she will need to request a consult."

"Isn't she too young for a pelvic exam?" Jessie asked.

"No, but I will modify it a bit. I'll get an ultrasound to check for ovarian masses and uterine size, rather than doing a bimanual exam. Also, they make small specula to use in children. Mostly, I need to see if there are masses or lacerations."

"Why would she have lacerations?"

"I doubt that she does, but we have to be sure." I avoided answering the question. "Most young women don't ovulate until they have bled for about a year. During that year the periods can be extremely heavy."

"What do you do about it?"

Before I could answer that question, Dr. Campbell came in with Grace's test results.

"Grace's hemoglobin is seven. I have scheduled her for blood transfusion of two units of packed red cells. The good news is that there are normal numbers and no abnormal white cells. I believe this is from blood loss not leukemia, so I'm going to consult the gynecologists."

"Dr. Campbell, do you remember my friend, Dr. Cara Land? She's a gynecologist. Would it be possible for her to do Grace's consult?"

"Yes, of course."

"I'll go have the nurses set up the exam room on the third floor," I said. "The sooner we check, the sooner we can get this bleeding stopped."

It is never easy doing pelvic exams on virginal twelve-year-old girls, but Grace was brave and Jessie held her hand. A small speculum is easily inserted as long as the child is not terrified and fighting the exam. If that happens, rather than force an exam that doesn't tell you anything, it is best to use a general anesthetic. Grace was able to relax enough for an adequate exam without anesthesia. Her cervix and vagina looked normal. The ultrasound confirmed normal ovaries and no uterine enlargement.

"Everything looks normal," I said when all the tests were done. "This bleeding appears to be due to immature pituitary-ovarian regulation."

"Can you make it stop?"

"Yes, Grace. The bleeding will stop with estrogen and progestin pills four times a day and IV Premarin. We'll add the Premarin to your IV as soon as this transfusion is finished. You will need to take the pills for three weeks. When you stop you will have another period, but it will be shorter and more moderate in flow. After that I want you to take birth control pills."

"Isn't she young to be on pills?"

"It will only be for three months, so she can recover her strength and have light periods. Then we will control the bleeding with synthetic progestin every six to eight weeks if she doesn't have regular periods on her own."

"I need to call your father, Grace," Jessie said. "Is there anything you want me to tell him?"

"Tell him he doesn't need to come. I'm fine and will come to see him next weekend at my usual time." Then, looking at me, she added, "I can go to see him then, can't I?"

"Yes."

When Jessie left the room to call George, Grace said, "I don't want Dad to come and see me since he didn't come to see Ellen. I'm afraid it would make her feel even worse. I can't believe he doesn't want to see Henry." *Only Grace would be thinking of her sister at a time like this,* I thought.

The medicines worked as predicted and Grace was discharged after three days.

On Thanksgiving Day, Jon and I went to dinner at Jessie's. Ellen was there with a healthy baby Henry. She had lost all of her baby weight and wore an outfit that she had designed and made. The pants were wide wale corduroy in a rich shade of brown, paired with a matching vest and ecru blouse. On the front of the vest she had appliquéd two small leaves in shades of rust with a larger one on the back. Ellen looked tired, but no one was surprised at that. She insisted on taking care of Henry, who was still waking at night. Henry weighed ten pounds and charmed everybody, including Jon.

Grace had been to her father's the weekend before so she was able to be present for all of Thanksgiving weekend, though she did have to spend part of her time catching up on school work she had missed while in the hospital. She looked grown-up, wearing navy slacks and a light blue turtleneck sweater.

Jessie looked more beautiful than I had ever seen her. She wore what had become her trademark gray slacks and pink sweater and hustled around attending to everyone's needs. She laughed easily and fussed over Henry. Both of her daughters were with her and past their frightening ordeals. After her prayer, in which she expressed thanks for those blessings and many others, she said, "In memory of Mr. Henry, I declare this the official opening of the eating season." As if on cue, Jon laughed, and I realized he was a keeper. Even Ellen laughed this year.

Jessie made a further announcement at that dinner. "I have decided to take a job at the Florence Crittenden Home after the holidays. They have an opening for a nurse." Jessie and I were familiar with Florence Crittenden Home from our days working in Labor & Delivery at the UK hospital. It was a home for unwed mothers. The girls got their medical care and delivery at the UK Medical Center and continued their education at the home.

"Ellen can still do homeschooling for the rest of this year, but she won't need me at home with her all the time," Jessie said.

"I've decided that I would like to take the GED test and skip my last year of high school," Ellen said. Before Jessie could protest, Ellen continued. "I think it will be better to be in college with a baby than in high school." Ellen had not discussed this with her mother, but it seemed to be a mature, well-thought-out decision. "I want to study fashion design and merchandising."

"What a good idea," Jessie said, smiling. "You'll be great at that." She walked around the table and hugged her daughter. "I am so proud of you, honey."

Jessie sighed as she sat back down. "Today would have been perfect if Jeff had been here."

"He wasn't going to be at Dad's either," Grace volunteered.

"Where was he going to be?" Jessie asked.

"Dad said last weekend that he called and told him he was going to spend Thanksgiving with his girlfriend's family."

"I didn't even know he had a girlfriend. Do you know anything about her?"

"Just that she lives here in Lexington and her name is Sara."

For the first time that day the smile left Jessie's face. Almost as if to herself, she said, "Right here in Lexington and I won't see him."

New Year's Eve and Valentine's Day had always been nonholidays for me. I may have had one date on New Year's Eve, and when I was an intern on the Internal Medicine service at the Veteran's Administration Hospital, one of my patients—a very charming alcoholic—gave me a box of bourbon balls for Valentine's Day. Other than that, the only valentines I had received were the boxed variety I got in elementary school. Things were different in 1978 and ever after.

Jon took me to a New Year's Eve party at the Lexington Country Club. We danced in the New Year and kissed at midnight. Then on Valentine's Day, he got down on one knee and presented me with a tiny black box.

"Cara, I know we haven't dated very long," he said, "but neither one of us is getting any younger. I love you, and I want to spend the rest of my life with you and your patients. Will you marry me?"

Both thrilled and shocked, I simply said, "Yes." He could not have made a more perfect proposal. He clearly understood how much a part of my life my patients were, and I understood how lucky that made me.

When I told Jessie that we planned to get married the following October, she immediately offered to help me with the planning. She knew me better than anyone and also knew I had no family to help. While I didn't want a big wedding, I still had to arrange church, ceremony, music, reception, invitations, flowers, cake, dress, and a dozen other things about which Jessie knew and I did not.

One Saturday in late March, I stopped by Jessie's home to work on the planning. When I arrived Ellen came in rather shyly and asked to show me something. After I agreed, she went to her room and came back with the design of a wedding dress she had drawn. It was beautiful. She knew my taste for simple lines, no frills, and natural fabrics. The fitted bodice had a deep jewel neckline that extended to the shoulders. The long sleeves were decorated with covered buttons at the wrist, the same buttons that extended down the back. The tea-length skirt had a flat panel in front with gathers at the back.

"If you like it, Mother and I will make it of silk and give it to you for a wedding gift," she said. "Only if you like it."

"What's not to like? The dress is beautiful, and it's perfect for me. You considered that I would not like strapless or sleeveless. The flat panel in the front with gathers in the back masks some of my figure deficits. I love cotton, wool, and silk. Ellen, this dress shows that it was designed for me by a very talented young woman who knows me, wants to please me, and wants to have me look beautiful at my wedding. Thank you. I love it."

"I'm going to start now," she chirped as she jumped up and left the room.

Grace sat by the window with a pair of binoculars and watched a robin build a nest in a box she had put in a tree last fall. "Mother is going to help me, and we're going to make the cake. I'm going to take a class in cake decorating this summer. What kind of cake do you want?"

"My favorite is carrot, and I think Jon likes everything."

"Carrot it is. It needs to have white icing, and carrot cake does."

At ten in the morning on October 28, 1978, about one hundred guests watched as Jon Parker and I married in a beautiful ceremony at Christ Church Cathedral. I wore Ellen's dress. Jessie was the single attendant. The church and country club were filled with calla lilies. Grace cut the cake that she and her mother had made, and Ellen kept the guest book. Jon's father was his best man. We were happy.

PART TWO

Elaine screamed. The sound pierced three doors and reached the top of the stairwell just as I did. It erased all hope of the New Year's Eve party I planned to attend that night. I rushed into the room and said, "Let's waltz. One, two, three, in, out, out, in, two, three." Almost immediately, she began to breathe with me.

"That's great. You can do it. That was the peak. It's beginning to go away."

Twenty seconds later, she smiled as she turned to me. "I'm glad to see you, Dr. Parker. The contractions are getting much harder." *What a difference a minute makes,* I thought as I smiled back at her.

The birthing room with cherry furniture and hardwood floors did not look much like the labor rooms of twenty years ago when I started practicing Obstetrics. Ruffled curtains covered the windows and flowered wallpaper added to the homelike atmosphere, a marked improvement over bubblegum pink paint. Thick area rugs invited bare feet to curl their toes, and on a small counter a coffeepot invited family and friends to sustain themselves while the patients had to refrain.

"Are we going to have a baby today, or do you want to have the New Year's baby?" I asked.

"I hope it's today. We could use the tax break, and if these contractions aren't the real thing, then I'm in trouble."

"Where's your husband?"

"He's gone to the car to get my bag, and then he's calling our parents. We're going to ruin everyone's New Year's Eve."

I thought how New Year's Eve is my least favorite holiday. "I would say you are going to *make* everyone's New Year's Eve. A new grandbaby is a great way to start the New Year. I doubt your parents will mind missing a party."

"I guess you're right. They seem pretty excited about this baby."

"It looks like the contraction is coming again. Let's get through this one; then I'll check your progress. Take a deep breath in and blow it out. Again. That's the way. When it gets too hard do the waltz breathing again." She started to breathe just as I had instructed.

While Elaine finished that contraction, her nurse assembled the supplies we needed to examine her. "This contraction is almost finished. Take a deep breath and let it out. Now relax a minute. When you're ready, turn onto your back for your exam."

Elaine did as I requested, and I noted that she had more bleeding than I expected. I tried not to appear alarmed by the bleeding as I considered all the possibilities. Having your first baby at thirty-six is old enough to be considered high risk. I knew from ultrasound that the placenta position was normal, so I continued with the exam and told her the findings. My concern was that increased bleeding might mean premature separation of the placenta, a dangerous condition for both baby and mother.

"The baby's head is well down into the pelvis and perfectly positioned," I told her. "The cervix is dilated five centimeters and completely thinned out."

At that moment a contraction started, bulging membranes ruptured, and clear fluid gushed out. It soaked my sleeve along with the pads on her bed. At least that time I missed the salty taste. The clear fluid brought with it reassurance of the baby's well-being. Extra bleeding was apparently due to very active labor.

"Your water just broke. You may get that tax break after all," I joked as we waltzed through another contraction. As Elaine turned to her side to rest between contractions, I said, "He has a lot of hair."

"He?" she asked, laughing.

"He, a generic term in preference to *it*." They had chosen not to be told the sex of the baby from ultrasound.

"Blond or brunet?"

"Hey, I'm just telling you this by feel. I can't see what color it is. Your contractions will pick up in both frequency and intensity now that your water has broken. If you feel you need medication for pain or want an epidural anesthetic, now is the time."

"I want to try to do this without medication."

"Fine, just let me know if you change your mind. I would like to use a fetal monitor. You're having a little more bleeding than I expect, so I want to observe the baby closely." She stiffened and I reassured her. "The amniotic fluid was clear so I think he's fine. The monitor is just a precaution."

Elaine struggled through the next contraction, her fear magnifying her pain. When it ended she leaned forward and her nurse dropped the monitor straps behind her back and tightened them around her abdomen. Immediately we were reassured by the rapid heartbeat, which increased slightly as the baby kicked.

"The baby looks fine," I said. "I'll be in the doctors' lounge if you need me."

With that I left the room, picked up a cup of decaf, and headed down the hall. After four thousand babies, I still liked to stay at the hospital once they were dilated five centimeters. I knew it could be anywhere from one to seven hours before delivery, but I hated to rush in at the last minute. My presence in the hospital had a calming and encouraging effect, as Elaine had just confirmed.

In the lounge, I settled down with my counted cross-stitch bell pull to stitch and wait. That bell pull, my first effort at counted cross-stitch, was a three-and-a-half-year project. Another patient and friend had loaned me the pattern, three scenes of Japanese women in beautiful kimonos, worked on Modena cloth with twenty-two stitches to the inch. Shades of pink and green were perfect for my home. I had just started that bell pull when I met Elaine. It was nearly finished. As I stitched I prayed that Elaine and her baby would be healthy and she would be spared a complicated labor. Soon, my mind wandered to the day I met her.

CHAPTER 10

Elaine Green was attractive, not so much that women were jealous or men lost their train of thought in her presence, nor so much for her strawberry blonde hair, big blue eyes, and great figure as for her expressive face, at once gentle and curious. Just watching her through the waiting room window, I liked her. Besides being early for her first appointment, which always garnered the favor of the office staff, she looked at an album of our baby pictures instead of *People* magazine. She turned the pages with a faint smile that broadened when she came to a particularly scrunched baby.

For the first visit I always saw patients in my consultation office while they were fully dressed. Intentionally small, my office had two walls made of windows that gave wonderful natural light but made it cold in winter. Neutral-colored drapes were closed for warmth, but that summer day they were wide open to let in the sunshine. A light oak burl wood desk, wicker table, and rattan chairs created a relaxed atmosphere, a place conducive to intimate discussions.

"Did you deliver all of those babies?" she asked as Anita, my nurse, showed Elaine into my office.

"Yes. I noticed you looked as though you were enjoying the photos. We used to have them stuck on a bulletin board but found the albums more popular and easier to peruse."

"I love children. It must be wonderful to be the first person to touch them."

"Well, their mothers are first, but attending birth is a wonderful experience. Do you have children?"

She dropped her gaze and shifted in her chair. "No."

Initially she said she was there for a routine checkup and denied problems, so the interview was short. We moved on to her physical exam. Her exam completed, she dressed and returned to the consultation office.

"Congratulations, Mrs. Green, you're pregnant." Usually when I say those words, patients respond with smiles and sometimes tears of joy. I thought that in light of our earlier conversation she would be happy; we could set a follow-up appointment and I would be on to the next patient, but her tears held no joy. I knew this would take a while.

"Mrs. Green, is something wrong?"

She made an effort to control her trembling and hide her expressive face behind her long blonde hair. "Dr. Parker, what am I going to do? My husband has had a vasectomy." Suddenly, concern about other patients' waiting seemed like nothing compared to this woman's problems. When she tucked her hair behind her ear and looked at me, her narrowed eyes and furrowed brow showed her distress.

"I am so sorry. Of course, I should have asked if you wanted to have a baby."

"I do want to have a baby more than anything." Sometimes it's best to say nothing and give people time to tell their story. I waited.

"I love my husband very much. He's a good man and would be a wonderful father. I want to have *his* baby. Dr. Parker, you know my husband. He's the one who wanted me to see you."

"Who is he?"

"Mike Green."

I wanted to cry. Not only did I know her husband, I loved him. His first wife, Sara, had been my patient. I watched him stand by her during her battle with breast cancer. I argued with the urologist over his agreeing to perform the vasectomy, and I still held it against the man. Mike was twenty-six at the time. We were all hopeful that Sara was cured but recommended that she avoid pregnancy. Since she had been through so much, Mike didn't want her to have a tubal ligation. I thought a healthy man so young should keep his options open and wanted Sara to have an intrauterine device, but they decided on the vasectomy. A year later she died after spending months in the hospital, during which time I got to know Mike very well.

He grew up in a small town in northern Kentucky. Spending summers with his paternal grandparents, who lived on a farm nearby, he learned to love animals and the outdoors. He and Sara had two Labrador retrievers with whom Mike ran every day. If being an attentive husband under such difficult circumstances were not enough to make you love him, there were his rugged good looks, his intelligence, and his manners.

Elaine continued, "I was one of Sara's best friends. Several months after she died, I started seeing Mike. I knew he had the vasectomy, but I loved him enough to give up having children if he wouldn't have it reversed or if a reversal failed. We married and have been very happy, but lately he has worked night and day. He does every tax season, but now he is so busy his work doesn't slow down much at any time." Her voice broke.

After a long pause she continued, "About three weeks ago Mike and I quarreled about his long hours and the fact that we had not made love in weeks. I told him I felt lonely and missed him. I had to go out of town to a meeting for a long weekend, and I begged him to go. He said he just couldn't with his work, and I thought I understood, but I was still angry and disappointed.

"Greg Miller, one of Mike's golfing buddies and my boss, attended the meeting. He is a very attractive man and the topic of much discussion at the office. We all laughed at one of the secretaries who almost got caught cruising by his house at midnight. She bought a new car that turned out to be a lemon. It died at the corner two houses down from his, and he came home while she was sitting there. He didn't recognize her, and she had to call Triple A from his neighbor's house.

"I had never thought about Greg in that way, so after dinner the first night of the meeting when he suggested we relax and watch a movie in my room, I agreed. I was still feeling angry and lonely. He brought a bottle of wine, and I had two glasses. I told him about the argument I had with Mike, and he took my side. I thought he was comforting me when he put his arm around me, and when he flirted I felt flattered. I was mad at Mike, but I knew nothing would happen. Greg was Mike's friend. Maybe I gave him the wrong impression.

"When he kissed me, I pulled away but he was insistent. He put his hand inside my blouse and I tried to push him away again. He stared at me with a cold, piercing look and said, 'I don't want any trouble.' I felt frozen to the spot, like I could see my breath in the chill. I was afraid, but I couldn't get up and leave. We were in my room. Neither could I think of a way to make him leave. I tried reasoning with him, reminded him that I was married, that he was one of Mike's best friends, that the office had a policy against sexual relationships among the employees. He said that no one would ever know. I said, 'I will know. Please leave.' His response was to pick me up and throw me onto the bed. I hadn't thought about birth control for three years. I guess Greg must have assumed I was on the pill."

"Are you saying you were raped?"

"Can you believe, I don't know?" Elaine said, her eyes wide. "I didn't want to have sex with Greg. I said no, but I didn't fight. I felt fear rather than attraction. I have since wondered what else I could have or should have done. It seems less painful to feel flattered and seduced than to admit I was assaulted."

"So you did not report this to anyone?"

"No, I still have to work with him."

"Elaine, did you suspect you were pregnant when you came to see me today?"

"Well, I guess I knew I could be. I was a few days late, but that has happened before."

Hoping the answer was no, I asked, "Have you discussed the possibility with anyone?"

"Well, Greg noticed that I was upset. I think he was worried that I might report what happened. I mentioned that I was going to the doctor. He knows I could be pregnant. He said he would help me if I am."

Though I couldn't say it, I thought he had helped his friends enough. Instead I asked, "What kind of help did he have in mind?"

"I guess he meant he would take me for an abortion. I believe abortion is wrong, and I always said I would never have one, but now I don't know. I've never demonstrated, but I've been critical of women who had abortions."

"Contrary to what some people think, abortion is not an easy way out."

Again she said, this time pitifully, "Dr. Parker, what am I going to do? I really want to have a baby, but I love my husband. Do you think I'm awful?"

I thanked God I was not premenstrual, tried to suppress my emotions and find the right words to say. I didn't know how responsible she was for this mess, but I felt very sorry for her and I believed her when she said she loved her husband. I loved him too.

"Elaine, I try very hard not to judge. Have you and Mike ever considered having a vasectomy reversal?"

"We discussed it at first, but I didn't want to have a baby then, and he seemed relieved. After I felt differently, I didn't know how to tell him."

"Can you tell Mike what you just told me and ask him to forgive you?"

"No," she said without a moment's hesitation.

"Are you absolutely sure of that?"

"He would never forgive me. When he was twelve years old his mother ran off with a man, deserting him and his sisters. Several months later, his parents divorced and he has seen very little of his mother since. He had been very close to her, being the oldest. He never forgave her, and he won't forgive me. I simply cannot do this to him. I don't want to lose him. I depend on him for everything. I can't imagine my life without him."

I tried a different tack. "Since you really do want to have a baby, abortion will be a very difficult option for you. Mike is going to notice you're upset. I would suggest you tell him as much of the truth as possible. Tell him you want a baby, and ask him to have the vasectomy reversal. Elaine, you're going to need someone to support you through this. Do you have family here?"

"No. I'm an only child; my mother is dead, and I rarely speak to my father."

"What about friends?"

"My best friends from church are pro-life activists. They do lectures and demonstrate. My next best friends are Mike's sisters. After them are the people from work, who also know the firm's policy against sexual activity among employees."

"I don't often come right out and tell my patients what to do, but I am making an exception here. Please don't discuss this with Greg. If you really want to protect your husband, do not give his friend any more knowledge of what is going on than he already has. Tell Greg you are not pregnant, and don't let him be your confidant. Think of someone else, or call me if you need to. Even though you didn't fight him off, he was not being your friend when he forced himself on you. I doubt you can trust him with this."

"Thank you, Dr. Parker. I'm sure that's good advice. I'll need someone to talk to."

"You're about five weeks' pregnant now. You have about five more weeks for abortion to remain a safe option. Please consider this decision carefully. Let's schedule a consultation visit next week so you can ask whatever questions come to mind after you have had time to think. I don't perform abortions, but this office can assist you with scheduling if that is what you decide. If I can help you in any way, please don't hesitate to call me." I couldn't remember a time when I felt any more helpless.

Elaine sat quietly a moment. "What kind of choice do I have? Either I choose to destroy my baby, or I choose to destroy my marriage." In that moment I understood why people feel like helpless victims. If the consequences of your actions are terrible either way, you don't realize you have a real choice to make.

A week later Elaine came to discuss her situation. Her shoulders slumped and she held her head down. Dark circles beneath her eyes said she had not slept and was no closer to a decision.

"You look tired," I said as she walked into my office.

"I haven't been sleeping, and I'm queasy all the time."

"Have you had any bleeding or pain?" I used the old doctor's ploy of dealing with physical problems when emotional ones are difficult to address.

"No, I guess it's just morning sickness."

"Have you made a decision?"

"No, I keep going back and forth. I went shopping for some shoes and ended up in the baby department. I ran into an acquaintance there, and she asked if I was pregnant. She was so excited that we might be pregnant together. I lied and said I was looking for a shower present."

"Have you discussed this with anyone?"

"No, but you were right about one thing. Mike did notice I was upset about something. I told him I wanted to have a baby, and he shocked me by saying he would go get a vasectomy reversal as soon as the late filing period is over. He said he had been thinking about it himself, and he wanted to have a baby too. I was elated, but the feeling didn't last long. I know I have to have an abortion. I guess I should go ahead and have your secretary help make the arrangements, but I'm just not ready."

"You still have some time. Do you have any other questions?"

"No."

About two weeks later Elaine called. "I can't have this baby," she said. "Mike would never forgive me if he found out. He will not tolerate infidelity."

"But, if you were forced . . ."

"I could never convince him of that. I haven't even convinced myself. No, I have to have an abortion even though I want to have a baby."

I gave her the name of a reputable doctor in Cincinnati, about ninety miles away. I explained that I could see her for her six-week postoperative visit if she did not want to repeat the trip to Cincinnati. A sense of foreboding washed over me when she said that Greg would be taking her. I wished she had not confided in him. I felt certain that it would increase the strain on her marriage. Maybe she was not as interested in saving her marriage as I believed. Still, she was having an abortion to save it—an abortion when she wanted to have a baby.

CHAPTER 11

_____

A few days later a red Corvette with a vanity plate, STUD, caught my eye as Jon and I watched the evening news. The Corvette was parked in front of an abortion clinic where a pro-life demonstration was taking place. The second abortion doctor had just been murdered on July 29, 1994, and more demonstrations followed. I listened with interest because the first doctor, killed in Florida, had been my medical school classmate. Already upset about his death, I was even more disturbed when I learned how unkind people had been to his family. Regardless of how people felt about his occupation, his mother had lost a son. How in the name of pro-life can someone kill? As I listened to the story, I realized this was the same clinic where Elaine had gone for her abortion and wondered if Greg drove a red Corvette.

Two days later the headline in the morning paper read "Local Accountant Kills Wife's Lover." The article said there had been a struggle and Greg Miller, a local attorney, was killed by Mike Green, the husband of Elaine Green, a paralegal for Miller's law office. The article alleged that Green had learned of an affair between Miller and his wife. I knew Elaine would suffer as a result of the abortion, but I had no idea how much, how quickly, or how much others would suffer as well. Somehow I knew Greg had betrayed her.

Six weeks later Elaine came into my office for her post abortion checkup. She was neatly dressed, wearing makeup, and had an attractive clasp in her hair. "You look good," I said as I walked into the exam room.

"Mike is out of jail on bond. I try to look my best, but he still won't speak to me. He stays in the guestroom."

I designed the tables in my exam rooms to be at standing height so as to be efficient with my time and not be tempted to talk too long. This time I just sat on my stool and looked up at Elaine who sat at the end of the exam table.

"Elaine, what in the world happened? I can't imagine Mike killing anybody."

She held my gaze only a moment then stared out the window and spoke in a vacant tone. "Because of the infidelity, they say Mike had a motive for killing Greg, but, Dr. Parker, it was an accident." She looked back at me. "Mike and I were watching the news and saw Greg's car parked at the abortion clinic."

"Not the red Corvette?"

"Yes, the red Corvette, you can't miss it. The day after the abortion, Greg stopped by the house, and Mike teased him about seeing the car. He said, 'Tough luck having CNN tell the world you knocked up your girlfriend. I saw your car on TV, buddy. You need to practice safe sex or drive an Escort.' Well, that made Greg mad, and he said, 'Why don't you ask your wife what she knows about it?'"

Elaine paused for a moment. "Mike turned to me with the question. I started to cry, and he said, 'What's he talking about; what do you know about it?' He still did not imagine the horrible truth. He trusted me completely.

"When I said nothing, he turned back to Greg who said, 'If you took care of your wife, none of this would have happened. I took her to have an abortion.' I shouldn't have been surprised that Greg betrayed me that way, but I was.

"I will never forget the stricken look on Mike's face as he just stood there. Greg moved over to him in a threatening sort of way and said, 'Well, what do you say to that?'

"Mike looked at me and said, 'How did you get pregnant?'

"'Unsafe sex with your buddy.' Greg snarled and shoved Mike in the chest.

"Mike shoved back and caused Greg to trip over an ottoman. He fell, hit his head on the corner of the raised hearth, and was knocked unconscious. As he called 911, Mike said, 'Get a blanket and a pillow.' He covered Greg with the blanket and laid his head on the pillow. When the ambulance arrived, Greg was still alive but died within seconds. They tried CPR then called the coroner and the police. We both gave the same statement, but they arrested Mike. The prosecutor is trying for a second-degree murder charge, but Mike's attorney would only plead guilty to manslaughter."

Elaine looked away again. I could feel the warmth in my face and my clenched jaw. I felt like I was listening to Tchaikovsky's 1812 Overture with stereo headphones. War raged between my ears. *Poor Mike,* I thought, *he's going to spend his life in prison over this. Poor Elaine, she's a victim too. She was probably raped, and now she's going to lose her husband and her baby.* The sympathy troops even got reinforcement from a kind thought for Greg's mother, *she's lost her son too*—but the fury force fought back. *I told Elaine not to trust Greg.* I wanted to scream at her. *Why didn't you listen to me?* In the end the professional won. "I am so sorry. Is there anything I can do to help?"

Tears streaked her perfect makeup, and, not hearing me, she continued, "I'm not sleeping or eating. I don't know if I can go on."

The makeup told me the answer to my next question was no, but I had to ask, "Elaine, have you considered harming yourself in any way?"

"No, I don't deserve to live, but I won't ever do that. Somehow I have to make this up to Mike. His suffering is my fault. Having sex with his friend was wrong. Having an abortion was wrong. Trusting Greg was wrong. And taking my own life would be wrong. I have to begin doing the right thing sometime. I just don't know what it is."

"Elaine, when my Uncle Henry needed guidance for something, he looked up key words in the concordance portion of his Bible. He would read the verse and the whole passage, trying to get the right context. Uncle Henry was a wise man."

She nodded. "I could try that."

We discussed antidepressants and counselors, and she agreed to see a clinical social worker who could help her work through these problems. She also agreed to take an antidepressant which was known to benefit sleep. I gave her an appointment in two weeks to check her response to the medication.

When Elaine returned in two weeks she looked more depressed and worried.

"How did you do with the medication?" I asked.

"I took it for a few days but felt so dopey I quit."

"Are you sleeping now?"

"No, and now I have a new problem."

"What's that?"

"I lost my job. They reminded me that policy prohibits sexual activity among employees, and everyone knew what had happened with Greg. I was given two weeks' notice. I told them he forced me, but since half the people in the office are hot for him, they didn't believe me. They said I would have reported it if I was forced, but I know that's not true. Thousands of rapes are never reported."

"Has the situation with Mike improved at all?"

"No, he still refuses to talk to me."

"Are you looking for another job?"

"Not yet. I have some money from my mother's estate so I don't have to work immediately. I need some time to figure out what I'm going to do. I probably won't be able to get another job as a paralegal. I may try to go back to school for something. I just don't know right now."

"Are you willing to try a different antidepressant?"

"Yes."

Over the next several months I saw Elaine at least once a week to adjust her medicine and evaluate a number of stress-related illnesses. She was not doing well. Mike had not moved out, but he slept in the guestroom, saying he would wait until the trial was over before he found his own place, if the state did not provide one. He left for work early in the morning, ate all his meals away from home, and returned late at night. He refused to discuss anything with her.

Only one of Mike's sisters prevented Elaine's total isolation. His youngest sister was away in college, and another of his sisters, who lived in town and had been very close to Elaine, took Mike's side. The other sister, who according to Elaine was beamed down from heaven, tried to offer support to both of them.

"Mike's sister took me to lunch, said she knew I loved him."

"Did you tell her what happened?"

"Yes. She wants Mike to listen to me, but she hasn't been able to convince him."

"At least she listened."

During this time, I worked late in my office one evening doing paperwork when the phone rang. I felt the muscles at the back of my neck tighten as they do when alarms are raised. I answered. Bill Tarter identified himself as Elaine Green's father. "Are you Elaine's doctor?"

I hesitated then wondered if something had happened to her. "Yes."

"I saw Elaine on her birthday and she referred to her doctor as 'she.' I've called every female gynecology practice in Lexington trying to find her doctor."

"Has something happened to her?"

147

"That's what I want to find out. I've called her repeatedly since I saw the article in the paper, but she doesn't answer."

"Mr. Tarter, I am not at liberty to discuss Elaine with you."

"I know, but I want to know how I can help her."

"Perhaps you could tell me something about your relationship that might help me help her." I guess he needed to talk, and that was the invitation he needed.

"I love Elaine, and I've tried to be a good father, but I made some bad mistakes, and she's not willing to forgive me. Elaine's mother was an alcoholic. I tried to protect her from that as much as I could. Her mother never got up before noon, so I always got Elaine up and off to school. We were very close at one time. Linda, her mother, was a very likable person and she did love Elaine. They had a lot of fun together, and Elaine was very close to her as well.

"When Elaine was little, Linda would put her to bed at eight o'clock and start drinking. After she got older, Elaine realized her mother had a problem, but she tried to cover for her. I guess we both did. When Elaine left for college, her mother stayed drunk all the time. I started spending more time at my office; then I started seeing Beth, a woman who worked in my office. On the night that Linda was killed, she got drunk and called Elaine at school to tell her about my affair. After she hung up the phone, she drove to my office and Beth's house looking for my car. She ran into a tree down the street from Beth's house and was killed instantly."

He paused. "Elaine blamed me for her mother's death and has had very little to do with me since. The truth is I blame myself too. She did allow me to be part of her wedding. I guess she thought that was easier than explaining why she hated me so much. Thank you for listening, Dr. Parker. I guess I needed to get that off my chest. Maybe it will help you understand Elaine a little better. I'd do anything I could to help her, but she doesn't answer my calls."

"How did you happen to see her on her birthday?"

"I just showed up at her door."

"That seems to have worked."

"So it did. Thank you, doctor."

About a week after I talked with her father, Elaine came for an appointment to evaluate her antidepressant. Wearing a bright yellow dress and smiling, she looked as if a burden had been lifted. She said she was getting some rest and thought she was tolerating this medicine okay, but she admitted that most of the improvement was due to a visit from her father.

"On Saturday, he just showed up at my door."

"What happened?"

"He said he loved me and wanted to be there for me. He said what he did was wrong and he wasn't trying to make excuses, but he hoped I would find it in my heart to forgive him. He said that he was sorry. He said he was lonely after I left for college, and I realized for the first time what a difficult life my father must have had, caring for me and covering for my mother. I remembered telling you I felt lonely with Mike working all the time, but I didn't have half the problems my father had. I ruined my marriage with much less excuse than he did. Something about being guilty of the same thing makes you a lot more understanding of someone else's indiscretions. I forgave him and asked him to forgive me for the way I've treated him all these years. He said he understood, and he forgave me. I feel like I have my father back, and maybe there is some hope that Mike will forgive me too."

There is power in forgiveness, I thought. "What is going on with Mike?"

"The grand jury met last week. They returned an indictment. Mike will have to stand trial for second-degree murder."

"That's ridiculous. If the district attorney wasn't running for reelection, he would be a lot more sympathetic toward an accident." I could feel my hostility for our legal system rising.

"I'm sure you're right. I hope you don't have to testify."

"Why would I have to testify?"

"They may want to have you say I was pregnant and that it was Greg's baby in order to establish the motive for murder."

"Wouldn't I have had to do that at the grand jury if they were going to need my testimony?"

"I don't know. Maybe they won't need you."

"Do they have a date for the trial?"

"Yes, on April 2 they begin the jury selection."

"So quickly?"

"The election again."

"How could I forget? Well, I'm glad you're feeling better. I don't think we need to change your medicine. Let me see you in a month."

CHAPTER 12

On Tuesday, April 2, I had a high-risk obstetrics patient in labor and expected to be needed in the hospital all day, ready to perform an emergency C-section if necessary. I rescheduled the office patients for the entire day and was once again surprised by the patient, who delivered in four hours with no complications. With an unexpected afternoon off, I decided to call Jon to see if he could get free. Spending a weekday afternoon with my husband was a delicious thought. When Jon's secretary said he had committee meetings all afternoon, I decided to go to the courthouse for the jury selection in Mike's trial. I realized all I knew of the events were from either Elaine or the newspaper, and I wanted to see for myself how Mike was holding up.

Sheets of rain, driven by the wind, made both raincoats and umbrellas useless. I was soaked by the time I walked the half block from the parking garage to the courthouse and wondered why I hadn't gone home, made a cup of tea, and built a fire—my favorite time for a fire being rainy days in spring. The courtroom felt cold. Mahogany furniture and woodwork created a formal, uninviting feeling. I was surprised to find it only half-filled. The newspaper made it seem that this was a high-profile trial since Greg had been a prominent attorney.

Taking a seat on the back row, I noticed Mike looked tired and thinner. So did his curly black hair. I had not seen him for over five years, but he looked ten years older. His once kind face, while still handsome, looked harder, more lined, more ominous. I suspected he had sleepless nights too. He sat next to his attorney, Robert Brown, at a table left of the center aisle in front of the bench.

Brown had a considerable reputation as a defense attorney and looked more confident than anyone else in the courtroom. His slim physique, full head of gray hair, bronzed skin, and rugged features were attractive. He wore a charcoal pinstriped suit, white shirt, and red tie. His carriage said he was a man used to having his way.

A familiar looking older couple, apparently Mike's parents, sat in the first row behind him. I thought maybe I had seen them while Sara was sick. On the second row, Elaine and an older man sat talking quietly. I assumed this was her father. Sitting behind Elaine, I recognized Ellen Green Finch with her husband of twelve years, Joshua. *She looks terribly thin,* I thought. Sitting next to her was her sister Grace. *She looks great. They have the same name; I wonder if they are Mike's cousins?* In all the years I had known the girls and Mike I had not put this together, but then I didn't see nearly as much of them since I married and worked ninety hours a week.

Both Mike and his father gazed intently at one of the potential jurors, a lovely gray-haired woman dressed in a gray suit and light pink silk blouse. She sat very straight and stared at the back of the courtroom. She smiled faintly when she saw me, and I recognized my friend, Jessie Ferguson. I didn't realize until later, but someone else also stared at Jessie.

"All rise," the court clerk announced as the judge entered. Voir dire began as the judge explained the process. Mike's attorney and the prosecutor were each allowed two preemptory challenges, persons they could disqualify. Both attorneys asked a lot of questions of each potential juror, and you got the distinct impression they were already trying to establish the direction their prosecution and defense would take. Mike's attorney disqualified an older man who was a Baptist minister and said his son had been killed in an accident caused by a drunk driver. The prosecutor disqualified a young woman who wore a tight sweater and couldn't keep her eyes off Mike. Mike's attorney disqualified another attorney. The prosecutor disqualified a college professor.

When the time came to question Jessie, they asked her about her profession. Mike's attorney asked if she or anyone close to her had suffered accidental death. He asked her thoughts on adultery. When she said, "I believe adultery is morally wrong," Mike sneered and grunted so loud all eyes looked at him. Next the prosecutor asked if she had a relationship with any of the parties involved that might prevent her from being objective in her decision. She said, "Jeff . . . uh . . . Mike Green is my son," and people who had been half-paying attention suddenly stared first at Jessie then at Mike.

The judge dismissed Jessie. As she made her way down the aisle toward the back of the courtroom, I hoped the potential jurors were not looking at Mike. His flushed face, clenched teeth, and white knuckles gripping the arms of the chair all screamed his hatred as his eyes followed her. At that moment even I, who was totally convinced of Mike's innocence, believed he could commit murder. Jessie, trembling like a frightened child, sat down next to me and I put my arm around her. Mike, seeing that gesture, stared at me with shock and betrayal on his face.

At first I thought, *This can't be*. Then I remembered Elaine saying Mike's mother had run off with another man when he was twelve. Jessie's son, Jeff, had been twelve when she left. Suddenly I understood; Mike was Jeff. Mike's father told him Jessie had run off with another man, and Jessie never told him the truth about the abortion. It was no wonder that couple looked familiar; they were George and Mary.

As Jessie sat in the courtroom shivering, I realized I too was freezing. "Let's go to my house, make a fire, and get something warm to drink. You've been dismissed," I whispered.

"That sounds good." As she stood, Jessie waved goodbye to Ellen and Grace, who both looked back to see her leave.

Outside the rain had not abated. We both were drenched by the time we reached our cars. At my house I put on the teakettle, loaned Jessie a purple terry cloth robe and slippers, and changed into a sweat suit. We hung her clothes by the fireplace and made a roaring fire. At first we sipped tea in silence. Finally, Jessie said, "I was surprised to see you in court today. What is your interest in Jeff?"

"We became friends when his first wife was dying with cancer. She was my patient. He had recommended that Elaine see me as well. I had no idea Mike was your Jeff. As close as we are, I had only seen him as Jeff that one time at the middle school basketball game."

"His name is Michael Jeffrey. When he went to college they started using his first name, and he kept it. I was the one who wanted him called Jeff. I guess it was one more rebellion against me. Do you believe Elaine loves him?"

"Yes, I know it may seem hard to believe, but I think she does. She really wants to have a baby. I think that her strong desire to have children, coupled with her physiological drive at ovulation, was a factor in the infidelity, if that is what it was."

"Why would you say that?"

"I'm not convinced she wanted to have an affair. As a matter of fact I don't think she did. I'm concerned about her. Right now she is so distressed about Mike and what is happening with him that she has completely repressed the fact that she had an abortion."

"She'll have to deal with that sometime."

"Yes, I know she will."

"I wasn't prepared for today. I knew Jeff's trial was coming up, but my jury duty just started this month. This was the first day, and we didn't know what trial we would be asked to do."

"It must have been a terrible shock when you realized it was Mike. I'm so sorry."

"I'm glad you were there. I don't know what I would have done without you. Of course, this is not the first time that's been true."

"It was nothing short of a miracle that I was there. The lady whose labor I induced today delivered in four hours or I would not have been in the courtroom."

"I guess God puts us where He wants us to be. I am glad the girls showed up to support Jeff. It can't be easy for them, but thanks to you, they didn't have to worry about me."

It rained all afternoon as we talked. Jessie had just changed back into dry clothes when the doorbell rang, followed by loud, urgent banging. When I opened the door, Mike quickly stepped in out of the downpour.

Dripping on my floor, he shouted, "How could you know my mother and not tell me?"

Before I could tell him I didn't know she was his mother, he saw Jessie standing by the fireplace. He erupted, hurling words like volcanic ash and spewing anger and hatred like lava. I stood by the door, stunned. Jessie sank into the sofa before the deluge. Mike paced back and forth in front of the fire.

"You've got your nerve showing up in that courtroom today when you know I never wanted to see you again! What happened? Did you want to blame Dad for his son being on trial for murder? When you left we searched for you for weeks. I prayed every day that you would be safe and come back to us. Dad said he could understand why a woman like you would leave him, but he knew you would never leave your kids, so you must have been abducted or hurt. When that credit card bill came and we finally knew you were alive, I started hating you. Even then, Dad defended you. 'I wasn't man enough for your mother,' he would say. 'She left me, but I know your mother loves you,' he would say. Over and over, 'I know your mother loves you; I know your mother loves you; I know your mother loves you.'

"One day when the girls weren't around I screamed at him, 'Don't ever say that to me again. You don't know she loves us. You don't know anything about her.' He never said it to us again, but that night I heard him tell Mary he would never understand why you left your children; he knew you loved us. I can't believe he thought he wasn't good enough for you, you whore. Go tell the judge you can be a juror; you are not my mother."

With that he abruptly turned and walked out into the rain. We sat thunderstruck. Neither Jessie nor I had said a word to him. Only the crackle of the fire, ticking of the hall clock, rain on the windows, and harmonious chords of the tenor wind chimes saved us from silence.

Finally I said, "Jessie, he needs to know the truth. He still thinks you ran off with another man."

"Is the truth so much better?"

"Yes, I think it is. You did not choose another man over your children, and he needs to know that. I heard a lot of anger, hatred, and pain, but I also heard a question. Why would a mother who loves you leave you? You can answer that question, Jessie, and he needs it answered."

"I want to talk to him, but how? When? Where?"

I had no answer, and as the grandfather clock chimed Whittingham and struck six o'clock, Jessie left for home.

Jon got home around six-thirty. Tired as he was from his afternoon of meetings, he brightened my day as no one else could. While I prepared dinner, he shared hilarious observations of his day. I loved his sense of humor perhaps more than anything else about him. After dinner, Jon retired to grade papers and I thought about my day. I decided to write a note to Mike, got out my favorite Waterman fountain pen and best cream-colored note paper, and wrote:

Dear Mike,

I wanted to let you know that while your mother has been my dear friend and patient for many years, I did not know until today that she was your mother. Your anger is understandable, and it is healthy for you to deal with it rather than suppress and nurture it, but some of your assumptions about your mother are inaccurate, and it would be beneficial for you to know the truth. I would encourage you to talk with her. If I can assist either of you in any way, I will.

Cara Parker

Having finished the note, a bit worried about meddling, one of my tendencies, and feeling very tired, I had gone to bed early and was sleeping soundly when the phone rang. Elaine asked if Mike was with me.

"We all noticed when you left the courthouse with his mother, and I overheard Mike say he was coming to see you. I'm worried. It's two o'clock in the morning and he hasn't come home." She was even more worried when I told her Mike had come, found Jessie at my house, and left quite upset.

"We were all surprised you knew her."

"I'm sorry if my concern for Jessie left your family feeling betrayed, but she has been my friend for many years, and I didn't know she was Mike's mother until today. There is much more to the story than you know, but Jessie is the one who'll have to tell you. I pray she will have the courage and get the opportunity."

"I would like to talk to her."

"I can tell her, or you could call her. I can give you her number."

"Maybe after the trial is over." She apologized for calling so late and hung up.

I had trouble going back to sleep. I wondered where Mike was, how Jessie was, and what would happen at the trial. Jon was used to late night calls. He turned over and went right back to sleep. I kissed his cheek and that accomplished what the phone had not. Later we both slept.

The next evening, Jessie called to say she had spent the day at the trial. She had disguised herself with a blonde wig and sat in the balcony. No one recognized her, but she nearly ran into Mike as they both came in late. She said, "Mike looked terrible—unshaven, hair messed, and eyes bloodshot. He wore the same pants and blazer that had gotten soaked the night before. His shirt was open at the neck and the tie was missing. He looked hungover, like he had spent the night on a park bench."

"Maybe he did spend the night on a park bench," I said. "Elaine called last night asking if he was at my house. She said he hadn't come home. How did the trial go?"

"The prosecutor tried to establish Jeff's motive for murder at the very beginning. He called the doctor from the abortion clinic first. You know, I'm surprised they didn't call you. That doctor said Elaine came accompanied by Greg and had an abortion. Jeff's attorney on cross-examination asked him if Elaine revealed the father of the baby, and he said she had not."

"I'm glad they didn't call me. I would have had to say she did, and that would have helped to establish a motive for murder."

"Next the prosecutor called the EMT who answered the 911 call. He said Jeff had answered the door and then paced back and forth between the door and the fireplace. Elaine was sitting on the sofa. He found Greg lying on the floor next to the fireplace with a pillow under his head, covered by a blanket, and unconscious. He was alive but died soon after they arrived. In response to Jeff's attorney's question on cross-examination, the EMT said he didn't usually find murder victims with such attention paid to their comfort.

"The prosecution then called the police officer who investigated the case. He said he arrived soon after the EMTs. He said he questioned Elaine and Jeff separately, and they both spoke rationally and calmly and related the same story. He found blood on the corner of the hearth and on Jeff's hands. The blood matched the victim's. Both Elaine and Jeff denied having moved any of the furniture in the room, and the ottoman was near the victim's feet.

"Jeff's attorney asked if he found any physical evidence that made him doubt Jeff's story, and he said he did not. When he asked how they explained the blood on Jeff's hands, the police officer said Elaine told him Jeff had placed the pillow under Greg's head. Jeff's attorney then asked the policeman if he had ever seen a murderer put a pillow beneath the victim's head, and he had to agree he had not."

"That seems like a good point. Did the jury respond to it?"

Jessie paused, thinking about the question. "I saw two women nod to each other and a man shook his head like he agreed, but another man sat on the back row and yawned all afternoon."

"Makes you wonder about our legal system. What happened next?"

"The prosecution then called the medical examiner, who said the blow to the temple had been the cause of death. When asked about the weapon causing the blow, he said he found minute fragments of brick in the wound that matched the brick in the fireplace. Jeff's attorney made the point that there were no other injuries, which was consistent with Jeff's claim that he only slightly shoved Greg in the chest, causing him to fall over the ottoman."

"That all sounds hopeful to me," I said. "How can they say it is anything but an accident?"

"I don't think they can. I'm surprised they are trying. Tomorrow they begin the defense. I'll let you know what happens."

"Thanks."

The next evening Jessie called again. She seemed sad.

"Did something go wrong at the trial today?" I asked.

"No, I think it's going well. They put Jeff and Elaine on the stand, and they told the same story. Then they called three character witnesses: Jeff's partner, one of his college professors, and Sara's brother. His partner told a story about one of their clients who refused to use Jeff as his accountant, because Jeff wouldn't allow him to claim some questionable income tax deduction. His college professor talked about his commitment to the Big Brothers program while he was in college. Jeff taught a young teen to read and helped him get a GED after he dropped out of high school. Sara's brother talked about how kind and gentle he was when she was sick. He told how he cared for her at home with the help of Hospice and a day nurse."

"That sounds like the Mike I know."

"Cara, I was so proud of the man they say he is, but the contrast between that man and the one who came by your house made me even more ashamed of what I have done to him."

"Maybe it means he is more likely to listen to your story."

"Somehow I doubt it."

"I hope you have the opportunity to find out. Jessie, I have a confession to make. I wrote a note to Mike after you left the other night. I told him some of his assumptions about you were inaccurate, and I thought he should talk to you. I hope you don't mind."

"No, I don't mind. I just don't have much faith in it happening."

"What is the next step in the trial?"

"Tomorrow the attorneys do their closing arguments, and then it goes to the jury."

"Are you going tomorrow?"

"Yes."

"I'm off in the morning. Would it be all right if I sneak in with you?"

We sat in the back of the balcony. The closing arguments were short and the jury deliberated less than an hour. They returned a verdict of not guilty to the charge of second-degree murder. They found Mike guilty of reckless homicide which carried a sentence of five years in prison with eligibility for parole in one year. He was taken into custody immediately after the verdict was given. Hugging George, Mary, Ellen, and Grace before walking away, he only glanced at Elaine, his expression cold. She sat alone as the courtroom emptied, staring at the door where he left.

"Jessie, I forgot to tell you. When Elaine called the other night looking for Mike, I told her about him coming by the house and finding you there. She said she would like to talk to you. Do you want to meet her? She looks like she could use a friend about now."

"I guess it wouldn't hurt to meet her. We have several things in common."

"I have time for lunch. Do you?"

"Yes."

Jessie waited in the foyer while I invited Elaine to join us for lunch.

"Hello, Elaine," I said as I touched her on the shoulder. "You look lonely today. Was that your father with you on Tuesday?"

"Oh hello, Dr. Parker. Yes, that was my dad. He had to go to Columbus on business so he couldn't be here today. He has been at the house since Saturday. I'm so grateful we have been reunited. I can't imagine this without his support."

"I'm relieved the jury didn't find Mike guilty of murder."

"Yes, I guess reckless homicide is as good as we could hope for under the circumstances. Still, it seems so unfair that Mike has to go to prison for what Greg and I did to him."

"Elaine, I was wondering if you would like to have lunch with Jessie and me. You said you would like to talk to her." Sensing her hesitation, I continued. "She really is a wonderful person, and I believe you both love Mike. She knows you've hurt him, and so has she."

"What makes you think she loves him after what she did?"

"Things are rarely exactly as they seem. Why don't you let her show you how she feels about him?"

"I guess I could."

As we walked into the foyer, Jessie stepped forward, her hand extended. "I'm Jessie. Thanks for joining us, Elaine. Cara told me she believes you love Jeff, and I want you to know I do too."

Elaine hesitated only a moment then took her outstretched hand. "I don't know which one of us has hurt him more."

"I'm beginning to realize I hurt him more than I imagined."

"Dr. Parker told me I don't know the whole story."

"I'm willing to tell you, if you want to hear it."

"I do."

At the restaurant, I ate and listened while Elaine and Jessie moved their food around on their plates, talked, and ate very little. Jessie began her story, and with each word she seemed to fade as if someone had taken her photo into the sun. Her voice sounded hollow and empty—like a reporter describing footage she was watching on a screen. As I listened, I realized this was probably the first time Jessie had told this part of her story.

"The day I left home I bought a round-trip ticket, took a bus into the city, and walked ten blocks to an address I had been given. I took two hundred ten dollars in cash and a credit card. I paid two hundred dollars for an abortion and saved the other ten to take a cab back to the bus station after the procedure."

Elaine's eyes grew bigger. As comprehension dawned, she gasped, "But that was 1971."

"Yes," said Jessie. "It was illegal then. The address was a motel near downtown. There were two adjoining rooms. I waited with two other women in a room with a bed, sofa, and round table with four chairs. The other women appeared to be about my age, frightened, and poor. We stared at the dingy green carpet on the floor and didn't make eye contact."

"Weren't you afraid?" Elaine asked.

"Yes, but I knew someone from work who had done it, and she didn't really have a problem. I didn't know all that could go wrong or I would have been a whole lot more afraid. I had heard that you were sometimes sterile afterward, but I actually wanted that. It never occurred to me that I might not survive."

After the initial surprise, Elaine looked very sad. Tears welled up in her eyes as she listened to Jessie.

"Did they give you anything for pain?"

"No. As I waited I listened to the other women scream when they were taken to the room next door. I promised myself I wouldn't scream, and I didn't. I fainted. I don't know how long I was out, but it seemed that I was in and out for a long time. I heard the bed in the next room squeaking and a woman moaning. Later I heard a man and woman arguing.

"When I came to, the room was dark even though the curtain was open. I called for someone, and a thin woman who smelled of smoke and whiskey came to me. She handed me a glass of orange juice and said, 'Here, drink this.' I did as she instructed, but it was rancid and made me sick. I must have gone back to sleep because I was awakened later with sun coming in the dirty window. The woman returned and told me to get dressed and get out. 'I have to use this room,' she said. 'You've already been here too long.'

"After I was dressed she gave me some more juice, and I walked out into the hallway. I don't remember anything else that happened for nearly a month. Cara was a medical student then, and one of the doctors who took care of me, so you see our relationship goes way back." With that she smiled at me.

"Why did you do it?" Elaine asked.

As Jessie continued with her story, I noticed it seemed easier for her to tell it. This part I had heard. She looked sad but didn't cry. She had carried the shame and guilt of having an abortion and kept the secret from her children for so many years, it appeared to lighten her burden to share it.

After Jessie paused, Elaine said, "So there never was another man?"

"No, never."

"Then I don't understand why you didn't go home."

At this point I excused myself and left Jessie telling Elaine about all the complications associated with what she had done.

Jessie called that evening to thank me for introducing her to Elaine. She bubbled into the phone, "We spent the whole afternoon together. She invited me to their home, and I got to see where Jeff lived, photos of their last vacation, a windjammer cruise to the Netherland Antilles, his awards from Big Brothers, and his restored 1966 Mustang in the garage. I like her, Cara, and I agree with you. I think she does love Jeff."

"Are you going to see her again?"

"Yes, as a matter of fact, I wanted to ask you to join us. Could you come for lunch next Saturday? Elaine is going to try to see Jeff at the prison this weekend, but she can come next Saturday."

"Sure, I'd love to come." Jessie was a marvelous hostess whose food always looked as good as it tasted. "What time?"

"Come at noon. Thanks again for today. My mind is racing but my body is exhausted; I need to get some rest, so I'll get off the phone. Goodnight, Cara."

"Goodnight."

CHAPTER 13

Two days before the scheduled lunch with Jessie and Elaine, I got a letter from Mike.

Dear Dr. Parker,

Thank you for your note. I'm sorry for the way I acted in your home. Please forgive me. I was relieved to hear that you were as surprised as I to learn that your friend was my mother. Ever since Sara's illness I have trusted your opinion. I guess I might not be in this mess if I had listened to you about the vasectomy. My mother hurt me when she left, and I didn't think I would love anyone again. Without Sara I wouldn't have. I have been thinking of her a lot in here. Anyway, I am interested in your comment that there is more to this than I know. I don't want to forgive my mother, but I would like to understand what happened, especially since you seem to think it might help me. Elaine came to see me but I refused to see her, don't want to hear her excuses, and don't want to forgive her either. You have been more than my wife's doctor. You were our friend.

I know you are very busy, but if you could find time, would you
call or come to see me?

Mike

As I tried unsuccessfully to sleep, I reread Mike's letter in my mind.
I was in the middle of this mess, and it was going to be difficult to be
present for everyone who needed me and still protect doctor-patient
confidentiality. I was going to need every listening skill I had. Relief came
at four a.m. when the phone rang and I had to go for a delivery. *If I can't
sleep, I might as well work*, I thought.

Fortunately, this delivery was one any cab driver could have done.
She was a delightful thirty-five-year-old woman, gravida 5, para 4,
meaning five pregnancies and four deliveries. On her first prenatal visit
she told me she ate toilet paper. Pregnant patients often eat strange things;
for years Argo laundry starch was the most common. It usually meant
that something was missing in their diet or their ability to absorb nutrients.
When she told me what she did, I said, "I would recommend that you eat
white and unscented."

In her wonderful, direct way, she said, "Dr. Parker, are you making
fun of me?"

"No, I was just thinking that you should avoid the chemicals in
dyes and perfumes."

"Oh, okay."

"I do confess that I'm amused at the unusual things pregnant
women eat."

This bit of information went into her prenatal record, which was
copied and sent to the hospital to be available at the time of delivery. Part
of routine admission orders called for an enema. That night as I sat at the
desk making my notes, Ms. Short, a no-nonsense kind of nurse from the
old school, came out of the bathroom after giving the enema and said, "I
didn't know whether to give her the whole roll or just a few sheets." I
needed that laugh.

The next two days were very busy, so I didn't have much time to think about whether I would mention Mike's letter at the luncheon. Jessie knew I had written to him, and it would be easy to explain to Elaine. It might be good to see what they thought about my visiting him.

I arrived on time and found Jessie dressed in black slacks with a rose-colored shirt, a deeper shade than her usual pink. Orange and yellow tulips adorned her table. Chicken salad made with red seedless grapes, celery, and walnuts was the main dish. It was served over avocado halves with whole wheat banana bread and a fruit cup on the side. The English would have been appalled to find Fortnum & Mason's Royal Blend tea made into iced tea, but we Southerners love our iced tea, and Jessie's was the best.

Elaine had not arrived so we drank tea on the screened porch while we waited for her. After thirty minutes we began to worry. We tried calling her home and got the answering machine. Thinking she was on the way, we waited a little longer.

Finally Jessie said, "We should go ahead and eat. I guess she forgot." Her face showed there was no way she would have forgotten.

While we ate I told Jessie about the note from Mike and asked her advice about a visit. She seemed to think I should see him. While we didn't say it, we both hoped I would be able to convince him to see her. When I told Jessie that Mike had refused to see Elaine, we both felt guilty that we had not called her to see how the visit had gone. Neither one of us knew her well enough to know where she was likely to be if she wasn't at home, but we did know her well enough to know that Mike's refusal to see her would have distressed her.

"Jessie, you should open a restaurant or at least a catering service," I said as I finished lunch. It was delicious.

"I have all I can do with the home, but I'm thinking of adding some basic cooking and nutrition classes to the girls' curriculum." She was the director of the Florence Crittenden Home now.

"That would be a great idea."

Jessie was unusually quiet and, sensing her disappointment and worry about Elaine, I excused myself soon after we finished eating. Her introverted personality needed refueling by some time alone.

As I was leaving, I remembered I had Elaine's father's phone number in the office. I decided to phone him to see if he had heard from Elaine, and I promised to let Jessie know if I heard anything.

"Bill Tarter here."

"Mr. Tarter, this is Cara Parker. I wondered if you have heard from Elaine."

"Yes, she's right here. Would you like to speak to her?"

"Please."

"Dr. Parker, how nice of you to call."

"Well, Jessie and I were worried about you when you missed lunch today."

"Oh no, I completely forgot Jessie invited me to lunch. Do you think she will ever forgive me?"

"Jessie has become a very forgiving person. I don't think it will be a problem. We both felt guilty that we hadn't called you to ask about your visit with Mike."

"He refused to see me. I took him the newest Robert Ludlum and Wilbur Smith novels. He loves their books, and I thought the prison library might not have the newer ones. I left them with the guard, but I don't know if he got them. After I came home I cried for two days. Dad called and asked me to come here, so I did. He took a few days off work, and we've had a good visit. I'm not very good company, but he doesn't seem to mind.

"We went through photo albums and talked about Mom. You might want to put it in my record that she was hospitalized for two months with postpartum depression after I was born. That was one reason they didn't have more children. Apparently, she knew she was weak and shouldn't have children. I had no idea how many sacrifices Dad made to protect me from her drinking, or how much effort he put into protecting my love for her. I was so wrong to have judged him."

"Judgment is often wrong."

"I can't tell you what it means to have my daddy back."

"I'm so glad he is there for you. Elaine, I didn't tell you, but I wrote Mike a note the night he came by the house and found Jessie. I wanted him to know I didn't know she was his mother."

"Did he write to you?" Elaine said a little too quickly.

"Yes, he thanked me for writing, apologized for the way he acted, and said he was glad I hadn't known Jessie was his mother."

"Did he say anything about me?"

"He mentioned he had refused to see you. That was all. Elaine, he said he would like to talk to me. How do you feel about that?"

"You're connected to his precious Sara. That's why he wants to talk to you. She would never have hurt him like I did." The edge in her voice was sharper.

"We became friends during Sara's illness. You knew that. If it makes you feel any better, he did say maybe none of this would have happened if he had listened to my advice about the vasectomy."

"That's for sure."

"Elaine, maybe if I see him I can convince him to see you."

"I guess it's worth a try. I'm sorry. I'm not angry with you. I'm angry with him. He's never let me explain anything. He hasn't let me tell him how sorry I am about what has happened, about what I did, or about what Greg did."

"Maybe in time. You haven't given him any reason to think this was anything other than an affair, so he doesn't think he needs to hear any more, just like he doesn't think he needs to hear anything Jessie has to say."

Unlike Jessie, Elaine was determined to keep trying to see Mike. "I sacrificed the baby I wanted to save this marriage, and I'm not giving up. I am going to that prison every Sunday afternoon until he sees me.

Somehow I will convince him I love him and only him." Elaine knew her appeal, also unlike Jessie, who considered herself unattractive.

"Surely he won't refuse to see you much longer."

"I hope not."

"Have you decided when you're coming home?"

"Tomorrow is Sunday. I'll go to the prison on my way home. I'll call you when I get home and let you know how things go. I need to call Jessie too. I'm so sorry I forgot her luncheon. I know. Maybe you both could come for lunch to my house next Saturday."

"I think I can, but I'll check my calendar and let you know when you get home. I know Jessie would be pleased to hear from you, and I'm glad your father was able to be there for you. I'll talk to you soon."

On Sunday evening when Elaine called, I learned that Mike sent the books back by the guard and still refused to see her. We settled on lunch at noon on Saturday. She seemed relieved to have something positive to anticipate. Looking at my calendar for the week, I realized I had Wednesday afternoon off. *Should I go to the prison?*

On Wednesday morning I tried to add a new patient who urgently needed to be seen to my afternoon schedule. She couldn't come. I offered to induce someone's labor who was thirteen days late. She wanted to wait. I tried to convince myself I was getting a summer cold, but I knew I was fine. I admired Elaine's determination to continue her visits to see Mike. There was nothing fun about the prospects of a visit to prison even without the added risk of rejection. Difficult as the decision had been and hard as I tried to be busy when Wednesday afternoon came, I found myself on the road to Eddyville. After the visit I admired Elaine even more.

Doors slammed shut, locked behind you. Every footstep taken, every door closed, every word spoken, even the tick of the clock echoed off the bare walls and floor. Shivering, in a room with gray paint on the walls, no carpet, and no windows, I waited for Mike.

170

"I never thought we would be meeting like this," he said as he walked into the room. His appearance was a surprise. He looked younger, innocent, rested. The anger, pain, and tension on his face during the trial were gone. Even prison had not been as much strain as the uncomfortable silence in his home for months before the trial.

"Nor did I. How are you holding up, Mike?"

"Actually, better than I expected. This is not any worse than living on an iceberg in my home and wondering what would happen at the trial. I mark each day off the calendar. Fortunately, my sentence is not too long. What worries me most is how I will make a living when I get out of here. Even if the licensure board will let me, I'm not sure my clients will want a felon doing their accounting."

"They will know it was an accident."

"Will that matter?"

"I don't know."

He leaned back in his chair. "So what is so important that I need to know about my mother?"

"Mike, that's privileged information. I can't tell you, but I believe it would be good for both of you if you would let her tell you."

"People here don't get too many visitors; I guess I ought to see anyone who is willing to come."

"I assume you're referring to your mother, but isn't the same true for Elaine? I understand she has been here twice."

For the first time Mike dropped his head, no longer making eye contact. The chair squeak echoed around the room as his body stiffened and he stood, paced, and picked at the cuticle of his left thumb. I had seen this unconscious gesture many times during the stress of Sara's illness.

"She was pregnant, for God's sake. She certainly doesn't have anything to say that would change that."

"Well, actually she might."

"Oh come on, Dr. Parker. I know you like to think the best of people, but you would believe anything if you believe that. You know I had a vasectomy. She was pregnant, and unless she was raped . . ." He stopped pacing. His angry scowl changed to a thoughtful frown. One eyebrow rose, as if he remembered something long forgotten. Silence underlined the question on his face. I waited. Finally, he said quietly, with less visible anger and an expression of hope mixed with guilt, "What could she say?"

"You're right, Mike. I do like to give people the benefit of the doubt, and I believe Elaine loves you. Elaine made some mistakes, and a big one was not discussing what happened with you in the first place." Silence. "Do you want to share what just came to your mind?"

"No. I just thought about something else. If Elaine had something to say, why didn't she say it?"

"Think about it, Mike. She hasn't had much chance, and I think she was afraid you wouldn't believe her. She couldn't risk that."

"Maybe that's because what she told you is a lie."

"I don't think so, but then I have been fooled before. It's easy to lie to someone who wants to believe you. Mike, I need to go. Would you like your mother's phone number? It's unlisted."

"No, I don't want to talk to her on the phone. Do you think she would come here with you?"

"I think she would fly around the world if you would talk to her."

"Maybe she'll enjoy seeing me here. She can blame Dad for how he raised me."

"No, she would never do that. She was thrilled to hear the things the character witnesses said about you at the trial."

He looked up. "She was at the trial?"

"At the trial, at your graduations, at your basketball games, at your wedding."

"What are you saying? I never saw her at those things."

"She didn't intend you to see her, but she was there. Ask her when you see her."

"I guess I can do that."

"Is there anything you'd like me to bring you when I come again?"

"I could use some more books."

"Elaine said you sent back the books she brought."

With a hint of the old mischievous glint often seen in Mike's eyes, he said, "I read fast."

"Elaine will be pleased." I smiled.

"Don't tell her."

Driving home, my conversation with Mike played over and over in my head like a recording. Visiting Mike was the right decision. There is just no substitute for talking to people face to face. He was going to see Jessie. I could hardly wait to tell her, but I wanted to see her face so I decided not to call. And he was going to see Elaine sometime. It would just take a little time. What had he remembered that drained his anger?

I offered to pick Jessie up on Saturday, ostensibly so she could show me the way to Elaine's, but really because I wanted to talk to her about my visit with Mike. I didn't want to tell her about it in front of Elaine. I expected Jessie to be overjoyed, and she would not want that to hurt Elaine. There would be time to tell Elaine later.

"I went to see Mike on Wednesday."

Her face lit up. "How is he?"

"He looks surprisingly good. We had a nice talk, and I was glad I decided to go, though I tried to think of every possible reason to avoid it. I offered to give him your phone number."

"And?"

"He refused." Jessie looked so disappointed I was sorry I teased her. "He said he didn't want to talk to you on the phone—he'd rather see you in person. Would you come visit him with me?"

She was so excited she grabbed my arm, and I ran against the curb, scraping the alloy wheels on my car.

"Did you say yes?"

"I think I said something like you would fly around the world to see him."

She smiled. "When are we going?"

"How about Wednesday afternoon?"

"I can do that."

We rode the rest of the way in silence, Jessie's face a complex mix of joy and fear, faint smile and furrowed brow.

Elaine and Mike lived at the end of a cul-de-sac. Their lawn was perfectly manicured, with each tree mulched, mature boxwoods trimmed, and day lilies almost ready to bloom. I expected some deterioration in the gardening with Mike gone, but I learned that Elaine did the gardening. She called it her therapy.

The Cape Cod style house was made of stone with wood trim. As we entered, Elaine, wearing a pale green sheath and white sandals, led us past the living room where Greg had died and took us to a small den adjacent to the kitchen. There, she introduced us to her father, Bill Tarter. Our brief conversations had favorably impressed me, so I was happy to meet him. Jessie, who had been somewhat introspective in the car after our discussion about visiting Jeff, seemed agitated. I didn't think much of it at the time, but Bill appeared to hold her hand a moment longer than expected.

Elaine was not as comfortable as Jessie in the role of hostess. She had left too much to do after her guests arrived. After she excused herself to go to the kitchen for the second time, we offered to help. Jessie washed and dried basil leaves, I sliced tomatoes, and Bill set the table. Conversation was easy and superficial, avoiding the difficult events of the recent past.

Bill explained that unexpected business had brought him to the city, and he had taken the opportunity to see Elaine.

After lunch, Elaine showed us a scrapbook she had gotten from her father. It reminded Jessie that she had made a similar one for each of her children.

"Bill, did you make the scrapbook for Elaine, or did your wife do it?" Jessie asked.

"I did it. Elaine had forgotten, but she helped me. It was one of our projects for when her mother was out."

"Which was a lot," Elaine said. "There are many ways for a mother not to be there for her children." Fearing she had hurt Jessie, she quickly added, "I'm sorry."

"You're right, Elaine. It's your mother and I who should be sorry, not you. I did make a scrapbook for each of my children though."

"You did? But how did you do that since you weren't there?" Elaine asked.

"I was there as often as I could be. Cara and I went to one of Jeff's ballgames soon after I discovered who I was, and Jeff refused to speak to me. After that, I would either not try to speak to him or I would disguise and hide myself altogether. I was even there for your wedding."

"Were you sitting in the balcony wearing a purple silk dress?" Bill said, to everyone's surprise. "I saw you. Your hair was light auburn and shorter."

We all laughed as Jessie said, "Yes, that was me. I remember thinking maybe a purple dress was not a good idea for someone who was trying not to be seen. I rather fancied that auburn wig, though."

"You looked beautiful. I remember wondering who you were and why you sat alone in the balcony." An awkward silence followed.

"Now you know," Jessie said brightly, breaking the lull. "I missed Jeff's marriage to Sara. They married in a small country church with no balcony. There was no place I could hide there. I made a habit of visiting the site of each event before it happened so I would know if there was someplace I could sit and not be noticed."

"Dad, I had no idea you were so observant."

"Oh, I'm not observant. It's just that Jessie is a beautiful woman, and I do notice beautiful women."

Jessie blushed. "Thank you." That was the first time I had ever seen her blush. Quickly, she turned the conversation back to the scrapbook. "George gave me the school pictures each year, and his sister, Martha, gave me some photographs. She also went to some of Jeff's games with me so I didn't have to go alone. I appreciate Martha."

"I've never met Martha," Elaine said. "Do you know why the family shunned her? Mike said she was a flower child during the Sixties, got into smoking pot and free love. That embarrassed George's conservative family."

"Yes, that is true, but there is more to her story than that. She fell in love and planned to marry a young man who was sent to Vietnam. Nine months after he left she had a baby, and her parents forced her to give the baby up for adoption. Thirteen months later he was killed. She became vehemently opposed to the war and joined the protest movement. The pot and free love were her ways of dealing with the pain. She's still searching for that child. I've tried to help her through my connection with adoption agencies, but so far I've had no luck. Adoption was much more secretive then in Kentucky. Now the families know each other, and often the mother even chooses the family that gets her baby."

Elaine shook her head. "I had no idea. I'm sorry I didn't try to get to know her. Maybe, if we have lunch again we can invite her and make it a meeting of the Green Outcast Society."

"We would have to invite Ellen too if we did that."

"Yes, I almost forgot about Ellen. I wasn't part of the family when that happened."

"Interesting, isn't it, how all four of us did something different about our unwanted pregnancies, and we were all still outcasts," Jessie said.

"It's interesting to me how it was the men who did both the impregnating and the out casting," Bill observed.

"Seems to me everyone needs to be more responsible about birth control," I said.

"Seems to me that everyone needs to be more loving and forgiving," Bill added.

Jessie and I looked at each other as I thought, *That sounds like Uncle Henry.* "That sounds like something Mr. Henry would have said," Jessie said, then continued, "Elaine, would you like to see Jeff's scrapbook sometime?"

"Yes, I want to see it, and I bet he would like to see it too. He has often wished for a copy of various clippings about his high school sports activities."

"I probably have them," Jessie said with some excitement. "Maybe he will see them."

I was paged to the hospital for a delivery. Bill offered to drive Jessie home so she could stay. She later told me she stayed all afternoon. Bill played the piano and she and Elaine sang old hymns and Sigmund Romberg songs that Jessie had learned in high school.

Wednesday afternoon found me driving to Eddyville again. Even though I only worked until noon, the day was dark when I left the office. My heart felt heavy, like leaves weighed down with raindrops. I didn't like the barren prison and worried it was not a good setting for Jessie to meet Mike. Jessie, on the other hand, had high hopes for this meeting. Her heart seemed light, like a leaf floating on the wind. Clutching a bag, which I rightly guessed held the scrapbook, she talked the whole way about Jeff, how he loved to sing as a little boy, how he protected his little sisters, how he confided in her when he was afraid. There seemed to be such a bond between them, I couldn't imagine how heartbroken that little boy must have been when she was suddenly gone. *Would he ever forgive her?*

As we parked the car, Jessie grew quiet. Cement parking areas abutted gray walls with no relief by grass or trees. The austere prison loomed before us. The weight of those walls seemed to settle over Jessie. Her eyes widened as her skin grew pale and her hands began to tremble.

"What a horrible place," she muttered more to herself than to me.

"Unfortunately, the inside is no better. Are you sure you're up for this?"

177

"I've waited over twenty years for this day. Gray walls won't stop me."

Inside we followed the guard down long corridors, through locked doors, coming to the same room I had visited before. There was no waiting room for people accompanying visitors, so I was shown into the room with Jessie. I offered to wait in the car, but she grabbed my hand and asked me to stay. "I need you," she said.

Mike, dressed in his orange prison clothes, came into the room. He stood tall, his face defiant. Jessie remained seated. After what seemed like an eternity of silence, he spoke first. "Dr. Parker says there's more to your story than I know. I assume you have come to tell me."

"Yes, I'm here to tell you what happened, if you will listen."

"Do I have a choice?"

"Yes, of course you do. I've learned we always have a choice, even when we don't think we do."

"Go on." Mike sat down.

"I didn't leave with another man like you believed. I loved your father, and I love you."

Mike gave a grunt of disbelief as he stared at the floor.

"Do you remember what happened a few months before I left?"

"Yes, you had a stillborn baby boy. I felt like I lost you then."

"In many ways you did. I was depressed, forcing myself to go through the motions of life. Jeff, I got pregnant again, and I left that morning to have an illegal abortion. I thought I would be home by the time you got home from school, and no one would know. Dr. Parker was one of the doctors who saved my life when I was found unconscious and in shock. I had no identification so the hospital could not contact your father. When I regained consciousness, I had no memory of who I was or how I got there. I was in the hospital for months. When I got out, I became the housekeeper for Dr. Parker's uncle. It was eighteen months before I saw your father and remembered my past."

Mike remained silent, now staring intently at her.

"There was never another man, and there hasn't been in all these years," Jessie said.

"Is that supposed to make it all right that you deserted your family?" Mike said, the pace of his speech speeding up with his rising anger.

"No, Jeff. I am not making excuses. What I have done will never be all right. I just want you to know what happened and that I love you, that I never intended to leave you, and certainly not for some other man. I did a terrible thing, and you, your father, and your sisters have had to pay for it. I'm sorry. Will you forgive me?"

"I'll have to think about that." He abruptly rose and turned to leave. "I've heard enough," he said as he walked out and slammed the door.

Tears ruined Jessie's silk blouse as we called the guard to let us out. She clutched the scrapbook like a drowning man clutches shattered pieces of his ship which has been dashed on the rocks.

"He didn't say no," was all she said on the long trip home.

Several weeks passed before I talked to Jessie or Elaine again. Then one Friday Elaine came to discuss her antidepressant. She looked well, wearing her makeup and an attractive yellow sweater set with khaki pants. She had been lifting weights and running with Mike's Labrador retriever. She said she had seen a lot of Jessie and her father lately. Her father was planning to retire and move to Lexington.

"I have taken antidepressants for over a year now," she said. "I'm sure I needed them, but I don't like the way they make me feel. I'm numb."

"Seems hard to believe it's been that long. How are things going with Mike?"

"He still refuses to see me, but I did find a job. It's more receptionist than paralegal, and it pays a little more than half of what I was making. I put the house on the market. Without Mike's income and with my decrease in pay, I can't afford to keep it. It makes me sad to think of losing the home I shared with Mike, but I figure it's better to sell it than to have a foreclosure. My father is helping me keep it until the sale."

Remembering the living room where Greg died, I said, "I'm sure it has some sentimental value, but there are some unhappy memories there as well."

"Well, that's true."

"Have you decided what you'll do when it sells?"

"Jessie invited me to move in with her. She says that she rattles around in that big house since Grace, Ellen, and Henry left. I'm not sure about living with her."

"I lived with Jessie for a couple of years after my Uncle Henry died. I was a resident, working eighty hours a week. She was a wonderful roommate, used to have dinner on the table when I got home from the hospital. I don't remember her saying a cross word. It might be good for both of you."

"I'm just concerned that, if I don't have my own place, Mike won't have a place when he gets out of prison. I haven't given up on him, and I'm afraid he might not want to live with Jessie."

"Have you heard when that will be?"

"The parole board will consider his case after a year."

"Maybe you could stay with Jessie until you know what they say. A lot can happen between now and then."

"Well, I still have to sell the house. Do you think I can stop the antidepressant?"

"Yes, I think you can, especially since you're exercising and eating properly. Your father and Jessie are providing support that you didn't have when you started. You don't need to taper off this particular antidepressant. You can just stop. I'll see you back in three weeks to see how you feel off the medicine."

Three weeks later Elaine returned to my office looking a little tired. Since she did not need an exam, my nurse showed her into my consultation office. When we were both comfortably seated, she admitted that she had not slept well the night before.

"I feel better off the medicine. Even if I don't always sleep as well, I have more energy. You won't believe it; I sold the house."

"I'm not surprised. I would have bought it for the yard alone. You did a beautiful job with your gardening."

"I'm relieved to be out of that responsibility. The closing is next week."

"Did you decide about living with Jessie?"

"I've decided to take her up on the offer. I don't really need to be alone."

"I think it will be good for both of you."

Elaine nodded. "Jessie is a wise woman. She says I need forgiveness not just from Mike, but from others as well. I thought about that and decided to go see Greg's mother."

"You did? Did you know her?"

"Yes, Mike and I had seen her several times at Greg's home, and she's a member of our church. I told her I was sorry about what happened to Greg and sorry that I aborted her grandchild. I asked her to forgive me."

"What did she say?"

"She said she did forgive me. She said she had always liked Mike and me, and she believed us that Greg's death was an accident."

Amazed, I thought how difficult that visit must have been, both for Greg's mother and for Elaine. I didn't know what to say.

Elaine continued. "You won't believe what she asked me."

"What was that?"

"She asked me if Greg forced me to have sex with him."

"Really?"

"I asked her why she asked, and she said she was surprised that I would get pregnant with Greg's baby. She had always thought that Mike and I had a good marriage. I didn't respond, and she went on to say that Greg had been accused of rape in college. The grand jury didn't indict him because the girl decided not to testify. The charges were dropped. I told her I didn't want to have sex with Greg, but I didn't fight him. He was insistent, and I was afraid."

"What did she say?"

"She thanked me for not saying that in the trial, and she said she was sorry. She also asked me to tell Mike she forgives him too." The intercom buzzed. My nurse said L&D was on the hospital line.

"Excuse me Elaine, I need to take this." I gave routine admission orders for a patient in early labor and calculated I would have several hours before they needed me. Then I asked my nurse to call Jon's office and tell him I had someone in labor and would call him later. "I'm sorry, Elaine. That was someone in early labor. I guess you haven't told Mike about this conversation with Greg's mother."

"No."

"I wonder if Greg's mother would visit him."

"I don't know. I didn't ask her that."

"Elaine, maybe I should have told you this before now, but when I saw Mike we talked briefly about his refusing to see you. I told him you might have something to say that would make a difference. He was angry, saying nothing would change the fact you were pregnant unless you were raped, when he stopped midsentence like he remembered something. Do you think he knew about the rape charges?"

"He might have. They were friends from college."

"If he knows, maybe he would believe you."

"I hope I get the chance to tell him."

"Have you tried writing to him?"

"Yes, he refuses my letters too."

"Have you taken him any more books?"

"No. Why?"

"He read the others before he sent them back."

"He did? I'll take more. Maybe I could sneak a letter inside," she said with a faint smile, the first I'd seen in a long time.

"Did Jessie tell you she saw Mike?"

"Yes, she told me about it. She wants to see him again, but she's afraid he won't see her. She's not like me. She says she couldn't go week after week and have him refuse to see her. She's hoping you will offer to take her again."

"To tell you the truth, I was a little embarrassed being there the last time."

"Oh, you shouldn't be. She said she couldn't have done it without you."

CHAPTER 14

A few weeks later, I had a free Wednesday afternoon. A patient scheduled for a hysterectomy developed a bad cold and the surgery had to be rescheduled. Having no intention of making another trip home from Eddyville with Jessie in tears, I decided to go see Mike and learn for myself where he stood on forgiving her.

It was a beautiful fall afternoon; the trees were at that perfect color where there is still a little green mixed with the red and yellow. The bright sun made the colors even more vibrant, and I loved the crisp chill of sweater weather. Still, I dreaded the visit before me. I had no idea it would be one of my best afternoons ever.

When I arrived, the sunshine seemed to remove some of the gray from the place. I noticed a beautiful oak tree to the left of the entrance that I had never noticed before. The slamming, locked doors did not disturb me as much as they had on my first visit. As Mike walked into the visitors' room, I knew this was going to be a good visit. He looked me in the eye, and a big smile lit up his face. His step was lighter and quicker. Even the cadence of his speech was different.

"Dr. Parker, I am so glad you came. It's good to see you."

I returned his smile. "I'm glad to see you too. Why don't you call me Cara? I'm not here to be anybody's doctor."

"Okay, Cara it is."

"I guess this may sound like a strange thing to say to a man in prison, but you seem happier today."

"I am. I don't know if my mother ever told you, but she made me take piano lessons from the time I was five years old. We had an old ebony upright piano that weighed a ton and had the ivory missing from some of the keys." Mike looked past me, like he could see and that old piano. "We moved a lot when I was growing up, from one rented house to another. Dad always complained about having to move the piano, and Mom would just find more neighbors to help him. About a year after Dad married Mary, we moved to her house. Dad left that piano sitting in the house where my mother left it and us. I played until the day she left home, and I had not touched a piano since that day until about a month ago. The man who plays piano for our traditional chapel service is getting paroled next week, and the chaplain needed someone to play. He said that if anyone volunteered they could practice in the chapel whenever they wanted. Nobody stepped up, so I agreed to do it. I've been playing old hymns for hours every night, and they have changed my life."

"Why, Mike, that's wonderful. I love the old hymns too, but I'm surprised they use traditional music in the services here. I would have thought they would use contemporary music."

"Oh, they have a contemporary service too. They actually provide every kind of worship service that is represented by the population. They even have an outdoor place for Native Americans to worship. The chaplain is in charge of finding someone to lead all of the services, but he doesn't lead what is not of his faith."

"I'm glad to know they provide what people need spiritually."

"Chaplain Harrison is great. His mantra is, 'If you have to do time, do it right. Don't let doing time waste your life; have it make your life. Do time with your Lord.' His theme song is 'Take Time to Be Holy.' That's his idea of doing it right. I've practiced that one a lot, and the words are wonderful. We sing it every Sunday. I think he's taken that text and extracted the ideas so that even the other religions can benefit from the wisdom. As I sit and play, reading the words over and over, I feel the anger and fear going out of me, feel peace and joy coming in. I'm glad my mother made me learn to play."

"Speaking of your mother, have you given any more thought to forgiving her?"

"Yes, I choose to forgive her. Chaplain Harrison says forgiveness is a choice we make. We act like we forgive, and then the emotions gradually catch up with the conscious decision."

"Sounds like a wise man. Your mother wanted to show you something that she has been making all these years. I think it would be good if you could see it."

"Tell her to bring it. I'll look at it."

"I will. Is one time better than another? I understand you have a job."

"Yes, but I'm off on Wednesday afternoons, evenings, and weekends. Grace comes every weekend. Maybe Mom could come with her."

"I'll suggest it."

"What do you think about Grace?"

"What do you mean? She's an extraordinary young woman."

"I mean, is she okay?"

"It has been so long, I would think that she's cured. Childhood leukemia is cured now most of the time, but when Grace had it, cure was extremely rare. I read a paper, written in the 1970s, that reported only fifteen out of over fourteen hundred children had survived for five to seventeen years. Grace's survival is a miracle."

He looked pensive for a moment. "Grace is a miracle in more ways than one. I've never known anyone as loving. She sees the best in everybody, and everyone, male and female, loves her. There is no shortage of guys who want to date her, but she's just amused and refuses to go out with them. She's thirty years old. I wish she could find someone to share her life."

"Maybe she's still concerned about getting sick. She did see how hard it was for you to lose Sara, and she's the most sensitive person I've ever known."

"I hadn't thought of that. Do you think she could ever have kids?"

"I would think that she's fertile, but she might not want to have kids for the same reason she won't date. Do you have many other visitors?"

"Dad comes every weekend too." I guess my face betrayed me, because Mike quickly added, "Cara, being my mother's friend, you have seen my father at his worst, but he really is a good man. He's hard on people, but hardest perhaps on himself. He grew up with that rigid, judgmental brand of Christianity that turns so many people off. This thing with me has finally made him realize that you can and should still love people when they disappoint you. He told me last weekend that he feels bad about the way he treated Ellen."

"Ellen needs to hear his apology. He hurt her."

"He knows that. I suggested he go see her. He hardly knows Henry, and he will graduate this June and be gone from home."

"Does Ellen ever get here to see you?" I leaned back in the straight, hard chair and thought about how hard it would be to visit if you were as sick as Ellen.

"Rarely. Do you know that she was diagnosed with chronic active hepatitis?"

"Yes, I know that. She told me when she came in for her annual gynecologic checkup. I feel so bad about it. I'm the one who gave her all that blood. I thought she had been spared, but her initial hepatitis was so mild we missed it. We all thought she was just tired from taking care of Carl Henry."

"You shouldn't feel bad. Henry is the light of her life. For that matter, he's the light of Joshua's life too. Ellen thinks Henry would have died without you."

"I wonder if Joshua misses it that Ellen's disease kept her from having more children."

"Didn't you know? Joshua is sterile. He knew he couldn't have children when he and Ellen met. He was thrilled when he found out Ellen had a son already. Henry is just as much his son as Ellen's."

I did know. I also knew infertility procedures might have helped them if Ellen had been well. "I'm glad Ellen found someone who could love her and Henry."

"Joshua is the best. He brags about Henry even more than Ellen. Henry is brilliant, you know. He just found out that when he finishes high school, he has a full scholarship to MIT. He's going to study physics. Ellen and Joshua don't know whether to be thrilled or worried that he's going to be so far away."

"That's understandable; he may not come back this way. It sounds like you and Joshua are close to each other."

"Yeah. You know, Joshua is the same age as Mom's first stillborn baby would have been, a year younger than Ellen. He's like the brother I lost. He comes to visit at least once a month."

After Mike and I had finished catching up on all the people we knew in common, I decided to address a touchy subject. I squirmed for more reasons than the hard chair and my aching back. "I saw Elaine yesterday."

"How is she?"

"She looks good."

"The way she looks was never the problem."

"I hear you. I understand she comes every Sunday afternoon to visit you."

He nodded and looked at the floor. "Yes, she does. I'm thinking of seeing her next time. I might choose to forgive her too."

"It's good you're planning to see her, and I hope you choose to forgive her." Looking at my watch, I realized it would be late when I got home. Jon would be late for dinner, but there was barely time to pick up

Thai take-out. "Mike, this has been a wonderful afternoon, but I have to go. Jon will be home from work before I get there."

"How come you and Jon never had kids?"

"We both wanted them, but he was afraid they would have birth defects from his Agent Orange exposure. The Vietnamese suffer the most disabilities, but American veterans suffer as well.

"I didn't know he was in Vietnam."

"Yes, in the Air Force. He helped drop the stuff."

"Wow. I'm sorry. With as many unwanted children as there are in the world, it's a shame for people to want them and not have them."

I agreed.

As soon as I got to the car, I called Jessie. "I just visited Mike."

"How is he?"

"Jessie, you won't believe how good he is."

"Really, in what way?"

I began relating the afternoon's conversations as I pulled out of the parking lot. We talked on the phone most of my way home. Finally, I told her that he said she should come with Grace to see him.

"That won't work," she said.

"Why not?"

"Grace's visits usually intersect with George's. I don't want to risk having George color my visit with Jeff."

"Well, I can understand that. Maybe you should just go when it suits you; I'm sure this will be a good visit. Jeff said Wednesday afternoon, Saturday, and Sunday are the best times."

"What are you doing next Wednesday?"

"I can check, Jessie, but I really don't think you need me."

"Please, just once more."

"Okay, I will check. I'm getting back to town so I need to get off the phone."

As I glanced down to disconnect the phone, I rear-ended the car in front of me. I knew I should not have been on the phone. I've lost count of how many fender-benders I've had. The combination of sleep deprivation and distraction can be deadly. Fortunately, no one has been hurt in my accidents, including me, unless you count being embarrassed and poorer. The last time I took my car into the body shop the owner recognized my voice from the other room. My car insurance costs a lot. After I called the police, I called Jon and asked him to pick up the Thai take-out for an even later dinner.

The next day Jessie called to tell me that she had talked to Grace and learned that George was not going to visit Jeff that weekend. She would be going with Grace.

"Don't forget the scrapbook," I said. "I didn't tell him what you had, but I told him you had something to show him, and he wants to see it." I was a bit sorry I was not going to see Mike's reaction to the scrapbook, but I was confident that I would hear about it.

On Saturday evening, Jon and I had just gotten home from a concert at the university when Jessie called.

"Cara, thank you for arranging today," Jessie said, somewhat breathless.

"Jessie, I didn't arrange anything. Mike had already decided to forgive you. I take it things went well today."

"Oh, yes. Grace and I had a wonderful day. The weather was beautiful for the drive. Jeff seemed truly glad to see me."

"What did he say about the scrapbook?"

"He loved it. As a matter of fact, after we looked through it page by page, he gave it to the guard to go through, hoping he would be able to keep it. They didn't find any files or weapons, so they let him keep it. He seemed really grateful to have it."

"What about it did he enjoy the most?"

"Well, he loved the clippings from his games. They let him relive some joyful times, but I think he liked the photos that I had taken of the games and important events the best. He had never seen those pictures, and they proved that I had cared enough to come. I should not have tried so hard to hide my presence. He needed to know that I cared about what he did. I should have known that."

"Don't second-guess yourself. That time we went to see him after the middle school game distressed even me. I can imagine how you felt. The important thing is that he has forgiven you, and you can begin anew."

"Yes, thank God. I told him I'm going to start coming to visit on Wednesdays, and he said that would be fine. You know, Cara, he even thanked me for making him take piano lessons."

"Did he tell you about the chaplain?"

"Oh, yes. He sounds like a remarkable man."

"Who represents a remarkable God."

"Indeed. Well, I'll let you go. Tell Jon I said I'm sorry for keeping you so long."

"Oh, don't worry about that. He's watching UK's first basketball game of the season. It's just an exhibition game, but it's still on TV. I could be on Mars and he wouldn't miss me. Jessie, I am so happy for you."

The following night Jon was working on a guest lecture he had been invited to give at his Alma Mater, Wharton School of Business, and I was washing dishes when Elaine called.

"I saw Mike today," she said. "We talked all afternoon."

"Elaine, that's wonderful! Sounds like it was a good visit."

"He didn't want to talk about what happened, but I did say I was sorry and asked him to forgive me. He wanted to talk about his mother. I told him I was living with her now. He didn't know that but agreed that selling the house was a good idea. He said he didn't want to ever see that raised hearth again."

"I can understand that."

"He wanted to know all about Jessie's house and her work. It seems that every time someone had tried to tell him anything about her, he had refused to listen. When I told him how big the house was, he wanted to know how his mother had gotten that. He didn't even know she had inherited the house and money."

"Amazing how clueless we can be when we refuse to communicate with people."

"In the end he wondered if Jessie had been the source of the money he needed to go to college. His father never told him where the money came from."

"I know Jessie offered, but Mike refused her money. I don't know that George refused."

"I told him about visiting Greg's mother. He seemed relieved that she didn't blame him for what happened. He said we could discuss our issues next time. At least he's going to see me again."

"That's a start. I'm glad you talked."

Jessie and Elaine saw Mike every week for the remainder of his prison term. That Thanksgiving was the first time in more than twenty years that Jessie did not cook Thanksgiving dinner. She, Elaine, Grace, George, Mary, Erin (Mike's youngest sister), and Bill all spent the day at the prison with Mike. Ellen, Joshua, and Henry spent the day with Joshua's parents so Ellen could rest if necessary. Jon and I went to Florida to visit his parents, who had retired in Sarasota. Jon's mother loved the artistic community in Sarasota, especially the opera.

On April 1, 1996, the parole board met to consider Mike Green's case. The chaplain testified that Mike's conduct had been exemplary. Greg's mother came to say that she believed her son's death had been an accident and Mike had been punished enough. The board voted unanimously to approve Mike's parole with release planned for Wednesday afternoon, April 10. On April 3, I received an invitation from Elaine and Mike to attend his release. I thought that was a little strange, but it was a Wednesday afternoon and I could arrange to be off.

When I arrived at the prison entrance, I left my purse at the desk and went through security as usual. Then I was escorted in the opposite direction from the room where I had always visited. After passing through countless locked doors, I arrived at the prison chapel. Mike and Elaine were there. She was wearing a beautiful champagne-colored linen suit.

Mike was also dressed in a suit. Jessie, Bill, Grace, Ellen, Joshua, Erin, George, and Mary were there. I was introduced to Chaplain Martin Harrison, whose bald head shone under the fluorescent light and whose eyes twinkled like Santa Claus.

"Would everyone take a seat?" Chaplain Harrison said. "Jeff and Elaine Green have invited you here to witness as they renew their marriage vows." Jessie was obviously surprised to hear Mike called Jeff. As if Chaplain Harrison could read her mind, he said, "Jeff has requested that he be called by that name in the future. He remembers an innocent, happy time before age twelve when that was how he was addressed. As he enters this new phase of his life, he wants to return to his former name. He wants this name change to help him leave behind this time in prison and to symbolize the change in him.

"Over the past four months Elaine and Jeff have had weekly counseling sessions with me. They have dealt with marital issues, communication issues, and spiritual issues. They have both expressed their desire to repeat these vows. Elaine and Jeff, come and stand here in front of me. Jessie and George, they have asked that you stand with them."

Jessie beamed as she stood beside Elaine. How different this was from their first ceremony when Jessie sat alone in the balcony! It was equally different for Elaine and Jeff. Whereas the first ceremony was in a huge church, filled with flowers devoid of fragrance, the only flowers in this small chapel were three gardenias grown in the prison greenhouse and set into a wrist corsage for Elaine and a boutonniere for Jeff. Their heavenly scent filled the room. Elaine's formal white wedding gown, complete with twenty-foot train, and Jeff's tuxedo were replaced by the simple suits, their Sunday best. Whereas their love had been blind before, now it had been tested and made stronger by failure and forgiveness. I thought of Uncle Henry and Aunt Edna.

Elaine turned to Jeff, took his hands into hers, and repeated her vows after Chaplain Harrison. Jeff did the same. It took only a few minutes, but it felt as though they saved a lifetime, and perhaps they did. Chaplain Harrison closed with a prayer.

"Dear God. I ask that you bless this union between Jeff and Elaine. While difficulties will doubtless come again, I pray that their love for each other and for You and their newfound commitment will lead them through any trouble. I pray that You fill all the remaining days of their lives together with peace and joy. As You are their witness and ever-present help, remind them of these vows and keep them faithful. Give them a home filled with Your presence. Help them to love as You loved. Lead them to the life that You have planned for them to live, and whatever comes their way, give them an ever greater capacity to love and forgive."

Jeff walked out of prison with Elaine by his side. They went to Jessie's house, which was now Elaine and Jeff's home as well.

CHAPTER 15

On an unusually warm day in May, Jeff and Elaine came to my office. Jeff looked tense, picking at the cuticle of his left thumb. He was dressed neatly in khaki pants and a green golf shirt, though I knew he was not playing golf. Elaine looked radiant in navy and white polka dot pants with a navy shell and white shirt. Her smile was so broad I guessed the purpose of their visit.

"We want to talk about having a baby," she said as soon as they sat in my inner office. "We know the first thing is Jeff's vasectomy reversal, and you won't do that, but we want to know who you would recommend."

"I'm still mad at him for doing this vasectomy in the first place, but I think Dr. Daniel Day is the best in town. He's done more reversals than anyone else, and that is especially important in microsurgical procedures."

"Will it work?" Jeff asked.

"Dr. Day can give you his statistics, but across the board there is a 92 percent chance of normal sperm counts and motility. It usually takes about three to six months for the normal counts to occur. Of course, success is in pregnancy. Just over 50 percent of reversals result in pregnancy within two years, about 75 percent if you look at longer time periods. I do know that the sooner you do it the better. There is some decrease in success if it has been over five years since the vasectomy was first done. You are past that."

"Is it expensive?"

"Yes, it is, and your health insurance will not cover it. It's less if they don't find much scarring and the procedure can be done easily. More complicated procedures cost more, and they can't tell you ahead of time if it will be complicated."

"Oh, dear," Elaine sighed.

"If I were you, I would ask Dr. Day for a discount. He may be willing to help." *He ought to*, I thought to myself. *He had no business doing the vasectomy in the first place.* "Even so, that will not help with the facility bill. It is done as an outpatient procedure now so that will help some."

"We're going to use some of the equity we had in the house to pay for it," Elaine said.

"My mother also wants to help. I hope she doesn't have to, but we may have to let her. Will I need a lot of recovery time? I still haven't found a job, but I want to get back to work as soon as possible."

"I would think you could work after two to three weeks."

"How soon can we get pregnant?"

"We don't consider couples infertile until they have tried for a year."

"That long?" Elaine looked as though yesterday was not soon enough.

"You could do some simple things like keep a basal body temperature chart just to help with timing. I'll ask Anita to get you one. You just use an old-fashioned thermometer and take your temperature for five minutes before your feet hit the floor every morning."

"I suppose you also mean before any other morning activity." Jeff winked at me. Elaine's face turned the color of the roses that sat on the corner of my desk, and I laughed.

On Monday, June 3, 1996, just one day before Jeff's thirty-seventh birthday, he was scheduled for his vasectomy reversal. Dr. Day had agreed to do the procedure for half his usual fee. I had a tubal ligation scheduled at the same time in the operating room next door. When I finished my short procedure, I stopped by Dr. Day's operating room. "Worlds Apart," a song from Vince Gill's new country music album, blared from the radio, and Dr. Day sang along with a rich tenor voice that seemed better suited to "Nessun dorma."

"We could use that tenor voice in my church choir," I said.

"Not me. I'm usually on the fifth green about the time church starts."

"How's it going?"

"Good. When I did his procedure originally, I took a very short segment of the vas deferens. I do that when the men are young and may be making a mistake having the vasectomy in the first place. He was so sure his wife was cured; I didn't have the heart to tarnish his hope."

I have judged him unfairly, I thought to myself. *When am I ever going to learn?*

"I just have to attach vas deferens to vas deferens," Dr. Day continued. "It's much simpler than if I had taken a longer segment, like I do with old farts who have eight or ten children with four or five different women. I wouldn't even want their reversals to work. Are you going to the waiting room?"

"Yes."

"Would you tell his wife that Jeff's doing well? She looked like she was scared to death."

"They've been through a lot. I'll tell her." *What a colorful character,* I thought as I left for the waiting room, feeling much more kindly toward Jeff's urologist and walking a bit lighter not carrying my heavy load of judgment.

In mid-July Jessie invited Jon and me to share her table for Picnic with the Pops, a popular August activity in Lexington. People bought tables and chose a theme for decoration and menu. During the meal the Lexington Philharmonic played popular music and the tables were judged. Jessie, who had bought a table every year since the first one, usually chose her theme based on the movie that won the Academy Award that year. She did the decorations and cooked the food for the table of ten. Often others had the meal catered, but not Jessie.

"I'm not sure what to use for my theme this year," she said as we had coffee one Saturday morning. "What kind of food would you choose with *Braveheart* as a theme? The nominees aren't much better—*Apollo 13, Il Postino: The Postman, Sense and Sensibility*, and *Babe*. I guess I could use *Sense and Sensibility* and cook roast beef with Yorkshire pudding, but that would be a difficult meal to make into a picnic."

"You could do *Babe* and have pulled pork barbeque."

"Somehow it doesn't seem right to serve the star of the show." We both laughed.

"I'm sure you will think of something."

She did. In the end she chose *Babe*, but instead of pulled pork barbeque she had a completely vegetarian meal with eggplant Parmesan, a garden salad, multigrain garlic bread, and carrot cake for dessert.

"This meal is in honor of all the farm animals," Jessie said. "We aren't eating any of them."

She decorated with a red checked oilcloth tablecloth, a centerpiece of flowers arranged in a container made of barn siding, and stuffed barnyard animals of all types. She served the salad from a bucket onto metal plates, and we drank white wine from plastic glasses. In addition to Jon and me, Jessie had invited Bill, Ellen and Joshua, Jeff and Elaine, and Grace, who brought her first boyfriend, a hematology resident from the university.

"He was the first person to use the word *cured* in relation to my leukemia," Grace said when she introduced Grady Davis. "Everybody else said that I had the longest remission they had seen. I decided that if I was cured, it was okay for me to date." I thought how hard it must have been for the young girl to live with the fear that her remission would end. No wonder she had chosen not to share that fear with someone she loved.

"I had no idea the word *cure* got me the first date," Grady said. "I thought it was my good looks." He had a deep chuckle not unlike Jon's.

As we settled into our places, Jessie asked Jeff to pray.

"Thank you, God, for food, family, and friends. Amen."

Over dinner, Jessie seemed quieter than usual. Finally she spoke and I understood why. "I'm not going to dwell on this, but it was twenty-five years ago this week that I left my home and my family. I destroyed my marriage, lost precious time with my children, and nearly lost my life. I have dreamed of having my three children around the dinner table with me for twenty-five years. Tonight that dream has come true; thank you all for being here, and most of all thank you for forgiving me."

Bill, who was sitting between Elaine and Jessie, took Elaine's hand. "There are many reasons why parents and children become estranged. While it hasn't been twenty-five years, Elaine and I spent far too many years not speaking. I longed for her forgiveness, and I am grateful that dream has come true, as well."

Elaine looked at her dad. I guessed what she was about to say. "Amazing, isn't it, how it takes realizing your own need for forgiveness to make you willing to forgive someone else."

Jeff sat next to Jessie. "I'm sorry, Mom, that it took me the longest to forgive you. It's been my loss."

Ellen, who looked happier than she had in years, said, "Speaking of forgiveness, guess who came to see Carl Henry last Saturday."

I looked at Jessie. I knew who Jessie and I hoped it would be. She said, "Who?"

"Dad. He said he was sorry for how he had treated Carl Henry and me and for all the years he had lost with us. He said Grace had told him all about Carl Henry, and he wanted to see him before he left for school. He asked us to forgive him and we did."

"Oh honey, that's wonderful," Jessie said. "We will always need to love and forgive, but here's to a future where it doesn't take us so long." She raised her plastic glass.

Jessie and I sat in the backseat as Bill drove us home. He and Jon talked about this season's football team and wondered how many games they would win.

"I can hardly believe it's been twenty-five years since we met in that ER," I said.

"We've been through a lot, my friend." Jessie patted my hand.

"Thanks for letting us share this special time with your family."

"Cara, you are family."

"Our Uncle Henry would have loved tonight."

Neither Jon nor I wanted a television in our bedroom. We both liked to read and discuss the day before sleeping.

"I noticed you talking with Jeff this evening," I said.

"Yes, he is a most interesting young man. He seems very bright. He was telling me how hard it has been to find a suitable job. His old accounting firm offered him an entry-level job doing the accounting work, but not being exposed to clients. The salary was less than half of what he made before. He just didn't think he could be there under those circumstances. He would be reminded every day of what happened. Most other places look at his felony conviction and just say their positions are filled. He seems discouraged."

"You can't blame him."

"He said he guessed he should take a minimum-wage job and give up his dreams. I asked him if he thought he might like to go back to school and do something totally different."

"What did he say to that?"

"He said he didn't see how he could with them trying to have a baby."

"Jessie would help them."

"I'm sure he knows that, but I don't think he really wants to go back to school. I wish I could help him somehow."

About a month later, Jon came down to breakfast, looking very handsome in his navy blazer and light gray pants.

"Good morning, dear," he said.

"Good morning. You know I love you in that outfit."

"I know you love me, period."

"Well, that's true. What are you up to today?"

"I'm going to the September sales at Keeneland."

"Is there a particular horse you want?"

"Actually, there are two fillies and one stallion whose bloodlines interest us. The issue is whether those with deeper pockets are interested in the same ones." Jon was part of a five-man group that had equal interests in a few racehorses. Two of the men were Wall Street friends.

"Are Nathan and Craig here from New York? We should have them over for dinner if they're in town."

"No. Just Joe, Charlie, and I are going this time." After quickly downing a cup of coffee and a piece of toast with peanut butter, he grabbed an apple, kissed me on the cheek, and headed for the door. "Wish me luck."

That evening the house smelled wonderful when I got home. I had left a roast, carrots, and potatoes in a crock pot. I was in the backyard picking a tomato for salad when Jon drove in.

"Well, are we the proud owners of a new horse?" I asked as he got out of the car.

"Afraid not. The Saudis were interested in both fillies, and the Irish contingent wanted the stallion. We did bid for a while just to keep some of their money in Central Kentucky, but it was pretty clear that we wouldn't get them."

"I'm sorry. Are you hungry? Dinner is almost ready."

"Yes, I actually missed lunch. I do have some good news, though."

"Really? What's that?"

"Let me wash up and I'll tell you over dinner."

"I just need to add this tomato to the salad and we're ready."

When Jon came back, he said, "Do you want to eat outside on the screened porch? I'll set the table."

"Just get napkins, knives, and forks. We can fill our plates in the kitchen."

As we sat down, I asked, "So, what's the good news?"

"I have an idea for what Jeff can do."

"What?"

"I asked Joe if he was aware of anyone who needed an accountant, and he said he might be interested in changing. I told him about Jeff, and he seemed interested. We decided that we might be able to recommend enough clients that he could start his own business."

"Do you think he kept his license?"

"Yes, I know he did. He told me last month."

"That sounds like it might work."

"I know Jeff's old firm did work for some of the larger farms, so I think he would be familiar with tax laws affecting horse farms."

"Would he have to have an additional license to practice on his own?"

"I looked into that this afternoon. Yes, he would have to make an application as a sole practitioner, but I don't think having the felony prohibits his getting it. The key would be some of us being willing to trust him and recommend him. After all, his felony is about a terrible accident. It's not like he embezzled some client's money."

I smelled the dinner roll burning in the oven. "I'm sorry, dear; I forgot your bread again."

"I don't need it anyway. I thought we could invite Jeff and Elaine to dinner this weekend and talk about it. In the meantime, I'll call the accounting board and make sure this could work."

"Sounds like a plan. I think the weather is supposed to be nice. Would you grill steaks?"

"Sure, Jeff and I can talk while they cook."

When they drove down the lane to our house, Jeff and Elaine had the same response as everyone else.

"What a beautiful place! You must love it here," Jeff said. "I could just feel my tension slipping away as I got farther from town."

"It's so quiet," Elaine said.

"I love that, perhaps best of all. I think our bodies react to sirens even if we don't consciously register hearing them. Come on out to the porch. Jon is starting the grill. We're making this a very informal dinner."

"Would you like a drink?" Jon offered beer, wine, soda, or water.

"Just water for me," Elaine said. "Always hoping, you know."

"That's wise. What about you, Jeff?"

"I'll take a beer."

"Bud or Heineken?"

"Bud's fine."

When Jon came back with the drinks, he invited Jeff to go with him to the grill. Elaine and I chatted about the Picnic with the Pops, Ellen, Carl Henry, Grace, and her new boyfriend, but throughout the conversation she fidgeted with her bracelet, crossed and uncrossed her legs, and asked me to repeat things I had said.

"You seem tense, Elaine. Is something wrong?"

"Jeff is discouraged about the job situation, and I'm no help. All I do is fret about getting pregnant again."

"You need to relax. Maybe Jon will help tonight."

"Jon. What can he do?" She did not relax, but she did listen.

"He has an idea about what Jeff can do. He's probably talking to him about it as we speak. It was his idea to invite you for dinner. Why don't you help me carry out my part of dinner, and I'll explain."

By the end of the evening, Jon and Jeff had a plan. Jon would try to find clients, and Jeff would look into the required license, office space, and financing.

That Thanksgiving Jessie was again hostess. This time Jeff joined Ellen and Grace at their mother's table. All three of them plus their families planned to spend the following Sunday with their father. I was amused to see that Jessie was filling Uncle Henry's antique table a little more every year. Jeff, the largest of the men, sat at the end of the table, Uncle Henry's seat. Jessie invited Elaine's father to offer thanks, after which she announced the opening of the eating season. This time it was Jeff and Grady who laughed at the traditional pronouncement, hearing it for the first time.

"It's official. I move into my new office space on January 2," Jeff announced over pumpkin pie. "I'll even make it into the new phone book, which is important."

"I've secured eight clients who will have Jeff doing their payroll, accounting statements, and taxes beginning in January," Jon said. "I'm sure I'll be able to find more once Jeff has proven himself with these."

Jessie sat in what had been Aunt Edna's seat, at the end of the table closest to the kitchen. She smiled and jumped up and down the whole meal to serve more food or fill empty glasses. Each time she would touch one of her family on the shoulder or cheek. She asked questions of each of us to make sure everyone was part of the conversation. Jessie had always been a great hostess, but this was her crowning performance.

Jeff cleared his throat. "When my family came to share Thanksgiving with me at the prison last year, I never could have dreamed how much would take place before the next Thanksgiving. I just need to say to all of you that of all the things in the world, I am most grateful for you. Thank you for being there for me, even when I was shutting you out. Mother, thank you for all you've done, not just this year, but over the years. You have us living here at no cost, and last week Dad told me about the college 'scholarships.' Now you're helping me start this business. I can never repay you."

"There's no need for you to repay me," Jessie said softly.

But in fact Jeff did repay her. On the first day of December, Jessie began to read the Gospel of Luke. This time Jeff joined her. Just the two of them met each morning, and Jessie shared with him how the practice had started. The bond that had existed between a twelve-year-old boy and his mother was being rebuilt, one verse at a time.

On March 12, 1997, a Wednesday, Elaine came to my office for an appointment.

"It's been nine months," she said. "Jeff's semen analysis shows normal counts and motility. Dr. Day said that I should get pregnant."

"I told you it might take a year."

"I know, but I wondered if there was anything else we could do. I'm thirty-six years old. I'm not getting any younger."

"Have you been keeping your temperature chart?"

"Yes."

"Did you bring it?"

"Yes." Elaine's hands shook as she fumbled in her purse for the chart. "Here it is."

The chart showed a biphasic pattern consistent with regular ovulation. "This is good. It looks like you are ovulating regularly. I suppose there is one thing we might do before I send you to an infertility clinic. Sometimes after a procedure like the abortion, you can get scarring or adhesions that might affect the tubes. A hysterosalpingogram is an X-ray procedure where we force some dye through the cervix and check to see that it spills out the tubes. Sometimes it actually helps you get pregnant by breaking little adhesions."

"Can we go ahead and do it, please?"

"It is done ten days after the first day of your period, before you ovulate. Your chart looks like you have already ovulated this month. Call if you get your next period, and we can schedule it."

"Thank you."

"The procedure causes a little cramping, but it won't be too bad. It's done in the X-ray department at the hospital. I do think it would be good if someone drives you."

"Jeff is really busy with tax season. I'll see if Jessie can bring me."

March 24, 1997, was the date of Elaine's next period and her last period. Her due date was December 29, 1997.

CHAPTER 16

I had been thinking about Elaine and Jeff's story and stitching for about forty-five minutes when the phone rang. "She wants to push," the L&D nurse said when I answered.

"I'll be right there."

I hurried down the hall thinking how quickly some prayers are answered. So far this had been a model labor, something I never expect for a first delivery of a thirty-six-year-old mother.

"Elaine, I need to check you again before you push. Just try to blow over the urge. When this contraction ends, turn onto your back." Looking at the monitor, I could see that the contraction had peaked. "This contraction is going away. Maybe you can push next time. It will feel better to push."

Elaine gave a long sigh at the end of the contraction and turned from her side. "Jeff, could I have some ice chips?" He was quick to provide them.

Her cervix was completely dilated and the baby was in perfect position, its head well down. "You're ready to push."

"The contraction is coming," Elaine said, a frown creasing her brow.

"Take a deep breath and blow it all the way out. Then take a deep breath and hold it. Bear down like you are trying to push the baby out." Elaine did just as instructed and pushed perfectly, an advantage of not having an epidural anesthetic.

When the contraction ended, I asked, "What are you going to name the baby?"

Jeff answered, "If it's a boy, William Martin Green for Elaine's father and Chaplain Harrison. You may remember his name is Martin. If it's a girl, Sara Elaine Green, for my two wives." He chuckled.

"Jeff and I both loved Sara." A contraction interrupted Elaine's comment. After pushing for 45 seconds and taking a cleansing breath she finished her thought. "She was my best friend. Actually, we both came up with the name Sara independently."

"Do Sara's parents know? I think they would be pleased. It's an honor when babies are named for you or those you love."

"We thought we would wait and see if we have a girl before we tell them."

"That makes sense."

"Elaine didn't really want to, but I wanted Elaine in the name too," Jeff said.

"Seems only fair, considering how hard she's working to get her here. Speaking of which, here comes another contraction."

Within five contractions we could see some dark curly hair. "I can just begin to see some hair when you push," I told Elaine. "You're doing great. Rest between contractions while you can. You won't have much time. I'm going to run by the waiting room and give a progress report. Then I'll be right here at the desk."

In the waiting room Bill sat with Jessie in one corner. George and Mary Green sat in the opposite corner. Mary looked like she had lost weight. *I hope she's not sick,* I thought. They all looked up anxiously as I walked in. As the room was empty other than the two couples, I stood in the middle and addressed them. "Elaine and the baby are both doing well.

Her cervix is completely dilated and she's beginning to push. We should have a baby within a couple of hours."

Forty-five minutes later, Elaine was ready to deliver—we just needed to break down the bed and let her keep pushing. The nurse did a sterile prep of the perineum. While Elaine pushed, I massaged the area. After three more pushes, Elaine delivered without an episiotomy.

"It's a girl!" I said as I laid the baby on Elaine's abdomen. Her Apgar score at one minute was 9; that was perfect. Babies really aren't supposed to have 10s. I put a plastic clamp and a large hemostat on the umbilical cord and cut between them. The nurse helped Elaine put the baby to her breast while I released the hemostat and obtained cord blood for tests. Almost immediately, Elaine pushed out the placenta. After checking to make sure the placenta was intact, I looked for tears and was amazed that there were none.

"Well, I'm done here," I said. "Everything looks good. I noticed that just your parents are in the waiting room. Are your sisters coming, Jeff?"

"Actually, no. Erin is in Alabama. She's in college there now and left after Christmas to spend New Year's Eve with her sorority sisters."

"Roll tide."

"Yeah, Mary's from Alabama."

"What about Grace? I would think she would be here if she could."

"You're right about that, but the little miracle girl is in Haiti on a short-term mission trip with her church, and Ellen isn't getting out much. Did you hear? They put her on the liver transplant list."

"I did hear that. I ran into her gastroenterologist last week, and he said she got accepted with the group in Pittsburgh."

"Yeah, they're sort of a regional center. I just pray they can find a liver before hers makes her too sick to have the transplant."

"I hope they can." I still felt that little question of myself that always came when I thought of Ellen.

"The great thing is that Ellen's boss likes her work so much that he allows her to work at home whenever she feels like it. He says there's no reason you can't design clothes from your sickbed. It allows Ellen to contribute, and she loves her work."

I thought of that kangaroo maternity top and my wedding dress with a smile. Ellen's pregnancy had blessed her life in more ways than Henry. It led to her career.

"Would you like me to go talk to your parents, or do you want to do it when the baby goes to the nursery?"

"Just tell them it's here and they're both all right."

I noted through the window in the waiting room that George was sitting by the door, talking with Jessie. Mary Green and Bill Tarter were still sitting in opposite corners of the room. As I started to open the door, I heard George say, "Jess, I owe you an apology." I stopped. I didn't really want to eavesdrop, but neither did I want to interrupt this conversation that had been years in the making.

He continued. "I've called you a whore, said you were a terrible mother, and nursed Jeff's anger toward you. I was wrong on all counts, and I am truly sorry. Will you forgive me? I've seen how much happier Jeff is since he forgave you, and I can't deny what you have done for the girls."

"I need you to forgive me too," Jessie said. "What I did was terrible to everybody I loved. I haven't deserved it, but somehow God has allowed me to be reconciled to my children. I am grateful, and I would love for us to have peace between us too. I can certainly forgive you, if you can forgive me."

"Deal," George said. Jessie offered her hand. George took it and then embraced her. Bill Tarter and Mary Green looked at each other and smiled a smile that said they understood the power of forgiveness, that it would spread throughout their circle of acquaintances and make everyone's life better.

I opened the door and they all looked at me anxiously. "Mother and baby are fine," I said. "Jeff will come by and show you the baby on their way to the nursery."

"Is it a boy or a girl?" George asked.

"He wants to tell you, so you'll have to wait a while longer."

As I was going to see Elaine the next morning, I ran into Jessie, who had come to visit before work.

"I have a twelve-hour shift today, so I thought I would sneak in and see my grandbaby first." We walked to Elaine's room together. When we entered we found Elaine crying. Huge tears dripped off her chin and fell onto Sara's face as she nursed.

"What is it, Elaine?" Jessie said. "Is something wrong with the baby?"

"Not this one," she said. "I was just thinking about my other baby."

I was glad that Jessie was with me that morning; I would never have come up with what she said. I had seen this many times; a woman has an abortion, and it's not a baby to her until she has a child. What can you say to comfort someone in that situation? I watched as Jessie sat on the side of Elaine's bed and took her hand. Wisdom born of experience and inspired by the love of God gave her words I never would have had.

"There is nothing wrong with the other one either, Elaine. That baby went straight from your womb into the arms of God. He's perfect. He's happy. Yes, you cheated him out of this life, but he has eternity, and that is what's important."

"I wish I could believe that."

"Trust me, you can, but it isn't easy," Jessie said. "The reality of what you have done rises up to choke you at the most unexpected times. That won't go away no matter what you believe, but I have found that picture of my child in the arms of God to be a comfort. Elaine, the other thing you need to know is that God loves you and me as much as He loves those babies. We aren't innocent, but He will forgive us for what we've done. We just have to ask Him."

Elaine whispered, "Oh, dear Lord, I am so sorry for what I've done. I was selfish. I did not consider my innocent child. I did not consider Your laws. I deserve nothing from You, but please forgive me."

"Now, perhaps the hardest part is that you have to forgive yourself."

"I don't know how I can."

"One of my friends told me that in Japan there's a Shinto temple with thousands of dolls where mothers who have aborted babies go to grieve. Grieving is part of the work you have to do now," I said.

"How wise of Shinto believers," Jessie said. "I wish the Christian voice in America was more loving and less judging."

I remembered a review I had read. "*Rachel's Vineyard* is a new book about a spiritual journey of post abortion healing. Some churches are using it as a model for retreats, so finally the church is offering some help and hope instead of judgment."

"The judgment will always get the press."

"That's too true," I said.

"I wonder if the demonstrators are right. Would it stop abortion if it was illegal?" Elaine asked.

Jessie shook her head. "Elaine, I am living proof that making abortion illegal does not prevent it."

"And I am living proof that making it legal does not prevent the consequences."

Elaine stopped crying and moved Sara to her other breast. A smile came to her tear-streaked face as Sara grasped her index finger in her tiny hand. "I don't deserve her," she said as though to herself.

"And Sara is living proof that God loves both of you."

By the elevator as Jessie was leaving for work, I said, "I'm so glad you were here. I wouldn't have known what to say to help her. Do you mind if I share the picture of the baby in the arms of God with other patients?"

"No, of course not. Do you know where I got that picture?"

"No, where?"

"When you went to call the doctor, Mr. Henry gave it to me the night I came in from the window ledge."

CHAPTER 17

In mid-January, Jon and I had just gotten home from visiting his parents in Florida when Jessie called to say that she needed to talk. We met for coffee the next day. When I arrived at the restaurant, Jessie was pacing back and forth in front of the seats in the waiting area. Tension elevated her shoulders, and her fists were clenched.

"Cara, I'm so glad to see you. I hope you had a good trip."

"We did. Jon's parents are a joy. I hope we are that active when we get to be seventy."

"Thank you for taking time to meet me today. I know you're always busy when you get home from a trip."

"True, but I'm never too busy to see you. What's up?"

"George and Mary stopped by the house to see Sara. While George and Jeff were talking sports, Mary told me she had an abnormal mammogram. She wanted to know what I thought she should do. She hadn't told George yet."

"What did you say?"

"I told her she needed to tell him. Then I told her I would help her find a surgeon if she wanted to come to Lexington, but she said there was a surgeon at home that people liked."

"When Sara was born, I noticed that Mary had lost weight. Has she been trying to lose?"

"I asked her. She said no, but she has lost twenty pounds since October."

"That's not good. How did you leave it?"

"She said she would tell George on the way home. I told her to call me if she wanted to come to Lexington, or if she needed me to help in any way. I'm worried, Cara."

"With good reason."

January 31, a Saturday, was Sara's one-month birthday. Jessie decided to have a party and invited the family, including George and Mary. She admitted that she wanted to give Mary an opportunity to talk to her if she needed a shoulder. While the men watched a basketball game and Grace, Ellen, and Elaine played with Sara, Jessie, Mary, and I talked.

"I told George about the mammogram, and he went with me to the surgeon. I had a lumpectomy, and it's cancer. I started radiation last week."

"Are you getting that here in Lexington?"

"Yes, at the University Hospital."

"Just remember that you can stay here with us if you need to because of the weather, or if you don't feel like the trip. There's plenty of room."

"Thank you, Jessie. That's very kind of you."

"Mary, it's a small thing for me to do. I don't think I have ever thanked you for all you've done for my children."

Mary cried. "Maybe someday you will need to be there for my Erin."

Jessie moved to sit by her on the sofa and took her hand. "I will, Mary. Rest assured that I will."

"Did your doctor take lymph nodes, Mary?" I asked.

"Yes, there were ten of twelve positive for cancer. I have to take chemotherapy after the radiation."

Mary stayed with Jessie for the last two weeks of her radiation therapy. She first stayed because a giant snowstorm made travel dangerous, but then she stayed because she did not feel well enough to make the trip. George stayed at home to work, and it was Jessie who took Mary back and forth for the treatments.

When Mary finished the radiation, she was able to get her chemotherapy at home, so we didn't hear from her for a while.

On April 1, 1998, Jessie and I celebrated her sixtieth birthday at the Green Tree Tea Room. We had been wrong about her age when we guessed in 1971. She had been born in 1938 instead of 1940. She had not looked her age then, nor did she now.

We both loved the Green Tree, as we called it. Located in an old house on Short Street, there were smaller rooms on the right of the entry used as dining rooms and a large room on the left where you could browse for antiques while you waited. Jessie and I agreed that theirs were the best scones we had ever had anywhere, and we'd both had high tea at several places in England, including Harrods and a number of charming little tearooms in the Cotswolds. The Green Tree served the same menu to everyone and changed it once a month.

"I love coming here," Jessie said as we were seated in the front room next to the window.

"Me too, and you have to admit that your sixtieth birthday is a better excuse to come and celebrate than some of the others we've come up with."

"We have even more than that to celebrate today." Her eyes twinkled.

"We do? What have you been keeping from me?"

"Grace is getting married. She got a diamond for Valentine's Day. Can you believe it? I have never seen her so happy. My baby, my miracle, my only child who never once stopped loving me, who has been through so much pain and worry, has found someone to love her, whom she loves in return."

"Does she want a big wedding?"

"No, they want a small service with close friends and family. Grace is thirty-three this year, and she thinks big weddings are for young brides. Besides, they don't want to wait and take time to plan a big wedding."

"When will it be?"

"They're looking at September 12th. The weather is usually beautiful then and Grace wants to have the reception in the garden at my house after a morning service. She says she wants to be married all day on her wedding day and not spend it worrying about getting ready for the ceremony."

"That sounds like Grace." I thought Jessie's excitement would have settled some after she shared the news, but it did not, perhaps because she wasn't finished.

"I don't want a big ceremony either," she said.

"I'm a little surprised. I would have thought you'd want to give Grace a big wedding, especially since Ellen didn't want to have one."

"You don't understand. I don't want a big ceremony for me."

"You? Bill?"

"Yes, he proposed one night two weeks ago after we came home from having dinner with Grace and Grady. I accepted."

I rose to give her a big hug. As all of the difficulties of Jessie's life flashed before my eyes, I thought, *Nobody deserves this more than her.* "Jessie, congratulations! I know he's always been crazy about you, but I guess I had given up on you allowing yourself to fall in love."

She shrugged. "I guess I just didn't feel lovable when my children hated me. After Jeff forgave me for deserting them, I felt like I needed new goals for myself. Since Elaine lived with me, Bill and I saw a lot of each other without having to date. I probably would not have dated him if I hadn't seen him in the context of family events."

"You deserve to have some happiness." Jessie and I had been through so much together that we had the kind of friendship where you could be direct; ask awkward questions if so inclined. "Have you considered that George may be free again?"

"I'm sorry that he may lose Mary, but I honestly believe she was a better wife for him. I wouldn't want to go back there."

"Are you and Grace having a double ceremony?"

"Oh no, I want her day to be special for her alone. Besides, Bill and I aren't getting any younger either. We're looking at June 6."

"Jessie, that's two months away."

"You won't believe what I found in the attic. It's your Aunt Edna's wedding dress. It had been carefully packed away, and it fits me perfectly. I wouldn't have to change anything to use it, but I have to ask its owner."

"Jessie, Aunt Edna has been dead for over thirty years."

"Cara, the dress belongs to you."

"Oh, I guess it does. Well, of course you can use it. Uncle Henry would love that. I think he had a crush on you."

"I still miss him, Cara."

"So do I."

"Did you attend his and Edna's wedding?"

"No, they married before I was born. I've never seen the dress."

"Do you have time to come see it after lunch? You can help me get ready for a wedding in two months and another one in five."

"I'm sorry. I don't have time today. I have to do a hysterectomy at two o'clock."

"Well, in that case, I have one other announcement."

I laughed. "No wonder you've been rising off the chair. What else?"

"I'm retiring. I gave my thirty-day notice two weeks ago after Bill proposed. He is retired, and we want to travel."

"I'm jealous. Where are you going to live? Is Bill moving in with you?"

"No, I think Jeff and Elaine need some privacy. I'm moving to his condo."

"It will seem strange not having you at Uncle Henry's house."

"I hope that's all right."

"Of course it is. It's your house."

"It's more than my house. It was the sanctuary I needed when I had nothing, and it has been home and sanctuary for all three of my children. I wish Mr. Henry could have known what he did for me."

"I believe he does."

On June 6 at four in the afternoon, Jeff and Jon stood next to Bill Tarter and watched as Elaine and I walked down the aisle. Elaine was Jessie's maid of honor and I was a bridesmaid, the first time I had been so honored. Like Elaine for her vow renewal ceremony, Jessie chose gardenias for their beauty and fragrance. Two lovely vases flanked the altar, and the three of us carried them.

Jessie stunned when she entered in Aunt Edna's dress. Her once long black curls were chin length and highlighted with silver. She once said that women paid good money to have blonde highlights, and God highlighted her hair with silver for free. She thought it was too hard for brunettes to color their gray hair without going too dark, and she thought her eyebrows were too dark to go blonde.

Aunt Edna's dress was made of white satin with a lace overlay that had tiny silver threads throughout. The bodice had a high neck with mandarin color and satin-covered buttons down the back. The same satin-covered buttons adorned the sleeves from wrist to elbow. The A-line skirt reached to the floor, and a short lace veil completed the picture. No one could have designed a more perfect dress for Jessie, a more perfect partner, or a more perfect day. As we walked out of the church, the sun was low in a cloudless sky and the temperature was seventy-two degrees.

Bill's condominium was at the Woodlands, a beautiful building downtown on Main Street that had a spacious parlor beside a caterer's kitchen. It was a perfect place for residents to hold a wedding reception. Jessie had planned on a small wedding, but her church choir wanted to sing for her. That added forty people. In addition to her three children and their families, her father and brother came with their spouses. A few of Bill's colleagues came from Columbus. Several friends from Bill and Jessie's Sunday school class came. Other friends from the staff at the Florence Crittenden Home came. In the end over a hundred people celebrated the wedding of Jessie Ferguson to Bill Tarter.

"I have one regret," Jessie said at the reception.

"What's that? I thought everything was perfect."

"Sara was too little to be a flower girl," she said with a smile.

Jessie and Bill honeymooned in Maui. When they returned at the end of June, they were both tanned and relaxed.

In September Mary finished her chemotherapy, and Grace married Grady Davis in a simple morning ceremony in the chapel at their church. One of her fellow teachers was her single bridesmaid. Grace looked lovely in a tea-length white dress made of silk—designed and made especially for Grace by Ellen, who had started as soon as Grady proposed. She had less energy each day as her liver disease worsened, and she wanted to be sure she finished it. The dress, perfect for Grace, shouted to the world that the designer knew and loved her. Its simple lines accentuated her petite figure, and the bodice with a semicircle of darts across the chest led your eye to Grace's beautiful face. It was unique, like Grace.

Thirty people attended the brunch reception at Uncle Henry's house. Those who didn't care for mimosas had lumumbas made from brandy and chocolate milk. Grace appeared to have more fun than anyone. There were few enough people that she managed to talk with everyone long enough to find out about them. With Grace few things were about her.

During our moment she said, "I wish Mr. Henry could have been here today. I loved him."

"He loved you too. You gave him great joy in his last months."

"You know, he told me my leukemia was cured."

"He did?"

"Yes, one day in the library he put his hands on my head and prayed for me. He said, 'Dear God, You have promised that if we ask according to Your will, whatever we ask will be done. I know that it is not Your will that this child should have leukemia. I am asking You to cure her of this disease.' When he finished, he said to me, 'Gracie, you believe that you are cured.' Every day after that, when we prayed, he thanked God for curing me."

Grace and Grady honeymooned on St. Eustatius, a tiny island in the Caribbean. When the travel agent suggested they might want to try someplace else due to hurricane season, Grace told her she wasn't worried about hurricanes. God wouldn't ruin her honeymoon, and He didn't. The hurricane hit three days after she got home.

That Thanksgiving Mary wanted the family to come home, so that is what they did. She invited Jessie and Bill too, but they had planned a trip to Europe. Jessie had only been to England, and Bill wanted to show her other places he had visited. Jon and I took the opportunity to visit his parents in Sarasota.

Mary did well for six months. Then she developed back pain. Scans showed that her cancer had metastasized to her spine. She stayed with Jeff and Elaine while she had radiation to her back lesions. This gave her good pain relief for a few weeks, but by the time Erin got home from college, she had liver metastases as well. She decided against more chemotherapy, which she thought would make her feel worse even if it gave her more time. She wanted her last summer with Erin to be as good as possible. They went through all of Mary's photographs and made scrapbooks. Mary told Erin stories about ancestors that she had never met.

Elaine came for a prenatal visit on June 28. She was thirty-nine weeks by dates and by ultrasound, which also confirmed a footling breech presentation. When I came into the exam room, Elaine sat patting the baby's head, which rested just beneath her heart.

"It looks like the position hasn't changed," I said.

"No, the little head is still pushing on my stomach."

"Your ultrasound showed that you have a fibroid tumor just above the cervix. I think that is keeping the baby from turning, and I don't want you to go into labor with the baby in this position."

"Why not?"

"Because there is a risk of having a prolapsed cord which is very dangerous for the baby."

"What do we do?"

"A Caesarean section before labor begins."

"When?"

"What are you doing Wednesday afternoon?"

"Having a baby?"

"Works for me."

"Could you tie my tubes at the same time?"

"It's easy. Only adds five minutes to the procedure, but what if something happens to this baby?"

"Something can always happen. There is never a guarantee, but we have enough, and I would not ask Jeff to do the vasectomy again."

On Wednesday, even Mary and Erin came with George to be present for the birth of Jeff and Elaine's second little girl and last child. While they waited, Erin showed the family one of the scrapbooks she had made with her mother. Jessie looked at the old photos with pleasure; some of them had been hers. Ellen missed it as she was even more ill.

The University of Pittsburgh called on July 5—they had a liver for Ellen. Jessie and Bill drove Ellen and Joshua through the night to Pittsburgh so that Ellen could be there for surgery the next morning. For someone who had the most complicated pregnancy possible, Ellen had the most uncomplicated liver transplant. The surgical procedure was uncomplicated as was her postoperative course, and she tolerated her antirejection drugs well. Jessie and Bill found a furnished apartment where they could all stay for the six weeks after Ellen got out of the hospital. She had to have frequent follow-up and so could not go home to

Lexington immediately. Jessie stayed to oversee Ellen's nursing care, and Bill stayed to be with Jessie.

Erin decided to take a semester off from college so she could be with her mother. As soon as Jessie came home from Pittsburgh, she was off to Washington to help Erin care for Mary.

"I wonder what I would have done if I hadn't retired," Jessie said on one of her brief trips back to Lexington.

Mary Green died late in the day, September 26, 1999. Visitation for family and friends was held at the funeral home three days later. Jon and I drove to Washington for that. I watched Jessie in amazement as she made decisions and watched for the needs of Erin as well as her own children. They had all loved Mary. Bill Tarter and Martha Green provided the most support for George, who seemed to be going through life in slow motion. Almost everyone in the small community came to the funeral home that night to offer their condolences.

On the way home, Jon said, "It was wonderful how the whole community turned out for George and the family. I guess there are advantages to living in a small town."

Jeff invited his whole family for Thanksgiving, and Jessie helped Elaine prepare the food. Uncle Henry's antique dining room table had the last leaf added. In addition to Jeff, Elaine, Sara, and baby Mollie, Jessie, Bill, Ellen, Joshua, Carl Henry, Grace, Grady, Jon and me, we were joined by George, Erin, and Martha, who had not yet shared this feast at Uncle Henry's table.

I looked around the table and wondered at the suffering, love, and forgiveness it had taken to bring them all to this place. I watched Martha listen as Erin talked about going back to school in January. I realized that while Jessie would keep her promise to Mary and treat Erin like the rest of her children, Aunt Martha was likely to be special for Erin like Uncle Henry had been for me.

I watched as George placed his hand on Carl Henry's shoulder and gave him a loving pat as he talked about living in Boston. I wondered if George appreciated the irony that his only grandchild who could carry on his family name was Carl Henry.

After Jeff offered thanks, he said that Jessie had an announcement to make. Martha, Erin, and George all looked at her anxiously, as though something else terrible was going to be announced. When Jessie said, "I declare this the opening of the eating season," we all laughed.

What seemed like a perfect day was made more perfect when at four o'clock in the afternoon, Grace said, "I think I need to go to the hospital." A caravan followed her.

Grady went to the office to admit Grace while I accompanied her to Labor & Delivery. I could not imagine that Grace would be ready to deliver; she was thirty-four years old and pregnant for the first time, but this was Grace. Her cervix was completely dilated, the baby's head was at a plus-two station, and the membranes were bulging. During my exam her water broke, and with the next contraction some dark hair was visible as she pushed.

"We're going to have a baby soon," I said. I took a quick trip to the waiting room to tell the family they would not be waiting long. I looked through the window as I approached and was stopped still. There, seated at the table in the middle of the room, was Jessie with George on one side and Bill on the other. They had settled to look at the scrapbooks they had made. Jessie had one for each of her children; Bill brought Elaine's, and George brought the ones that Mary had made after she became ill. All of the children, spouses, and grandchildren stood around them and looked over their shoulders. They talked and laughed as they looked at the old photos and clippings.

"Grace labored while we ate Thanksgiving dinner," I said as I opened the door. "She's completely dilated and pushing. We'll have a baby soon."

My trip to the waiting room almost caused me to miss the delivery. When I got back to the labor room, one nurse had Grace trying to blow over her contractions and not push; one nurse was on the phone paging me, and still another nurse rushed around trying to get the room ready for delivery. One look showed me that their effort was futile; Grace was ready whether the room was or not.

"Grace, push gently," I said. With bare hands I controlled delivery of the head as she pushed out a screaming, healthy baby. While she held their daughter in her arms, Grady arrived from admissions in time for the birth of their son. Grace was fertile.

THE END

ACKNOWLEDGEMENTS

I owe a debt of gratitude to my patients who have taught me much of life and love, not to mention medicine. In this work of fiction I have tried to show some of the compassion I feel for them in their real suffering.

I am grateful to my editor, Angie Kiesling. This is a better novel because of her. My gratitude goes to all of the staff at Morgan James Publishing, but especially to Terry Whalin, the acquisitions editor who first believed in me and helped get my manuscript accepted.

At the risk of leaving out some very important people, I need to name a few for whom I am particularly grateful. Ted Andrew Purcell, a talented designer and my nephew, helped with the concept and design of the front cover. I appreciate his contribution and willingness to listen as I talked about my story.

My beautiful and talented cousin, the late Nancy Henry Chadwick, was very supportive and encouraging as I struggled with lack of confidence in my ability to complete this project. She was a better writer than I will ever be, and she was the person who said she wanted to know more after reading the first page.

Carroll Hunt Rader, an author, editor, and my friend, was a great source of encouragement and the first person to read the whole manuscript.

I am grateful for her support and practical writing advice. I am also grateful to Janet and Steve Bly who were mentors in my writing apprenticeship.

Others of my family, friends, book club, needlepoint group, yoga class, prayer group, and church family have helped in many different ways. Thank you one and all. May each of you have honey from the thistles in your life!

CPSIA information can be obtained
at www.ICGtesting.com
Printed in the USA
JSHW052017060622
26758JS00002B/162